Tell Me
Something True

Tell Me Something True

◇ ◇ ◇

Leila Cobo

GRAND CENTRAL
PUBLISHING

NEW YORK   BOSTON

Copyright © 2009 by Leila Cobo

Grand Central Publishing
Hachette Book Group
237 Park Avenue
New York, NY 10017

Visit our Web site at www.HachetteBookGroup.com.

Printed in the United States of America

First Edition: October 2009
10 9 8 7 6 5 4 3 2 1

Grand Central Publishing is a division of Hachette Book Group, Inc. The Grand Central Publishing name and logo is a trademark of Hachette Book Group, Inc.

Library of Congress Cataloging-in-Publication Data

Cobo, Leila.
Tell me something true / Leila Cobo.
     p. cm.
ISBN 978-0-446-51936-6
1. Colombian Americans—Fiction.   2. Family secrets—Fiction.   I. Title.
PS3603.O26T45 2009
813'.6—dc22
                                2008054425

To my mother, Olga, who inspired this story,
and to the Hanlon circle: Arthur, Allegra,
and Arthur III.

Tell Me
Something True

There is a picture of my mother. She's kneeling in front of a bed of roses in the garden of our Los Angeles home, one hand holding down a huge straw hat against an obvious gust of wind, the other clutching weeds and roots she's just dug up from the moist soil. Her long, curly hair is blowing around her face, and she's smiling and she looks beautiful and impossibly happy.

I had that picture in my bedroom, and it was my favorite for many years, before I learned that my mother hated gardening. That every plant she ever touched died. That the beautiful day in that beautiful garden was a fluke. That at the time that picture was taken, she was probably already thinking of another life, another place, far from me, far from us.

Gabriella

The air feels sweet and moist and just the slightest bit warm when you get off the 9 p.m. flight to Cali. It clings to your skin, but in the faintest, most tenuous way, like the sheerest of gauze blouses touching but not touching your arms as you breathe. When Gabriella tries to explain the sensation to her friends, they just don't get it.

"How can you feel or smell any air," they always ask, "if you arrive into an airport terminal?'

"It's not a real terminal," she is forever responding. And it isn't, to her at least. It's a building with open windows and no air-conditioning, and if it's raining, drops of water sweep in, like a mist, and it makes her feel as though she's arrived somewhere real and tangible and alive, so far from a carpeted airport terminal you feel like you're in another world.

Her friends from up there never come down here. They're afraid of getting killed, or worse.

"I don't know what's wrong with these people," she complained to her father as he watched her pack the night before. "It's extraordinary, really. They go to Singapore, to Turkey, to Peru! But Colombia is too dangerous."

Leila Cobo

Her father didn't say anything, because he's as guilty as they are, absent from her trips for over a decade.

"They'll go down," he finally contributed. "They'll fall in love with a Colombian, and then they'll have to," he added with a laugh, a laugh that tried to tell her it's okay that once again she's going without him.

She could sense his unease, could see it in his worried blue eyes, in his tall lanky frame that tonight was coiled tight, his legs crossed, his arms crossed, sitting on her bed, trying to look nonchalant but swinging his foot incessantly, making her nervous as hell.

"Try and use your time there wisely, Gabby," he said. "Think about where you want to be a year from now. You have to make a plan."

Gabriella wanted to say that maybe it could be wise *not* to have a plan for a change, that plans interfered with creativity, but he interrupted her thoughts before she could put them into words.

"And remember, I don't want you driving alone, okay?" he said for the third time that evening. "And I don't want you walking around without Edgar," he added, referring to her grandmother's bodyguard. "And I want you to call me as soon as you land and as soon as you get into Nini's house. And I want you to keep that cell phone on at all times."

"Daddy!" she finally exclaimed, exasperated. "Daddy," she repeated softer, picturing him alone in their big house for a whole month while she's gone. "It'll be okay. Nothing bad's gonna happen," she said placatingly, even though they both know bad things can happen, bad things *have* happened.

But they happen to other people, not to her.

"I'll be fine," she added, sitting next to him on the bed, her dark, curly head close to his straight, blond mane. She ran her fingers through his soft hair, twirling it at the nape of his neck, like she used to do when she was a little girl. "I'll be fine."

Thinking of him now reminds her she has to call. A quick call.

"Two dollars and fifty cents a minute," he's reminded her a dozen times, because she is a fiend with her cell phone and her text messages, and roaming fees to Colombia are outrageous, even for someone like him. When he answers, she speaks rapidly, almost furtively, and he laughs just to hear her voice, because she always makes him laugh. And she laughs, too, happy that he's finally happy, that she's arrived, that she's fine, and that now she can embrace her days here without guilt.

Tonight it smells like rain, and the wind carries a whiff of sugarcane from the refineries in the valley. She breathes deeply, taking in the burned, bittersweet smell, a smell most people can't stand but whose familiarity she embraces. For a moment, she feels physically lighter, feels the weight of her worries loosening their grip on her: what she wants, what she's supposed to do, who she's supposed to be in six months when she graduates.

"Extraordinary." That's what they say about her. Her father, her grandparents, her teachers. They say it to her face, and they talk about it when they don't think she's listening, ticking off the long list of potentials she could be. And if she could get off the treadmill of endless expectations, maybe she could focus for a moment, but she never seems to have the time.

She looks out at the airstrip from the open window and gets the strongest urge to go out there and run into the darkness, caution be damned, beyond the point where the airport lights end and the planted fields abruptly begin. She suddenly remembers one summer afternoon, several years ago, when they parked the car on a dirt road and climbed up to a grassy knoll, where her cousin Juan Carlos and she watched the sun set and the planes take off. The sky was stunning, with sweeps of orange and purple and pink, and for a few minutes, they felt like the only people alive, the only ones who knew that such beauty existed and was available free for them.

They stayed there until it was dark, and by the time they got home, it was nine and Nini was so mad.

She'll be here for four weeks. Same as it's been every Christmas, for as long as she can remember.

"Gabriella," says the immigration agent, looking at her American passport, then speaking to her in Spanish. "Razón por la cual viaja?"

"Vacaciones," she replies.

He grunts. Thumbs through the passport. Stamps. Then finally looks up at her. Unsmiling but polite, and yes, gratified that she's there, a foreigner in a city that discourages foreigners.

"Bienvenida a Cali, Gabriella," he says and hands her the passport.

Outside, Cristina Gómez waits. She waits and she frets, her perfectly glossed lips pursed, both arms clutching her handbag, even though Edgar is standing right by her side. Cristina hates airports in general and this airport in particular. Because it's hot and chaotic. Because the cement outside of customs is always slick with rain and aguardiente and trampled fruit. Because hordes of people, wound tightly together like spools of yarn, strain against each other to get a glimpse of the arrivals through the tinted glass, their shouts of recognition blending with shouts of drunkenness as bottles are passed back and forth, back and forth over her head.

Because she's petite and claustrophobic and always thinks she'll suffocate while she waits, and because it invariably reminds her of the accident. For years, she couldn't bring herself to come here. Regardless of who was arriving, she would dispatch Edgar and go out someplace else—never staying home—so as to dispense with any semblance of waiting. But when Gabriella turned ten and started to fly alone, she took it as her cue to take responsibility again.

Before that, Marcus would bring Gabriella for a week or two, in a gesture of solidarity with Cristina, even though they lived in Los Angeles and the trip was long and involved two flights. If Cristina had a soft spot for her son-in-law before the accident, she became his fiercest advocate afterward, supporting him through what she would teasingly refer to as his "dissolute lifestyle"—one girlfriend after the other. He never remarried, he didn't have any more children. She had never demanded that he give her time with Gabriella, but he had understood it was the correct thing to do, and she was grateful. As the years passed, he stopped coming altogether. But he never denied her Christmas, even the few times Gabriella herself had begged not to come because she was dating one boy or another.

Eleven years she's come to pick this child up. Always at this time, from this gate, from this flight; the same flight her mother used to take. The wait takes place outside, and it involves throngs of people, all anxiously leaning against the railing that leads to the exit door. They hold signs, toddlers with flowers and gifts, cameras. Moisture sticks to her skin, and she feels something wet on her face. Panicking, she swats her hand against her cheek, then stops, feeling foolish as she realizes it's her own perspiration damaging her matte makeup.

Someone in the crowd recognizes a passenger exiting the glass doors, and the bodies heave against her. Edgar firmly takes her arm and steadies her, his huge presence shielding her from the others, his right hand gently resting on the gun at his waist.

She sees Gabriella before her granddaughter sees her, and she doesn't say anything for a few moments, not until she can quell her tears. She is so tall, so striking, this girl, with her straight black eyebrows, pale skin, and slate gray eyes. How had her tiny daughter managed to produce such a specimen?

"Not to brag, but you haven't seen a more beautiful girl" is her mantra, repeated through the years at countless luncheons, dinners, and tea parties. She knows her love for this girl borders on the pathological, but she simply doesn't care. Eleven months of the year she devotes to Juan Carlos—her twin soul, so old and proper inside that boyish exterior—the son of her only son.

But Gabriella.

With Gabriella she only has four weeks to make up in

every way for the other forty-eight without her, and she caters to her every whim. The only daughter of her only daughter. She is entitled.

"There she is, Edgar," she finally tells him, and he immediately clears a path for her to walk through the crowd.

"Gabriella!" she shouts, waving frantically.

"Nini!" Gabriela pushes through the crowd, the porter behind her lugging three bags and her laptop. "Nini," she repeats, crushing her small grandmother and rumpling her linen suit with her hug.

Helena

Querida Gabriella:

You were born today, July 7, at 7:32 a.m. Weight: 8 pounds, 6 ounces.

A big girl! A perfect baby girl, the doctor said.

Wow, you came into the world with a bang!

I think you wanted to make a statement. We were at a gallery opening and my water broke. Oops. In the middle of the show. I was wearing a black dress, so it wasn't that obvious, but obvious enough. I mean, I literally dropped a bucket of water to the floor. I thought your daddy was going to have a heart attack as he drove to the hospital. He thought he'd have to deliver you himself!

But you waited, my sweet. Very patient of you. I even had a chance to get an epidural (I'll tell you what that is someday). And here you are. Your hair is black, your eyes are blue, but they tell me that can change. Will they be like mine? You have your father's mouth—a big, fat Cupid's mouth. You look utterly beautiful to me.

You are, dare I say it? Not what I expected. I didn't know what to expect. An alien, perhaps. A creature bent on tearing my body apart, on changing my life beyond repair. I always wondered how these calm mamas did it: Push a living child out of your own body. How it must hurt!

But here you are, looking up at me with those bizarrely huge eyes. I already forgot the pain!

Your name is from the Hebrew Gabriel, which means "Strong Man of God."

And you're a woman! Strong woman.

Like Gabriela Mistral. Like Gabriel García Márquez.

Like you, my Gabriella Richards.

Do you notice how easily you can say Gabriella in English and in Spanish? Because you're going to have to speak both.

You notice I'm writing to you in Spanish?

Spanish only in this book! This is your book. From me to you, so you don't forget who you are and where you came from.

So, my love, good night on this first night.

Bienvenida, querida Gabriella.

Te adoro.

Mamá

I had never been a writer. My means of expression had always been visual, out there for everyone to see. Then I got pregnant, a totally unplanned occurrence. At first I was truly furious with your dad, even though I knew it wasn't his fault. It was the last thing I wanted, a baby. I mean, yes, I knew one of these days I'd be a mom. I just didn't figure it had to be quite now, when things were just starting to happen, when I had finally lined up shows and assignments.

And then, you started to grow inside me. It's quite extraordinary, really. One thing is to get pregnant and intellectually know that you'll have a baby in nine months. Quite another is feeling that baby evolve within you.

"There is a maternal instinct," I told your dad one night as I rubbed lotion onto my ever-growing belly, "and it's been awakened!"

I began writing this diary the day I felt you move inside me for the first time. Quite a jolt. Your dad was away and I was lying in bed, watching TV. And then, the barest of flutters, like butterfly wings. I thought it was my pregnant mind's imaginings. And then it came again, so soft but so persistent. My belly was almost flat still. But now, the truth was undeniable. Something alive was inside me. I'll have you know that I quit smoking cold turkey. I quit drinking, too.

I'll admit. All my life I've gotten exactly what I want. But you. You made me responsible.

I bought a red diary because it's my favorite color and because I figured it would contribute to generating a strong personality for my Gabriella.

Marcus thought this writing kick was funny at first. Then he thought I would drop it in a few weeks. He humored me, because he always does, but I knew he thought it was a short-term project.

Ha!

I'll show him, you'll see. I'll write you. Forever. So you and I can remember everything that happened today, and ten, twenty years from now, we can laugh together.

Or cry.

Just joking!

Gabriella

"Can we go see Mom?" she asks, snuggling against Nini in the backseat, letting her stroke her hair.

"Of course, princess. Whenever you want."

"Did you fix the squeaky pedal on the piano?"

She hates the squeaky pedal that whimpers every time her foot rhythmically pumps it, bringing back memories of sagging beds in college dorms.

"Yes. I told you I did last week," Nini says patiently. "You can play until your fingers fall off, you won't hear a thing from the pedals."

Gabriella doesn't say anything for a moment. She wants the pedal fixed, even though the last thing she wants to do right now is lay her hands on the keys and practice endlessly for something she can't pinpoint.

"Is Juan Carlos home?" she asks instead.

"No, he went out tonight. But he's taking you to some party tomorrow," answers Nini.

"Ooh. Nice," she says, contented. Juan Carlos knows the right people. Always. And he always knows the right parties. "Is there soup for me tonight?"

"Of course. Vegetable soup. And shredded beef."

"And my Diet Coke?"

"Yes. I got you a whole case."

"Can Edgar take me to the club tomorrow?" she asks, sitting up straight in her seat. "I need to go running."

"Of course. I also reserved a horse for you to ride, if you wish."

"I'd love that, Nini. Thanks. Thanks, Edgar," she adds, leaning forward toward the front seat and patting his arm. Edgar emits a half smile, half grunt. He's been making this drive for as long as Nini has, seeing each year pass by on the face reflected in the rearview mirror. When she was thirteen, he taught her how to drive stick shift, making her learn in reverse first, one hand on the steering wheel, her other arm draped around the passenger seat to easily allow her to turn her head back. That, said Edgar, was the way the pros drove.

Gabriella smiles, settles back. Nini is a wealthy, patrician woman. Her dad is even wealthier than that, she knows. But in L.A. there is no driver, no army of cooks and maids, and certainly, no grandmother taking care of every single detail in her life. Since she can remember, she's done things on her own, down to meticulously scheduling her piano practice so it wouldn't interfere with her father's activities at home.

But for one month of the year, she needn't think about a single responsible thing. Someone else takes care of her. Completely.

Heaven.

Helena

Querida Gabriella:

Today you took your first step. You're nine months old! Do children walk when they're nine months old? No. They don't. That's what the nanny told me.

"No other child I've had has ever walked this quickly."

Well, you did.

So you walk, but you don't talk.

"Tete," you say when you want your bottle.

And I'm sure you say "Mama" although your dad swears it's "Dada."

And your eyes. They've lost all the blue and are now a most marvelous shade of gray, like a stormy sky over the Pacific Ocean. Big eyes. Expressive eyes. I love to take pictures of you when you're solemn and the eyes are biggest. Even in black and white, you can see the gray.

Te quiero,

Mamá

Gabriella

Gabriella, just put on something normal people would wear," says Juan Carlos.

Juan Carlos is twenty-four. He's her uncle Julián's son; the only son of her only uncle on her mom's side. Gabriella knows he loves her, because he has to—he's three years older and responsible for her while she's down here. He's taken her under his wing even when he hasn't wanted to, like the year he dated Marisol Vázquez, who hated her and still hates her now.

He also thinks she's weird, because she studies piano, which in his mind is useless. And that's cool, he always points out, since she's well off and should be able to do whatever the hell she wants with herself. Except that she practices eight hours a day, and he figures if anyone is going to put that much effort into anything, shouldn't it be something a little more practical?

"Tennis," he says. "Tennis, I get. If you played eight hours of tennis a day, you'd be the best player in the world, and you'd make tons of money. But all this practicing to have one hundred people go hear you? I mean, play guitar in a band or something."

"Really, Juanca, you are so incredibly superficial some-times, I have to wonder if we're even related," she snorts, although lately she's been wondering herself if all this piano playing is worth the grief.

"Gabriella is my crazy cousin," Juan Carlos often tells people, and compared with his other cousins, who are all MBAs, she knows she is. And she loves it. She does things just to provoke him, like the time she visited him at the New York firm where he was working as a summer intern, wear-ing a dress with oval cutouts along the sides.

"Gabriella," he muttered under his breath as they rode down in the elevator. "Could you try not to look like an art-ist for just one day?"

One night, in a moment of weakness, she tried to explain the psyche of the musician. "We dress like musicians to hide our insecurities, Juanca," she explained earnestly after smoking half a joint. "All musicians are nerds, and all clas-sical musicians are bigger nerds. We need to make it up, somehow."

Ever pragmatic, he really looked at her as if she were high. "Insecure people don't get onstage," he said quite logically.

"They do. They have to," she countered. "That's the only time they can show off."

"But you don't even like getting onstage, Gabriella," he said smugly. "I'm the one who likes it!"

Gabriella always waves him away dismissively when he says things like this, but she knows he's right. She is like her father, more comfortable behind the scenes than on the spot. And yet, everyone expects her to be in the forefront: her grandmother, who considers her perfect, her father, who tells her anything she wants to do is fine with him, and yet, she can almost touch the voids he wants to fill with her actions. He may not say it, but he wants her—no, he *needs* her—to shine.

When she's down here, she can physically feel the pressure of perfection easing from her chest. She is almost someone else; a glamorous stranger whose depths are rarely plumbed, who is never here long enough to make an impact, who can glide effortlessly in the shadow of an older cousin with just the right connections.

Juan Carlos has the golden eyes and pixie, youthful looks of her mother's family. He looks so young sometimes he'll go without shaving for days at a time, like tonight. He really, really thinks this makes him look tougher, more manly. She's always thought it makes him look like an overgrown school-boy, and that's why girls cling to him. They want to take care of him. She has never told him this, because he would genuinely be offended; more so because he is her designated protector. A traditional kind of guy who will still open the car door for her.

Gabriella likes it.

She thinks it's the Nini in her. Maybe her outfits are crazy, but she likes guys who dress like prep schoolers and intro-duce her to their parents.

So she lets Juan Carlos be a little dictator about her outfit tonight. It's his party, not hers. And he's playing it safe, with an untucked, dark blue polo shirt over his jeans, loafers, and a handwoven bracelet that all the preppie guys are wearing, the kind they think makes them look cool.

Gabriella wanted to go all out and wear this very, very

little, very, very red dress, partly because she's really stepped up on her running and her legs, with all due respect, she thinks, look fabulous.

But Juan Carlos thinks she'll stick out like an athletic gringa in a red dress, plus she'll be taller than him with her high heels. She likes to provoke him, but not make him look bad.

"Jeans?" she asks.

"Jeans is cool," he says, looking at his watch.

"Relax," she tells him. "I won't embarrass you in front of the new girlfriend."

"Oh, please," he says scornfully. "She is not the new girlfriend, and I could give a damn what she thinks. All I ask is normal. Normal. Is that too much? Hooker dresses aren't normal for a party."

"Hey, I'm wearing the jeans," she informs him good-naturedly from the walk-in closet. "And it's not a hooker dress," she adds huffily, considering it. I mean really, as if he were some fashion plate. "It's Juicy Couture."

But she puts on her jeans, tight, very expensive jeans, and a white T-shirt and a studded black leather belt. A dozen necklaces and her Celtic silver cross. She looks as normal as she can possibly look.

Juan Carlos stares at her hair, but she anticipates it.

"Don't even mention it," she warns.

He shrugs. "You look like a lioness," he snorts.

"Well, roar!"

Gabriella loves her hair. It's very curly and long and thick, and she likes streaking it in multiple shades of silver and blonde and brown. Drying it straight, she finds, is a pain in the butt. Plus she thinks it makes her look like a Cali Stepford wife, which she simply will not contemplate, no matter how much she identifies with Cali.

It's also the single physical trait she's inherited from her mother.

Gabriella likes to think that people who knew her mother will look at her hair and be reminded of her. No one has ever told her that. But still, she likes the thought.

Helena

Querida Gabriella:

You turned two today.

Incredible.

You used to fit in the crook of my arm.

Today, you opened the door for the guests!

We had 20 two-year-olds. Remember this piece of advice from your mom: When you have kids, NEVER invite 20 two-year-olds to a party. Invite eight, maybe. Tops.

NOT TWENTY!

Well, thank God for backyards. You have a best friend, it turns out. Someone called Melanie. She's a terrorist. Managed to uproot all the petunias.

But you were so, so happy.

This was your first bona fide party. You ran around like crazy in that yard. Did the swing set thing, ate cake, cried (boo-hoo) when another little girl took your seat at the head of the table. Poured pink punch (that will NOT come out) all over the brand-new, handmade dress I brought you from Colombia. All that good stuff.

And I must say, I was the perfect mom. I actually chatted with all the other perfect moms and baked a cake from scratch.

No, I'd never done that before, in case you were wondering! But, you see, becoming a mother is nothing. *Being* a mother. Now, that is definitely an act of love. Sometimes I'll watch you sleep. For hours and hours. I like taking your picture when you sleep. It's innocence upon innocence, your arms splayed open, your legs splayed open, your mouth open. You are not afraid of anything.

Grown-ups never sleep like that. They're always afraid of something. They hug themselves or fold their hands over their chests, like dead people.

I always sleep on my stomach, with both my hands tucked under my pillow. Your daddy sleeps sideways, with the pillow tucked against his chest. He stopped using the pillow after you were born. You would sleep in bed, between the two of us, and he was afraid he'd accidentally smother you during the night.

Gabriella

She now thinks she's been roped into going to this crazy party, and they're almost there and she knows already it's a mistake.

Juan Carlos is driving, and he's excited because of his new babe. He's set up his buddy Camilo with the babe's friend. But Camilo's sister, Angela, who's Gabriella's friend, couldn't make it. So now Gabriella is supposed to find someone to talk to once she gets there. Alone. She has a headache just thinking about this.

Why, why did I agree to come? she thinks.

Everything is warped about the evening, Gabriella muses. They're crashing the party via the babe, who doesn't live here, but in Cartagena. Turns out she studies in Boston, where Juan Carlos met her, and she's here visiting her friend—the one Juan Carlos has set up for Camilo—who's friends with this guy who's having the party.

And the place is far, far, far. If she gets bored, finding someone to drive her back will be next to impossible. There's nothing to see as she stares out the window. Nothing. Pance is Cali's most suburban suburb. You might as well be in the middle of the jungle, it's so dark there. They've already passed Juan Carlos's old high school, which is as far up the hill as Gabriella's ever gone.

It's a really beautiful school, like nothing she's seen in the States. Set up in the middle of this pasture—cows graze there in the afternoon—and with a real river that runs right through the middle of the soccer field.

Gabriella came here for one semester, when Marcus put his foot down because her Spanish was slipping. The houses around here are massive, too, she remembers. Big pools, huge trees, ponds, huge gardens. It's just so far. And so dark. It's funny how the entire world changes with the light. Her father always says that.

Damn, damn, damn, Gabriella chastises herself, her thoughts racing ahead. Is there something in my DNA that says I have to go to every single party that crops up? Is staying in on a Thursday night so terrible?

"Hey, I think we're here!" says Camilo from the backseat, pulling her out of her reverie.

She looks up and figures they're somewhere because there's a veritable army of guards with machine guns at each corner of the street they're about to turn into. One of them nonchalantly comes up to the car.

Juan Carlos slows down and rolls down the window.

"We're going to the party?" he says, a question mark lurking at the end of his sentence. It occurs to Gabriella for the first time that they don't know whose party this is.

"Open the trunk, please," the guard says in answer.

Juan Carlos pops it, and when the guard goes back to check, Camilo leans forward, and Gabriella sees he's visibly perturbed.

"You know, Juanca, this is a bit over the top," he says nervously, lighting up a cigarette. "Do we know who this guy is? I mean, are we cool here? This has mafioso written all over it."

Juan Carlos shakes his head.

"It's cool, man, don't be such an idiot. It's her friend's cousin. It could be anyone. And if it's mafia, well, big deal. We'll stay a little bit and leave. Hey, it's an adventure, right, Gabriella?" He's speaking heartily, which tells Gabriella he's not that certain about it all.

She shakes her head. They've been driving for forty-five minutes.

"At this point," Gabriella says, "we have to go on and at least check it out. But I'm telling you, if this is some mafia bash, I don't want to hang out all night."

They're all whispering furiously, and Gabriella practically jumps out of her skin when one of the guards outside taps her window. Did he hear?

Juan Carlos rolls it down and the guy—huge guy—just nods.

"You're okay," he says, looking directly at Gabriella, letting his eyes wander over the T-shirt. "Enjoy."

Juan Carlos gets the car in gear and drives up to a gate, where another guard greets them, with a clipboard in hand.

"Names, please," he barks.

"Ca—" Camilo starts to say from the backseat, and Juan Carlos cuts him short.

"Felipe Gómez, Andres García, Ana Gómez," he rattles off, giving fake names.

The guard obligingly writes them down and opens the gate.

There are so many cars there already, parking has moved to the huge lawn, and Gabriella's high heels sink in the grass as they plod their way up the hill to the house.

"Man, oh man," she says, picturing her lime green Coach shoes turned to dust. "This better be good."

The party is on the roof of the house.

The roof is reached via an elevator. Yes, an elevator.

Juan Carlos, Camilo, and Gabriella look at each other uncertainly as it goes up. They've already been frisked at the door to the house, which gives Gabriella a semblance of security. At the very least there shouldn't be a gunfight in here tonight.

"I heard Oscar D'León is coming to play at midnight," someone says excitedly.

"Great," says Juan Carlos stiffly. Gabriella tries not to giggle. He hates anything *nouveau riche*.

Gabriella tries to casually check out the blonde beside her, who wears a tight, short, strapless black dress and dominatrix lace-up black and silver boots.

"Very cool," Gabriella tells the blonde as Juan Carlos raises an eyebrow incredulously, the irony completely lost on him.

"I know," says the blonde happily. "You know Manolo Blahnik?"

Gabriella nods politely. "Yes, I do," she says nicely.

"They're Manolo Blahniks. Three thousand dollars!" she adds for effect.

"Wow," says Gabriella, trying to look suitably impressed.

"You gotta pay the big bucks to get the good stuff," says the blonde conspiratorially as the elevator doors open.

"Unbelievable," mutters Juan Carlos under his breath.

But moments later, he has no compunction in waving Gabriella a quick good-bye when he spots his babe.

"You'll be okay?" Juan Carlos asks, eager to leave her. "You'll find someone you know, I'm sure."

"Yeah, yeah," says Gabriella nonchalantly, though she can see this will be a very long night.

"We'll leave in a couple of hours," Juan Carlos reassures, backing away.

"Cell phone," he shouts as an afterthought, pointing to his, pointing to hers as he disappears into the crowd.

Gabriella asks for a vodka with orange juice from the bar and walks the perimeter of the terrace uncertainly. She can't see anyone she knows, and she doesn't want to walk around like she doesn't know anyone.

Oh, God.

She pretends to look occupied, nursing her drink as she shifts uncomfortably against the railing. Fifteen minutes later, her glass is empty and she's still alone. Unconsciously, she begins to gnaw on her thumb, absentmindedly peeling the edge of a nail that has grown too long for her to comfortably play the piano, tearing an edge of skin in the process.

Gabriella winces and looks guiltily at her finger, automatically balling her hand into a fist.

Bathroom. She doesn't really need one, but it'll give her something to do.

But the nearest one is locked. She puts her ear against the door, hears giggling. And sniffing.

Oh, God. The last thing she wants tonight.

Gabriella goes up to the bar and orders another screwdriver. Walks around some more, feeling like an idiot. Tries another door.

A staircase!

She walks down to a different level. The family area, she thinks uncomfortably. She tries one door, then another. Both are locked. She suspects she shouldn't be here. The doors are locked for a reason.

As if reading her mind, a voice makes her jump.

"You lost something?"

She turns around guiltily, even though she's done nothing to feel guilty about.

He's tall and wiry, with Indian-straight black hair and bronze skin that's pulled tautly over chiseled cheekbones. It's his eyes that startle her, sly and incongruously light, light green for a face this color. She knows immediately, in the way people like her always know, that it's his house, his party, his money, and yet, he couldn't be further removed from her.

"I'm sorry. I was looking for a bathroom," she says, distracted by his eyes, the way he looks at her, as if he could read her mind but finds everything slightly amusing. It sounds lame, so she babbles on. "The one upstairs was taken, and I really needed one ...," she trails off.

He doesn't say anything but walks past her, his bare arm brushing against hers, and opens a door that's not locked.

"You can use this one," he says, with a calculating half smile that tugs up one side of his mouth, leaving his arm extended against the door so she's forced to come up close to him to go inside. "You know your way back?"

"Yes," Gabriella says, infinitely uncomfortable. "Thanks," she adds quickly, shutting the door behind her, severing the connection.

When she comes out, he's gone.

Helena

Querida Gabriella:

I'm going away. It may seem like a long time, but it won't be. Six weeks, that's it. Really, I'll be gone for maybe thirty days.

Oh, I'll miss you, I'll miss you, I'll miss you.

But I have to do this, you know. It's a book. A book of photographs. A book of beautiful photographs of Cali and Colombia. It will be a precious, beautiful book, and when you grow up, you'll be so proud because your mami did it all! You'll look at it, and you'll know a little part of you is from one of these places.

Now, I must tell you, you've become a very big girl. A very responsible girl. You dress yourself for school. (Yes, you do!)

I want you to know these things. I don't want you to grow up and have anyone tell you differently.

Today you chose blue shorts and white top. In other words, you have good taste.

The socks and the shoes, we still have to do that. But the outfits, you pick.

You like to wear a little bow in your curls. So we have all kinds of bows. Hundreds of bows, in all different colors, just for you.

I've spoken with Daddy, and he's promised to pick a new bow for you, one for every day that I'm away. I'll call every day, I promise, and you can tell me what color bow you're wearing.

Your daddy loves curls. And bows. And making girls with curls look pretty with bows.

When he met me, he was getting his master's in film at USC. He was an L.A. boy, through and through: the son of a documentary producer and a TV exec, raised in a sprawling house north of Sunset. Tall. Blond. Handsome. Entitled. The kind of guy you watch in daytime soap operas.

But he really wasn't like that. He was smart. Well-read. An intellectual. My father adored him after the first conversation. He was too prepared, really, to go into film, and yet, there was never any doubt that he would be in "the business." He wasn't into the way things worked but the way things looked. He made little movies as a boy, learned how to cut and splice on his own. Even in his first year at USC, he knew what he wanted to do. Not direct; he couldn't deal with actors. But photograph.

He already had several film director credits under his belt when, almost as a whim—because he liked school, really—he took the job as TA for Horwitz's Rudiments of Photography class, the must-take for film and photography majors.

I was neither of those things. I was a history major in my senior year. But I had convinced Horwitz to let me take the class, even though it had nothing to do with the credits I'd taken before and even though most of my classmates were freshmen and sophomores. I didn't care. I wanted to be in that class, come what may. I was just an amateur photographer, but Marcus didn't know that at the beginning. He didn't know that the history degree was what my parents had pressured me to do, thinking I'd become a professor. Photography was what I really wanted to do. And that's what I did. Remember this, Gabriella. You are entitled to do what your heart desires.

Marcus says I have a "way." That I make people do things for me. I don't know about that. I just know what I want, and back then, I wanted that class. And then, I wanted him.

Marcus often says he fell in love with my hair first. But his gift has always been to discern people's true essence, their truly beautiful qualities. My beauty, he finally concluded, was not in my hair but in the shape of my head.

Oh, he was after me to cut that hair for months. But he convinced me only once, when I graduated, and that was only because I doomed his TA-ship. When people found out we were dating, they considered the relationship "inappropriate" (as if professors don't carry on with their students all the time). Anyway. I felt the least I could do was sacrifice the hair to whatever gods had brought us together in the first place.

To Marcus's credit, he kept his distance in the beginning. He was skeptical of my academic background—he was a purist, who felt the coveted slots in Horwitz's class should go to bona fide film and photography students. But I surprised him. My background in history had given me an eye for detail and an entirely different aesthetic from those one-dimensional students of his. Most of them were interested in portraits or photojournalism. I photographed architecture and landscape. *His* architecture and landscape, I should say. Because I was a foreigner in his town. Then again, that's why I could look at things in a different way.

But on the first grading period, for my shoot of the Venice Boardwalk at different times of the day, he gave me a B, for "failing to elevate the mundane to the compelling."

I felt wronged.

Wronged by someone barely two years my senior, this Los Angeles pretty boy who, I admit, was good at what he did, but who wasn't even a real professor.

The worst part was he liked me. I knew he did.

I was convinced that stupid B had deeper meaning.

So I asked for an appointment.

He looked shocked. I supposed students didn't ask for appointments with their TAs, because he wanted to have the conversation right there, in the middle of the hallway.

"No," I said adamantly and angrily, because my English became more accented with each word. "I need more than a few seconds, and I want to know exactly why I have this grade. I am asking you for fifteen minutes of your time."

Marcus was annoyed. I could tell he thought I was some kind of emotional Latina throwing a little Latina tantrum. But he couldn't refuse the appointment. So he made it as hard as he possibly could for me.

"You can come by my office at five thirty today or at eight thirty in the morning tomorrow," he said curtly after consulting his agenda, giving me the two single most undesirable time slots, way before or after any of my classes and right in the middle of rush hour traffic.

"I'll be there at five thirty today," I replied, cursing him inside. "Thank you," I added formally and went directly to the library, where I armed myself with a mountain of Venice Boardwalk photography books.

He was alone in the TA office when I got there, his feet propped up on his desk as he sipped coffee and read a novel, of all things. I wondered if he shouldn't be grading papers or something.

"What can I do for you, Helena?" he asked cordially, pronouncing my name "He-lee-nah," like an American. He wasn't annoyed anymore. Just amused, which made things worse.

"It's Helena," I said curtly, pronouncing it "Eh-le-na," as it's pronounced in Spanish, even though I was resigned by then to being a He-lee-nah instead in a country that insisted on vocalizing the letter *h*.

"Oh," he said momentarily nonplussed, but then more amused even than before.

"Helena, then," he repeated, drawing out the second *e* so it lingered on his tongue, long enough for me to want to taste it. No one had ever enunciated my name quite like that and I felt the barest of tingles up my arms.

"Marcus, I feel I don't deserve a B," I finally said flatly. "I've done well in all the projects, and I would like an explanation and I would like you to reconsider," I added all in one breath.

"Helena, you've done great stuff," he answered, and it was immediately obvious to me that he'd planned his words. "But in this case," he continued, "I have to tell you that (a) the Venice Boardwalk is not terribly original material and (b) because it isn't, you have to do something very, very special to make it appealing for me at this point, and you didn't. Different times of the day and different light and all that is pretty, but it doesn't do it for this subject matter."

Marcus didn't drop his feet from the desk, nor did he ask me to sit down, which was not only rude, but made me feel at a distinct disadvantage.

"I brought some books to show you," I said firmly, determined to win this one, like I had won my place in this class. "I'm sure my work can stand up to this."

I placed at least five books on the desk, all on the same subject, none executed with the same flair for detail or lighting.

He picked them up nonchalantly, feet still up on the desk as he thumbed through one, then the next. Then he stopped in the middle.

"I have something to show you, too," he said, getting up for the first time and going to the office next door.

He came back with a worn portfolio that looked a million years old and handed it to me.

When I saw the title, I felt my stomach sink a little bit: "The Venice Boardwalk: A Pictorial Study."

It wasn't a study of the architecture but of the people. But the juxtaposition of the faces against the buildings highlighted the architecture in a way that made my more complex project seem simply mundane.

I have a sturdy ego. But I truly also have a healthy dose of realistic self-critique. I knew when I was beaten.

"Yours?" I finally asked, still looking at the pages.

"No." He shook his head. "Horwitz's." He paused. "Look, it's an unfair comparison, I know. But you have a different kind of eye that can do much better things, with something that you know better."

I kept looking at the portfolio, trying to ignore the fact that, now that he was standing beside me, the top of my head didn't even reach up to his chin.

"When you're a photographer, half the work is in picking your subjects," he said gently, sitting on the desk in front of me. "You have to photograph what you know best, what you can make look the best. You have to make me see things in a way I didn't know they could be seen. You have to make me see things I didn't know existed."

I noticed then that his eyes were a deeper gray than I had thought before. That their irises were a shade darker than the pupils.

I was going to say it. "Your eyes are extraordinary."

But just then, the USC marching band started its practice in the field below the TA office.

I stepped back.

Picked up my books and got a grip.

"Thank you for your time," I said simply.

And then, because I realized he was much too proper to overstep his bounds and because I sensed the moment might not return and because, after all this, I really had nothing to lose, I put it out there: "Can I treat you for a coffee...you know, to make up for having made you stay for me?"

"No," he said nonchalantly. And then, he showed his cards: "But I'll treat you to dinner."

Gabriella

Gabriella walks around in a slightly tipsy daze. She's heard of houses like this, but she's never actually been to one. There's so much marble that it overwhelms her. Vast marble hallways, marble foyers, and spiraling marble staircases, like the one she walked down to find the bathroom. She opens a massive door and finds yet another staircase, this one going farther down. Maybe, she thinks stupidly, it leads nowhere. Maybe they built it just for fun, and if you go down, you'll just come up again in some other part of the house.

Maybe, maybe, she thinks, as she walks down, holding tightly to the balustrade because this marble staircase curves round and round, like a snail, and she feels like she could simply fly off at any second. Instead, she reaches the last curve and stops in surprise.

"Ooooooh," she says out loud, looking around her at rows and rows and rows of books. A library.

A library with old-world cherrywood floors and Persian throw rugs that jar with the glinting marble stairs.

She almost giggles. These people actually read?

But someone does, she sees, because there's a wooden ladder with little wheels, the kind bookstores keep to reach the top shelves. She walks around slowly and realizes there are books on one side, movies on the other. The giant screen, she guesses, is behind the closed doors of a massive wall unit. Automatically, she goes toward it, and stops at the coffee table. It's piled with books.

She takes in in one glance that there are too many to have been put there for effect. And they're of all sorts—paperbacks and hardcovers and magazines and coffee-table books.

She sees just one corner, sticking out from under the bottom of the pile, and recognizes it.

Gabriella kneels down, carefully picks up books and moves them to the floor, until she reaches her mother's book.

She lifts it slowly, reverently, feeling the sleekness of the cover, the ridges and grooves of the emblazoned letters. She knows this book well. But she hasn't seen it in someone else's home in years.

Las Haciendas del Valle del Cauca. Pictures of the state's historical farms and estates. "A labor of love," Nini would always say, shaking her head, dismissing it. "If it wasn't for that book, everything would have been different."

But Nini still keeps it in her bedroom, inside her nightstand. Sometimes after her nightly prayer, she takes it out and leafs carefully through the pages her mother never got to feel. The photographs she never got to see in print.

Gabriella knows her mother left her for nearly two months for this book. She knows rationally that she can't possibly remember a day that happened when she was barely three. But the story has been told to her so many times, she even knows the words by heart.

"Mi amor, I'm going to go away, just for six weeks. Six weeks

is nothing, Gabriella. Even if I'm not here, I'm still with you. In your heart. In your mind. Like an angel."

She had left her with her father in Los Angeles, and before her departure, she gave Gabriella the golden chain with the locket she still wears today. Sometimes, at night in bed, Gabriella closes her eyes and closes her hand over the little heart and is convinced she can feel the cool gold as it touches her neck for the very first time.

Her father told her it was a great six weeks. They went to the beach and to the Santa Monica Pier and to Malibu to watch the whales and the dolphins. Her father put her on a surfboard and filmed her as she splattered around in her mini–wet suit.

Her mother, he said, was doing important things in her country far away. She was taking photographs for a book, a wonderful book, a magical book, a book so special, the governor had commissioned it.

Gabriella now knows that there had been no money to be made from this book. That it was, as Nini said, a labor of love, important only for the prestige it generated in this one city, in this one state, in this one country.

When she was little, Gabriella would look at the book and try to divine these places her mother had captured with such care. It wasn't only the facades, but also the bedrooms, a corner footstool, the hammocks hanging from support beams on long, long porches, the verdant green that clung to everything in this valley. Everything was so very removed from her Los Angeles reality. So, so—*Colombian*.

She wonders if this is what Thomas Wolfe meant when he said you could never go home again. Or maybe it was the other way around. You could never leave home. You would forever be in a midground limbo, neither here nor there.

She turns the pages quickly now and stops at a double spread marked by a small, yellow Post-it note. The house is vast and sits at the foot of a hill surrounded by mountains. A winding road leads to a red wooden portal. Her mother shot it from the mountains above, early in the morning, Gabriella guesses, because dewdrops and mist still cling to the rooftop.

"Wow, you must be really bored."

The voice butts in through her drinks and her reverie, and she looks up guiltily.

It's him again, the guy with the eyes. Involuntarily she feels her pulse quicken slightly, and she brings her hand to her temple, certain he can see a vein throbbing or something. She now notices that he's wearing loose-fitting jeans and a black short-sleeved polo that looks worn and expensive. The look of someone who doesn't care how he looks because he knows he always looks good.

"No, no. Not bored," she says quickly. "Just...resting."

He walks closer, leans down to glance over her shoulder, and pulls up a stool next to her.

"We bought that house," he says matter-of-factly, pointing to the book with a glass that she smells has scotch on ice.

"Really?" she says, happily impressed.

"Yeah," he says nonchalantly. "My dad told my mom to pick whichever one she liked from that book, and she picked that one. I liked..." He leans over and flips the pages for her. "This one," he says, pointing to a smaller farm flanked by a decidedly modern pool.

"Well, tell your daddy to buy it for you," she says, slightly put off. As a matter of principle, she never talks about wealth. It's one of the few things her families on both continents see eye to eye on.

He laughs appreciatively, but not in the least bit mortified, she notes.

"Maybe I will," he says, taking a long sip of his whiskey. "Or maybe I'll buy it myself."

"Why that one?" asks Gabriella, curious despite herself. It isn't the biggest or grandest or the most anything, for that matter, house in the book.

"I went there once," he said. "It's really, really out of the way. Lost, almost. Not like these other places, which are just an excuse to be social with the neighbors. It's a place where you go to get away. And the view is amazing. I'm just waiting for the owner to lower the price. He's trying to gouge me just because he thinks I have cash."

Gabriella can't tell if he's bragging about his money or simply stating the obvious. Either way, it bothers her.

"I don't know. How many farms really does anyone need to 'get away,'" she says thoughtfully, her customary reserve gone with her drinks. "Can't you just lock yourself up in your room or something?"

She can read the surprise on his face, the vacillation between taking her comment as an insult or a joke.

"Anyway, look at your mom's farm," she says, flipping the pages back to the original photograph, slowly tracing on the glossy paper the path that leads from the portal to the actual house. "It's so beautiful. God, look at those colors! It makes you want to lie down on that grass."

Gabriella looks up and finds his eyes steady on her, and on his mouth is just the beginning of a smile; the kind of smile that comes with seeing something you like for the very first time.

She laughs suddenly. "I guess if you get up really close, it won't be nearly as beautiful, right?" she asks ruefully. "Nothing is."

"Actually, it's magical up there," he says slowly. "In the afternoons, the clouds come down, and they touch the house. It feels like you're walking in the sky." He shrugs. "Too bad no one uses that house," he adds, looking down at the photograph again, at her hands on the page.

"You bite your nails," he says suddenly, looking at her hands, but not touching them. "What's eating *you* up to make you do that?"

Self-conscious, Gabriella snatches her hand away, mortified. Her thumb looks raw where she tugged skin earlier, even to her.

"This is my mother's book," she says abruptly, changing the subject.

He looks at her blankly.

"I mean," she adds quickly, "my mother took the photographs. These are her pictures."

"Really?" he says, and she sees his eyes glimmer with a genuine spark of interest for her, one that goes beyond her face or her body. "Wow," he adds, lifting his eyebrows, but he says it like he means it.

He takes the book from her hands and flips the pages to the jacket's back cover where her mother's picture looks intently, seriously at them.

She isn't beautiful, or pretty, even, in a traditional sense. But she is riveting in her contrasts—a delicate face made up of a dozen tiny sharp angles: pointed nose, pointed chin, angular cheekbones, slanted eyes that look brilliant, even in black and white—all overpowered by the hair.

"You don't look like her," he says, studying Gabriella closely and putting the book back on the table by his side. He calmly cups a hand beneath her chin as he compares her with the black-and-white picture, turning her face this way and that. She is too taken by surprise to protest and lets him bring her face close to his, so close she can smell the musky mix of cigarettes and whiskey on his breath. He has smooth skin and very long eyelashes, almost like a girl's, and they're black and sooty and make his eyes look even greener.

"You're much prettier," he adds slowly, giving her that one-sided smile she now sees is his very own, making her pulse speed up again and making her grow warm, so warm she's sure he can feel it in his fingers.

"My hair is like hers," she blurts out automatically, wondering almost immediately why she's felt compelled to say this.

"So what?" he parries quietly, leaning even closer. "Eyes and mouth are what really matter. What does hair say about people anyway, except that they like to go to the beauty parlor, or they don't." He pauses for the briefest of moments then smiles wide. "You don't," he laughs.

"I . . . I really should get going," she says, flustered, pulling back from his touch, but not getting up, either.

"Go where, this time?" he asks. "You can't seem to find your way into the party."

"Well, you can't, either," says Gabriella, peeved. Is he following her, or what? "And it is your party and your guests, you know."

"I don't need to be in the middle of my party to enjoy it," he says, leaning toward her again, his elbows balanced loosely on his knees. "And you don't look like a wild partyer to me, either."

Gabriella looks at him inquisitively and against all logic feels a small pang of rejection.

"What, do I look like a dweeb who can't hold her own at a party?" she asks.

"Nah." He shakes his head. "Not a dweeb at all. I'd say, shy. Shy and aloof."

"Shy and aloof," she repeats, feeling herself being drawn in again. "Like you?"

He considers this for a moment, taking a sip of his drink. He finally replies, "Aloof, yes, shy—no. It's just that some people don't interest me and some people do." He looks straight in her eyes.

She knows, somewhere in the back of her mind, that if she were to repeat this conversation to anyone, they would laugh at the pickup line. But she is all alone here—Juan Carlos so far removed from her, he might as well be in Los Angeles with the rest of her life—and his eyes are so clear, almost like a piece of glass. She can actually see her reflection looking back at her.

She believes him.

"Let's go back together," he proposes good-naturedly, still smiling. "Oscar D'León is going to start playing any minute. You do dance, don't you?"

He gets up and holds out his hand to her, and she sees that he has a tiny tattoo of a cherubic angel inscribed on the inside of his wrist.

Gabriella wants to run her thumb across that angel. She wants to take that hand, and feel it again, cool and dry against her skin.

"Well, why?" she says, defiantly coy. "I don't even know who you are."

"Well, this is my house, and as you pointed out, my party, so I should be asking you who *you* are, don't you think?"

This time, she really blushes. Laughs to cover up her embarrassment, the flurry of adrenaline that's cutting her breath short and making her heart race, almost as if she were about to step onstage before a concert. "I'm Gabriella. Gabriella Richard."

"I'm Angel. Angel Silva."

He turns up the palm of his still extended hand.

"Now, do you want to go up? I'll make sure you don't get lost again."

"Sure," she says with a shrug, attempting to look as casual as he sounds. She thinks she probably doesn't sound casual at all as she puts her hand in his, letting him take her away from the book and the table and up the stairs and to the roof and into the party she had watched but hadn't wanted to join until now.

Helena

Querida Gabriella:

I spoke with you today on the phone.

"Me traes un regalo?"

That was the mantra. Regalo, regalo, regalo. Your main concern is the gift. Missing me is not part of the equation (so, don't give me a guilt trip twenty years from now!).

You seem perfectly happy.

Papi is "bien."

Connie, your nanny, is "bien."

School is "bien."

When I asked you if you missed me, you said, "No!"

Of course you don't. You have fifty people doting on you!

But I miss you, sweetness.

Things are different here without you. Because of you. I am in another hemisphere. In another world. Ah! I'm drunk. Can you tell? I don't even know what I'm saying anymore.

The thing is, your grandmother insisted I go to this party. It was being held at one of the haciendas I'm photographing. But do you know how long it's been since I've been to a party here in Colombia? Five years. Five years! The time I've been married to your father.

Ay, Gabriella. I haven't been home in five years.

Why did I let that happen?

It feels strange now. Not everything. My house is the same. My room is the same. I even wear the same pajamas I did when I was fifteen!

But going to parties just makes me a little nervous. It was supposed to be a fiesta bailable, a dancing party, with a big band and all that. That implies sitting at a table and, well, not dancing because I don't have a date and your dad isn't here to ask me out (which wouldn't make a difference since he can't dance salsa anyway).

But I digress.

It was a beautiful house. And they had lit it up with torches, lining the entrance and all around the garden. I could have kicked myself for not taking the camera.

But Mami said it clashed with the dress—"It will look bulky, you can't take a backpack, why, oh why, must you always make an effort to look as bad and dowdy as you possibly can," blah, blah—and I suppose she had a point.

It was a beautiful dress. Lilac silk, very clingy. I bought it at a vintage boutique in Melrose. Mami thought it was awful, of course.

"It's—exotic," she said doubtfully. Yeah. I call it that, too. It came with a long, long scarf. Kind of Isadora Duncanish. I love that scarf. I felt very Hollywood in it.

And there I was at this beautiful party, sitting at this beautiful table with orchid centerpieces that matched my dress, looking at this utterly romantic courtyard, with the dance floor illuminated by torches that cast just the right golden glow on the dancers.

Alone.

Papi took me out for a couple of mercy dances. He likes how I dance. He taught me.

"Keep your back straight," he would tell me, "your chin high. You never, ever look down." And I never do. I follow his hand. The lightest pulse on the small of my back can make my waist turn, my hips swivel, my legs crisscross or glide. My American friends never got this, the concept of following a man on the dance floor.

"It's so submissive, Helena," my friend Angie always says, and she even has the temerity to insist that you can actually dance salsa and lead the guy.

But I love to follow and my papi taught me well. If there's something even Mami can't dispute, it's that no one follows like me. "Like a feather, ni se siente," my boyfriend Jorge used to say.

But Papi likes dancing with Mami better, and they make such a beautiful couple. He's so tall, so stately. And she's so tiny. Very Coco Chanel. Not exotic. With that perfectly coifed hair. Sometimes she slips her right hand from his, like now, and just holds it up shoulder height as she dances, like a doll in a jewel box, and she smiles with her eyes closed.

And you know how it is, people start dancing, and in the beginning, they try not to leave you alone at the table, but then it's just too tempting. They want to dance. Even Elisa, my best friend, left me eventually to dance with her boyfriend du jour, leaving me at the table, feeling like a bona fide wallflower. There's a phrase for that here: "Comer pavo," which literally means eating turkey, and please don't ask me to explain what eating turkey could possibly have to do with not being able to dance.

Jeez. I hadn't comer pavo since the sixth grade. I played with the orchid. With the matches. With the candle. I was mortified.

Do you remember how it was in high school? When you prayed for the night to end and someone to take you home? When you felt so soundly out of place. Was it your dress? Your hair? What happened between the time when you last checked in the mirror and went out feeling confidently beautiful and now, when your increasing desperation leads you to eat the fruitcake in an effort to look occupied? Well, of course, you don't remember—you're just a baby! But someday you'll understand.

I now felt grotesque in my purple dress with its outlandish scarf, and when Papi took me out for a second mercy dance, I felt it trail down my back with the gracefulness of a clumsy, thick woolen scarf. Not Isadora Duncan–like at all.

He cut in before we got to the dance floor.

"Doctor Gómez. I'll trade your daughter for my mother."

We laughed.

And, of course, who could resist such an overture? We traded.

I knew him. From way back when. But he'd never given me the time of day. Never looked at me twice, as far as I could remember. I had looked but never expected anything back. Girls like me—then—never got looks from guys like him. Guys like my brother, who played polo and wore khaki pants and dated girls with long, straight hair, who used makeup in the mornings.

Tonight, he was looking at me like I was one of those girls. I no longer craved guys like him. Guys who have become men with small aristocratic guts, too proper, too well kept, too boring.

But tonight, he was different.

Different from himself. And different from Marcus, who is tall and athletic and so beautiful and easygoing.

He wasn't much taller than me, and I felt his breath rising and falling against my cheek, warm with just a trace of the last smoked cigarette, his cheeks lending just a whiff of expensive cologne. He smelled authoritative, like Cali, like farmland. He smelled like a man who knows what he wants and gets it.

Maybe it was the way he held me when we danced. His hand so tight, so rightfully firm on the small of my back, making my feet go forward and backward, so effortlessly I really did feel like a feather, and my Isadora Duncan scarf once again felt like it was made out of silk as it whirled around and around us as we turned in the courtyard under the torches and the sky.

Gabriella

The phone wakes her up—it's past 11 a.m., but she feels surprisingly lucid given the evening she's had and the fact that she went to bed scarcely six hours ago.

Angel, Angel, Angel.

She's never met someone whose name is Angel. Why was he named that? she wonders. Was he supposed to be a redemption, a saving grace? Or was it to protect him? A talisman name that would shield him.

What is she going to tell Nini?

That she has the hots for a mobster's son?

Maybe she won't have to say anything. Maybe he won't call her.

She wouldn't care if he didn't call. Well, she'd care for a couple of days. She liked him, she liked him.

But what to do if he did call? But he won't call. Guys like that don't call.

Juan Carlos was furious with her. Never mind he'd been the one to take her there.

"You were fucking necking with a mafioso, in his house!" he shouted at her in the car.

"I wasn't," she began to protest, but he cut her off midsentence.

"You want to get us killed? Shit. We're not in stupid gringoland here. This is Cali. People get shot over stuff like this."

"As if I did stuff *like this* all the time. You, you are so out of line, Juanca," she finally said; she was so outraged at the injustice of it all. "You made me go there. *You. And* you!" she screamed accusatorily at Camilo, who was trying to disappear in the front seat. "You make out with your bimbas and you freak out because I'm *dancing*?"

"No joda, Gabriella. Don't make me say it," said Juan Carlos, banging on the steering wheel, turning violently around. "He was all over you. Everyone was looking. Everyone was talking about it."

"Everyone? Who's everyone? You didn't know anyone there except your two wenches who you just met. I never do *any*thing with *any*one here *any*way. God, you're so overbearing, you'd think we were in the Dark Ages the way you go on about every little thing. Like my reputation is going to be soiled because I slow danced at a party where everyone was snorting coke?"

"Gabriella." Juan Carlos now sounded tired. "He's Luis Silva's son. If you were my sister, I wouldn't let you go out with him. But you're not my sister. And he's a fucking drug dealer with a personal army, so whatever I say doesn't mean shit!"

Juan Carlos's voice rose as he screamed the last word, banging against the steering wheel once again.

In the backseat, Gabriella squeezed her eyes shut as tightly as she could and covered her ears with her hands. She wanted to undo the night now, but she couldn't.

"You know what," she said quietly, holding her hand up, shielding herself from this anger that she's never seen in him before. "He's not even going to call. I'm not going to see him again. You're freaking out over nothing."

"I hope you're right," Juan Carlos said, shaking his head, sounding subdued. "I hope you're right, Gabriella."

They hadn't necked. They hadn't even kissed. They'd only danced. But in the end, she felt as if she'd been made love to. He was holding her so close, breathing into her hair, his hand on the back of her neck, pressing her cheek against his, his other hand planted firmly on the small of her back, leading her hips and her waist through the dances; then quieting down and only locking her tight against him, barely moving, oblivious to the people around them and to the relentless beat of the songs as they melted one into the next.

In the daylight, she winces at the thought, at the shocking intimacy that's transpired between their fully clothed bodies. In the daylight, she wonders if he was really all she saw and all he felt like, if other people feel things like this? In the daylight, she tries to conjure the steady touch of his cool hands and wonders if they would pass muster under her grandmother's perusal. She tries to picture him eating in the dining room next door, with Juan Carlos and her uncle, but the image fails to materialize, like a painting she can't finish.

In the daylight, she tries to imagine the daylight with him, and she can't. The thought is embarrassing, uncomfortable. It only works cloaked by evening, hazed by drinks.

"Niña Gabriella?"

It's Lucía, the cook, at her door. "Phone for you," she says.

Gabriella feels her stomach dip. It's him, but now she doesn't want him. Now, the thought of him makes her cringe.

"It's your grandmother," adds Lucía, and Gabriella feels relief pouring over her like a salve.

He won't call. He won't call. And if he calls, she'll just say she's not home, and he'll stop calling, and it will be over, like it never happened. Like when she was sixteen and she and her friends would get fake IDs to get into the clubs on the Sunset Strip, picking up guys for drinks, then giving them wrong names and phone numbers.

Because she never does anything rash, not really. She is so careful, living on tiptoes because if she were to break, like her mother, then what would be left?

Come to think about it, he hadn't even asked for her phone number.

Aquí no pasó nada, nothing happened, she tells herself, picking up the phone on her nightstand.

"Nini?"

"Mi amor, what time did you get in?" replies Nini in greeting.

"Nini, you know what time. You were up," says Gabriella, knowing that she was. Nini can't sleep properly until Gabriella's home. But she still gets up at seven thirty the next day, like a little clock, and goes to her office downtown.

"Did you have a nice time?" asks her grandmother, unfazed.

"Yes. Yes. Great time. Interesting," she says noncommittally.

"Good, mi amor. Listen, get dressed, I'm picking you up in twenty minutes and we're going to see your mother. It's our last chance before the weekend crush."

"Okay," Gabriella says. "I'll get ready."

But she lingers in bed, uncertain. Can Nini tell that something isn't quite right? When she was younger, one of her friends swore her father could tell if she had smoked pot, even three days later. Impulsively, she picks up the phone again and dials her father, even though it's only six thirty in Los Angeles, but who knows when she'll get another moment alone.

"Gabby," he answers her after the first ring, his voice thick with sleep. "Can I call you back?"

"Mmm, sure," she says quickly, immediately sorry she's woken him with nothing specific to say.

"No. Wait!" he says, more alert. "What's up?"

He's always been uncannily perceptive, her downfall and her trump card. Who else has a father you can talk to about boys, about birth control, about fashion?

But now, as she looks out the window from her bed, at the tile and tin roofs that stretch out below her amid the trees and the still cloudy mountains pasted to the back of the horizon, she is assaulted with uncertainty.

He is in Los Angeles, where appointments are kept, curfews are respected, where no one smokes, where most people don't drink and drive. Last night now seems impossibly foreign, a mesh of unforeseens and unplanneds that her father wouldn't—could not—possibly understand, even if he were disposed to do so.

What *did* she want to ask him?

Have you ever met someone and felt that the world literally comes to a stop? And what happens if that someone is off-limits. No. Not off-limits; an abomination. Maybe a monster. What had Juan Carlos said? "A fucking drug dealer with a personal army."

Back home, they made movies about this. Or maybe someone gets shot in a ghetto somewhere, in a drive-by that becomes a little item in the Metro section of the newspaper. Here, they... She's not even sure. They shoot people, she knows that much. Do they burn them with cigarettes? Pull their nails out? She's heard so many stories through the years, it's hard to sort out urban legends from fact.

"Gabby, what's up?" he says again, insistent.

Gabriella closes her eyes, touches her face, her neck. All her dad's admonitions of caution, and she'd tossed them out the window on her second night here. If she were to say a word, he'd do an Internet search and come pick her up himself by the end of the day.

"Nothing, Daddy," she says softly. "Really, Daddy. Nothing that can't wait."

Helena

He fell in love with my hair, Gabriella. Even before he saw my eyes. He'd walked into the classroom and had seen the hair, laid out over the desk in a huge, curly mess. I was passed out. Okay, I was tired. I fell asleep.

He was not pleased. He was a new teaching assistant, and he didn't want his stupid students walking all over him before he even started talking. But he loved the hair. He thought it would be nice to film that hair with the right light.

The rest of the class was apparently laughing when he walked up to me and leaned over the hair.

"Boo!" he shouted.

I literally jumped, toppling my chair.

"Class has started," he said calmly but looked into my eyes, and really, right there and then, we both knew.

You love this story. You can't possibly understand it, but your father sits next to you in bed and recites it verbatim, night after night.

"It was love at first sight," he always says. "We got married, and we lived happily ever after. And then." He always

pauses here, looks at you, raises his eyebrows, and you fall for
it every time.

"What? What? What?" you squeal in that little pip-
squeak voice.

"And then," he says, "we had you."

Gabriella

When she was a little girl, Gabriella took for granted these two worlds she came from, so similar yet so completely alien to each other. She took for granted that her Colombian grandmother had a chauffeur, who would open the door of the car for her, who would drive impassively as she sat princesslike in the backseat. Even in her Los Angeles, in her Beverly Hills, these were luxuries. The only time Gabriella was ever chauffeured anywhere was for her dad's movie premieres, and even then, it was in a rented limo.

Here, she sits in the backseat with her grandmother as Edgar drives solo, in the front of the cream-colored Volvo, which, truth be told, is five years old now, and compared to Gabriella's little BMW and her father's Jaguar is, well, totally middle class.

But from the looks of Nini, she's the one riding in a Bentley. Gabriella has to smile.

She is impeccable, as always. Dressed in light blue linen pants and a starched white linen shirt that defies the heat and the malaise outside the tinted windows.

Gabriella has also always taken for granted the duality
of life in Cali. There's her family. The country club. The
maids. Nini with her beautiful fourteenth-floor apartment, overlooking that vast, impossibly green valley. From
the window of Gabriella's Italian-tiled bathroom, she can
see the mountain range—blue in the distance, with high
peaks dipped in clouds—as she takes a shower. In the evening, lights flicker on the hills south of the building, making one think of a little Bethlehem. But when you drive
along those foothills, as they do today, it's not cute or picturesque, but dirty and poor. The houses are shanties, their
roofs made of corrugated tin or cardboard. She knows that
when it rains, water pours down from these hills, taking the
unpaved rocks and dirt of endless trails, and wreaks a havoc
of mud on the road below. She knows this, but she's never
experienced it, no more than she would by reading the *Los
Angeles Times* in her Beverly Hills home. She's but a breath
away from all this, she thinks, looking intently for once. All
she needs to do is lower her window and reach out and touch
it, but all these years, she's been detached. What had he said?
Aloof.

Today it's sunny, and the midday stupor that permeates
Cali at this time, before the afternoon breeze sweeps in at
three, barely reaches them, impervious, inside their air-
conditioned car.

Gabriella rarely talks during this trip to the middle of the
city. Nini doesn't, either. They stop at a light and a little girl,
one of hundreds that show their stuff at stoplights around
the city, furiously juggles three balls. Nini automatically

reaches into her purse for a coin, opens the window a sliver, and hands it to her.

She quickly shuts the window and reaches for Gabriella's hand in the backseat, covering it carefully, comfortingly, with her own, small and manicured. In the sunlight, her wedding diamond glitters.

Helena

Querida Gabriella:

When you're older, I will bring you here every year. Every year. It's important to never fully sever the ties that bind you. You're probably wondering why I haven't brought you here before. I don't have a good answer, baby. I knew I could always bring you, you know? I knew nothing would change here. Everything would always be ready for you, exactly the way I left it. Even my house, my room, are the same. The same bed. The same bookshelves. My high school nightgown.

In the mornings, I stand on the terrace and look at the houses below. They're the same, too, and I still know what tiles are broken on their roofs.

Time stood still here and time just went by, and there was always something else. Like this summer. I've come home to work, but you've stayed with Daddy and Grandpa and Grandma over there. They have a house in Lake Tahoe. You love it there because you get to go out on the boat, and there are no boats here.

But we're coming next Christmas. I have it all planned out. We'll have big parties with your cousin and invite all the kids we know, and you'll decorate the manger with real moss.

Gabriella

There's no one here at this time of the day, and Nini has a parking pass that allows Edgar to pull up inside the gates, right in front of the chapel. It's full of trees here, old trees, solid and generous with their shade.

When they built this cemetery, over two hundred years ago, these were the outskirts of town. But the city has grown and swallowed the dead, who are now shielded from traffic and smog by walls of concrete. From the outside, only the trees peek out, and a guard zealously mans the gates, following a strict schedule, to prevent any pillaging from these tombs that house the poor and the not so poor and the patrons of the city.

No one gets buried here anymore. There aren't any more plots to be had. And it's not the thing to do, anyway. People prefer those pastoral cemeteries that are miles away, where each grave has its plot, like an endless garden, where the lines are clean and organized. Here, the caskets are piled one on top of the other, inside tall walls with simple nameplates, each indistinguishable from the next.

Gabriella's mother isn't there.

She's in the Gómez mausoleum, an ornate little monument

with marble slabs and a wrought-iron gate that you must open with a key if you want access to those inside.

Gabriella's great-grandmother is on the left, and on top of her is her great-grandfather, and on top of him, her grand-father's brother.

Her grandfather is on the right, and on top of him is her mother.

"It's a temporary arrangement," says Nini.

"When I die," she always reminds Gabriella, "you have to put me on top of your grandfather, and your mami on top of me." She always adds, by way of apology and explanation, "I have to be beside your grandfather."

Edgar wipes the gate clean with a moist rag before unlock-ing it. There are coins and flowers and paper icons on the floor, offerings her grandfather's patients keep leaving for him, even seventeen years after his death.

Nini collects them in a bag but takes them outside. She doesn't like to keep foreign objects in the family crypt. Then she instructs Edgar to sweep the little entryway, clearing it of dust and cobwebs, until it again looks shiny and visited. "These dead haven't been forgotten," she always mutters under her breath.

"You want to go first, Gabriella?" she asks matter-of-factly as Edgar walks back to the car, leaving them alone with their ghosts. "I'll go to the chapel."

"Okay, Nini," Gabriella responds, and gently kisses her on the cheek because she always looks so grimly cheerful here.

Nini used to go in with her. The first years Gabriella came here, she was terrified. Of the casket, of the crypt, of all the dead people in this place. The two of them would visit together then; Nini would talk to her daughter, Gabriella to her mother. Nini would talk about Gabriella's horseback lessons and her awards and what she had done with her hair. Gabriella would listen solemnly, and nod. But it never felt comfortable, what Nini did. Talking to a dead woman she couldn't see, who didn't answer.

And then, Gabriella can't even pinpoint when it happened, but it just did. She started to have her own stories to tell her mother.

Now, she likes to close the gate and sit in the middle of all the coffins. Nini has a little chair for her in there, and when Gabriella sits down, she's still tall enough that she can rest her head on top of her mother's casket.

Gabriella likes it there. She likes to lay her head on her mother's chest and picture her, sleeping, face up, with her hands folded quietly over her chest. Her hair is long—because it's been growing all these years—and it falls in endless, gorgeous curls over her shoulders and her breasts and down to her ankles. She looks beautiful like this, like a resting Lady Godiva. And she always smiles, because she's happy to see her daughter, to feel her and listen to her.

"Mami," Gabriella says, speaking very softly, very close to her so Grandfather won't hear. He'd be pissed. And then she tells her what she couldn't bring herself to tell her father. "I met a boy. His name is Angel."

She pauses, trying to bring it all back.

"It's a beautiful name, isn't it? But the thing is, he's the wrong kind of boy. That's what Juan Carlos says, and honestly, that's what I think today, too.

"But he felt so right. And . . . and I guess he could be right.

We danced last night, and he's a great dancer. And he's so tall. You have no idea how hard it is to find someone who's taller than me! And he's so, so beautiful. He's a beautiful boy, with beautiful skin and cool hands—not clammy! I hate clammy. Just really cool and firm, you know?

"I don't know how to explain it, Mami. I can't remember the last time I felt like this about a boy. I don't know that I ever have. It's—" Gabriella stops. She tries to rationalize if it was the drinks or the moment.

"It's like there was no one else," she says, shaking her head. "And, you know what? He had your book! He had your *Valle del Cauca* book in his library. He told me they'd bought one of the farms in the book because of your pictures. I think that's a good sign, don't you?"

Gabriella stops, feeling guilty. She can't bullshit her mom. She's dead; she knows everything. Gabriella sighs. She can't pretend not to know what her mother already knows.

"Mami, his dad is a mafioso," she continues, lifting her head up and looking down at the casket, trying to see her mother beneath the marble and the wood.

"Actually, I think he's a pretty big deal mafioso. And I wonder, Mami, if I should just walk away? Now you see why I can't tell Daddy. He'd make me fly back in a second if he knew.

"Although." Gabriella pauses, but even before she speaks, she can hear how unsatisfactory her explanation sounds. "I mean, *he's* not the mafioso. It's his dad. He's a victim of . . . of fate.

"Do you hold people accountable for what their parents do? People can change the circumstances they were born with, don't you think? It's what free will is all about. It doesn't seem fair, Mami," she says, shaking her head. "It's not his fault that he is who he is. I wish..."

Gabriella doesn't know what she wishes, but the wetness on her hands startles her. She realizes she's started to cry because the tears are sliding from the casket onto her hands.

"Mami, he might not even call me. He hasn't called me. It doesn't matter. But Mami. I still wish I could talk this out with somebody. I wish I could talk this over with you."

She stops for a bit. "Please don't tell anyone," she says, looking around.

Gabriella wipes her eyes and scrambles through her purse for a tissue. Long ago she learned she couldn't do without tissues when she came here. You just never knew.

"Anyway, Mami," she goes on, and this time she looks outside the gate at the trees and listens, for the first time that day, to the birds that are quietly chirping out there. It's a fine place to rest in, she always thinks. She imagines that at night, when everyone's gone, her mother and grandfather get into these big, lively discussions with the great-grandparents—who were supposed to be partyers—and if there's such a thing as afterlife wine, they probably drink gallons of it.

"I'm fine. I really am. I'm graduating this spring, and I'm making my mind up about what I want to do with my music, you know? Sometimes I think I should bag the classical stuff and just write jingles. Daddy says it will be inane, and I can make a ton of money and he can retire. Of course, he'd hate for me to do that. He thinks I'm some kind of prodigy, but it isn't like that at all, Mami. Sometimes I think it's pointless

to have studied music. I mean, who am I kidding, right? I'm
not going to be a serious classical pianist. God, I'm a wreck
every time I have to perform. But I'm going to score a short
film that my friend Patsy is directing in the film department.
Daddy thinks it's a great opportunity, and it can open doors
in the business.

"But Mami, I'd like, for a change, to decide on my own.
Maybe to not run it by anyone at all, because then everybody has an opinion, and it's not even about me anymore,
you know? It's about what they think I should do and what
they think I should want, and never about what I might
really like. Last year I told Daddy I was taking a semester off
to study Italian in Rome. Oh my God, he almost had a heart
attack!"

She sighs.

"Well, then he spoke with the conservatory in Rome and
set me up there for classes, and of course, I didn't want to do
it anymore. The whole point was to have a change of air, of
perspective.

"Anyway. I'm just going to try and relax here. Think
things over. Go to the club. Run. I'll let you know what
happens.

"And Daddy is well. He's shooting a movie right now,
and he's getting all these accolades. He was nominated for
a Golden Globe, you know? He could win. He really could.
It's this story about a gay magician. I know, very esoteric.
But the book was written by Ann Patchett—do you remember, Mami? She's the one who wrote *Bel Canto,* that book I
told you I loved so much. The cinematography is just beautiful. Daddy really has such a great eye."

Gabriella tries to think of all the things she would have liked to tell her mother this past year alone, but of course, they're lost now. Gone with the moment in which they happened.

"Record it now or lose it forever" is one of her dad's favorite phrases, what he uses to justify his ever-present digital cameras.

"He painted the house," she says suddenly, the image springing to her mind. "It's yellow now. It looks really, really dramatic, but stylish, because the bougainvilleas finally grew in, and they're purple and fuchsia. Great contrasts. You would like it," she adds with a smile. "At least, I think you would."

In the distance, Gabriella sees Nini walking toward them and turns to her mother one last time.

"Bye for now, Mami," she tells her, giving her coffin a kiss.

"Adiós, abuelo," she says, giving Grandfather a kiss, too. Today she's ignored him and now it makes her feel a little guilty. But she needed a girl-to-girl talk. She thinks he'd understand.

"I'll be back soon," Gabriella promises and steps out into the sunlight.

Helena

Querida Gabriella:

No, I will not let you forget where you come from. Half of you is from the Northern Hemisphere. Half of you is from the South, from here. It doesn't seem like a world away, but it is.

On a clear day, from this terrace, you can see the snow peaks that are three states away.

You'll see that the grass is greener and the sky is bluer, and no matter how long you stay away, you can always come back. There was a time when I thought I had lost this, when I was lulled into thinking that I didn't need it. I used to scoff at these people—the fake Latinos, I would say to myself—who stop going back.

And then I became one myself.

One year. Two. Three.

There is such comfort in predictability. It makes you brave, the capacity to function in a world that actually works, where there is little risk in getting up in the morning, where mundane tasks are truly mundane. You can be brave because you know nothing can hurt you.

You grow, because nothing prevents you from growing. Until you need something else again, and then you go back. I

*waited. For as long as I could. Until the colors started to fade
from my comfortable days.*

   *I didn't even know what I missed, or what I needed, until I
went back.*

He called at nine this morning.

What was it about these Cali men, I thought, who can go
to bed at 4 a.m., having drunk a liter of whiskey, and wake
up three hours later feeling as if nothing had happened?

"Helenita, telephone," my mother said, softly but insistently knocking on my door before pushing it open.

"It's Juan José, doll. I'm sorry, I told him you were asleep,
but he said it was urgent."

My mother, who is the most consummately considerate person I have ever met, had turned off the ringer on
the phone in my room and drawn the double blinds on the
ceiling-to-floor windows, so I'd never be woken up unless it
was absolutely necessary.

In bed, I lay still, considering the implications of this call.

There were none, I finally decided. Or none that I could
discern with just five hours of sleep.

"Helena," my mother insisted, from the door.

"Okay, okay," I finally answered. "I'm picking up."

And I did, holding the phone against my shoulder until
my mother, who looked more than a tad inquisitive, quietly
shut the door behind her.

"Hello," I said huskily.

"Hey, wake up, sleepyhead!"

"Isn't it too early to be this cheerful?" I answered crossly.
Was the man on amphetamines?

"Of course not. It's a beautiful day outside."

What was I supposed to answer to this? Chatting about the weather was not an urgent matter. This was ridiculous.

He sensed my impatience, because he started to speak, and I could tell he was a little bit nervous. I mean, he really was. Jamming his words together in one breath, like people do when they're given ten seconds to give a five-minute speech.

"Listen, I woke you up because I'm going to the farm in Ginebra this morning to take care of some business. I have to be back by five, so I have to be there by eleven. I thought it'd be good for your book. It's a great house, and you could look around all you want without anyone else there. We could stop in a couple other places on the way back if we have time. And"—he went on before I could say anything—"my mayordomo knows the area like no one else. He can tell you the history of every house. He can tell you about every legend and every ghost."

"Ghosts. What ghosts?" I laughed despite myself.

"Hey, if you want to find out, this is your chance," he replied. "I can pick you up in forty-five minutes. Can you make it?"

I curled my hair around my finger, my nervous tick.

Could I make it?

"It just happened," my brother Julián had told Mercedes the night she found out he'd been having an affair with his assistant.

"Things don't just happen, Helena," she told me later, after she filed for the divorce. "You allow them to happen. That's the difference between your brother and me. He thinks events are out of your control. But you always have a choice. And with affairs, it's about saying no at the beginning, by refusing to even let it be an option."

I wasn't like Julián. I wasn't like Mercedes.

There wouldn't be an end to say no to. There wouldn't even be a beginning to say no to.

Just a day that will come and will go.

My book. It would help my book.

Our family had never been into farms. They were doctors and architects and attorneys. I was photographing this book from an aesthetic, architectural point of view, but having the inside history would give it added perspective, no?

Why was I trying to justify my actions?

At my age, I didn't need to justify anything to anyone.

"Yes, I can make it," I said as I sat up in bed and looked around, wondering what to wear.

Gabriella

After three days, Gabriella no longer wakes up with a stab of apprehension in the pit of her stomach. After three days, she can forget the call and the what-if. There is neither to be had. The weight of the decision has been lifted off her shoulders, and she feels immensely happy and relieved.

In the evenings, she calls her father and talks about other things. Trivial chitchat. The kind that simply provides more comfort than silence. It soothes her to speak with him; it always has. They can spend hours digressing over a book, discussing a shoot. But now, for the first time, she's careful about what she mentions: her workout schedule, outings with Juan Carlos that are controlled and predictable—dinner, drinks, dancing one night—with people she's known for years and years. People who are safe, whom any father would approve of unless the surface was scratched too deep.

"Are you thinking about your future?" he invariably asks, because he just can't help himself.

"I'm thinking!" she says, trying not to snap at him.

She's thinking that what she's been doing all these years maybe isn't what she wants to do anymore. Sometimes music flows to her and from her, but sometimes it doesn't. Lately, that happens more and more, and she can't seem to find what she had and what made her special, and she wonders if one can simply grow out of talent. But she can't tell her father that because he'd be so disappointed in her, so disappointed to find out she's not extraordinary after all.

Lying on her bed, her feet propped up against the headboard, Gabriella gnaws at her thumb.

"What's eating *you* up to make you do that?" she hears Angel ask in her mind.

She tells herself she's already forgotten her one-night stand. But could you even call it that? A one-night dance, maybe. One night. Period.

In the beginning, the thought crossed her mind that Juan Carlos would bring it up in front of their friends.

"Guess who Gabriella's new boyfriend is," he'd say, laughing over drinks.

It is, she'd admit, perfect fodder for teasing.

Gabriella and the Thug.

But Juan Carlos doesn't do things like that. She constantly underestimates this man, because he *is* a man at twenty-four, with a grown-up's sensibility to social norms that paralyzes her and fills her with self-doubt.

It's always been that way, ever since they were children.

"Gabriella, you can't wear that!"

"Gabriella, I know in the States no one cares what you do or how you act, but here, we do."

She has always kowtowed to him. As a child she was painfully shy and awkward with people her age. Half of her schooling had taken place with tutors on movie sets, where her friends were child actors with overbearing moms—moms that she sometimes wished she had. In the evenings, she would put on headphones and practice on the Clavinova her father let her bring with her since she turned ten and it became apparent that piano lessons weren't just another distraction.

She doesn't kowtow to Juan Carlos anymore, though. She's beautiful now. But inexplicably, she still wants to please him.

"Well, he hasn't called me, just thought I'd let you know," she countered that morning at the club, while running around the golf course.

"Who?" he asked nonchalantly.

"Angel Silva, of course," she replies, laughing.

"Don't know him," Juan Carlos answers shortly, picking up his pace as he climbs the hill that leads to the ninth hole.

The view is breathtaking from there, sweeping down the fairway dotted with mango trees, along the river that borders the course, and down below to the stables.

But he doesn't stop or even break his stride, merely looking back at her and shouting, "You're falling behind, prima!" and just like that drops the subject and the name from his existence.

And she did, too. Well, at least she's trying, and by force of will, even the remarkable color of Angel's eyes starts to slip into oblivion.

Helena

Querida Gabriella:

Las Ceibas is a three-hundred-year-old home named after the ceibas—the weeping willows—that are planted by the river that crosses the garden in front of the house.

According to the legend, the trees were planted in honor of an Indian princess, Atuni, who lived in the area. The entire valley is peppered with Indian burial sites, and they say Las Ceibas was built near or on top of one. That's where the story comes from. The land was granted to the Montoya family by the Spanish crown. That's where the word hacienda comes from, you see? From the hacendado period of the fifteenth and sixteenth centuries.

The Montoyas claimed the land and built it up, even though the Indians fought them on it. It was sacred Indian land and shouldn't be touched.

But the Montoyas wanted the home along the river. They compromised. The house is built apart from the burial ground, although it's hard to say what is what any longer. The grounds have shifted during the centuries.

What everyone swears is true is that Gerardo Montoya fell

in love with an Indian girl—Araceli—the daughter of one of the caciques of the region.

She was baptized with a Spanish name, which means "altar from the sky."

Of course, it was doomed. They were split by religion—the baptism was really a front—language and ethnicity. He had stolen her people's land. But she. She loved him.

You can imagine. She'd never seen anyone like him. Tall—because even though the Spaniards of the day were tiny, they were still taller than the Indians—and bearded and what was most remarkable of all, he had green eyes.

And she was supposed to be sublime and graceful and, on top of that, a healer, widely respected even by the other tribes.

It is said that both went against their parents' wishes, meeting clandestinely at the waterfall that still lies within the hacienda's boundaries. She even cast a spell upon her father, so he wouldn't realize she went missing for hours on end.

But, of course, he found out, because people are envious of others' happiness, and they made sure he knew.

One evening, as Araceli went to meet her lover, she was intercepted by her father and his men. Would they have killed her because of her dishonor?

It's hard to say. But Araceli panicked. She ran along the river's edge, and in looking back, tripped on a rock perched high on a cliff and fell to the water and to her death.

Gerardo planted the willows in her honor, and now, the trees weep for Araceli every time her spirit passes from the waterfall down to the river that runs in front of the house.

They say Gerardo never married, and the Montoya name died with him. The hacienda was transferred to another Spanish noble, and through the years its lineage was lost.

But the story of Araceli and Gerardo has remained in local lore.

Those who stay overnight at the house swear that some evenings, you can truly hear the willows weep.

The house is now owned by a friend of mine. A friend from long, long ago, Juan José Solano. His family bought the hacienda a century ago.

They call him Jota Jota, which is JJ in Spanish. Isn't that funny?

Actually, it isn't. People are their names. If they're not, they become them. Like Araceli.

Frivolous people invariably have frivolous names.

But only a few, a very brave few, Gabriella, ever change their names.

I told you what your name meant, didn't I? A strong woman, close to God.

I hope, Gabriella, that you never change your name.

I hope, Gabriella, that you grow up to become your name.

I, on the other hand, am an Helena, named after my grandmother and totally unfit for my name. Helenas are gorgeous creatures; impassive, elegant, proper, in command.

I am none of those things. I'm askew, the antithesis of Helena. Surely someone must have seen that from the moment I was born with this Medusa hair.

But Juan José must have been born a Juan José. Dignified, aristocratic, traditional. Chivalrous, even.

How could they have reduced him to a banal JJ?

Maybe a real Helena would have looked for a JJ. A yin to her yang.

But because I wasn't a real Helena, I always looked for a Juan José. But I never knew he was there, until now.

Gabriella

She had rehearsed the meeting that would never take place a million times in her mind. In all the scenarios, she is right and he is wrong. In all the scenarios, she is impeccable, she looks like old money, and she has a guy by her side. In all the scenarios, he has a girl by his side, too. A girl like him. The kind that wears very tight white jeans, heavy makeup, and a Louis Vuitton bag that could be real or could be fake. In all the scenarios, she acknowledges him slightly, like one would a servant. She goes on her way, and he looks at her longingly, knowing she was right and he is hopelessly wrong.

She expected the meeting would never take place, but of course, it does. And in it, she's wrong and he's right.

She's sweaty and flushed and unappealing, straight out of a five-mile run, in for a quick stop at the supermarket, wearing over her spandex shorts loose sweatpants that make her butt look droopy. She sees him enter her aisle at the precise moment she's plucking a box of tampons from the shelf. Their eyes meet briefly, his move on, and it occurs to her, for the first time, that he might not even remember her.

But as quickly as his eyes move on, they move back, and

his mouth slowly, knowingly, curves into that sideways smile that reached her three nights ago.

"Gabriella," he says simply. It's not a greeting or a question, but a statement, and she knows, unequivocally, that she, too, has been a part of his waking days.

"Angel? Angel!" The voice interrupts the answer she's unable to give, and the girl that steps onto the aisle with his name on her lips is beautiful in the way well-kept girls with straight blonde hair and fake breasts can be.

With her box of tampons and her ugly sweats Gabriella is utterly at a loss.

Only the arrival of Edgar, competent, commanding, practical, reminds her that she's not a player in this contest. "It's nice to see you, Angel," she says demurely as she slides by him on her way to the register and out the door.

Later, many days later, he told her he'd had one of his bodyguards follow her home.

But that afternoon, he only sends the roses. Five dozen red roses that the doorman brings up through the back door with a card inside a sealed envelope.

"Some things are really more beautiful up close. Angel."

"Who is this Angel?" Nini asks when she comes home that evening and sees the outrageous bouquet.

"Just a boy I met, Nini. At the party," Gabriella says shortly.

"Do I know him?" presses Nini. She always presses.

"I don't know," says Gabriella, deliberately evasive.

"I need to know who he is for you to go out with him," says Nini, who thinks every stranger is a possible kidnapper.

Gabriella doesn't remind Nini that she's twenty-one years old and can go out with whomever she pleases. In this house, that wouldn't fly. And if Nini knew who Angel's father was... Well, Gabriella truly can't imagine what the reaction could be.

"Nini, I met him at the party," she reiterates simply. "With Juan Carlos. Juan Carlos knows him."

That night, she lies on her bed and looks at the roses, which she's insisted on placing in her room. No one has ever sent her five dozen roses before, and the extravagance of the gesture thrills her.

She turns on the light in her room and looks at the card once more. *Some things are really more beautiful up close,* it reads in bold, block letters, and she knows that he wrote it himself, that he can get anyone to do anything for him, but that this, he's done alone.

Helena

His face was framed by the lens of my camera.

He had black eyes and blacker hair that he combed straight back, exposing a widow's peak he inherited from his Spanish grandfather. From the passenger seat of his black Ford Explorer I trained my lens on him patiently, zeroing in on the thin nose that's very slightly hooked and haughty. But then he looked at me sideways and smiled, displaying a surprising dimple beneath his mouth, and the arrogance of his profile dissipated. He drove with his elbow propped on the open window, steering with one hand, smoking with the other, never taking his eyes off the road as he pushed in the cigarette lighter by the stereo, waited until it popped out, lit the cigarette, and inhaled deeply.

He liked to talk. To pontificate. I liked it. I was lulled by his running commentary. How the endless row of tall acacias that divide the road in two is the work of a group of radical, well-educated bourgeois women, who had raised the money to plant the trees after countless accidents happened at night, because drivers were blinded by the bright lights.

He told me how the sugarcane is not cut by machinery, but by the hands of dozens of shirtless men wielding machetes relentlessly under the Andean sun. How they were paid by the weight of their cut cane. How in their rush to cut more and more, accidents frequently happened: lost fingers, slashed calves.

How, how, how.

From behind my lens, I wondered how it was that I'd lived here an entire childhood and never knew these things, never saw them, and I inhaled his cigarette smoke with him, tuning into the cadence of his breathing, the rhythm of his words.

When I was a little girl, my mother would complain incessantly about cigarettes and the smoke, but now, I find it comforting. When I'm in Los Angeles, it reminds me of my father, and I can picture him, smoking and reading in the library. When I finally snapped a picture of Juan José, wisps of smoke clung to his hair as he talked and gestured with his glowing Marlboro.

Gabriella

Gabriellita, I've been meaning to tell you," Nini says over breakfast. "We're tearing the old house down."

"But why?" Gabriella says, stunned.

"I can't rent it. It's too big and in too bad a shape. I can't afford to just have it lying there. Mi amor, I'm not going back to live there again. Neither is your uncle. We're going to tear it down next month. Your uncle is going to make a building, and one of the apartments will be yours," she adds comfortingly.

Gabriella looks at her cereal bowl, the milk stuck at her throat. She feels like crying, even though she's never spent any time in the house. By the time she started coming here, Nini had already moved to the apartment and the house had become home to her uncle's architecture firm. He would let Gabriella visit, and she'd play with the turtles and the fish in the garden pond and go up and down the curved marble staircase that swept into the foyer.

"I'm going to live here when I grow up," she would always tell Nini, because she always yearned for a house with a sweeping staircase like this one. She had a picture of her mother descending the staircase on her wedding day, one hand on the balustrade, the other holding the long train of her ivory wedding gown.

The dress was Nini's, and Nini had promised Gabriella the dress would one day be hers, too. In Gabriella's mind, the dress went with the house, with the staircase, with the huge garden, with the fountain and the orchids that grew on the acacia branches.

"I'll buy it from you," she'd been saying about the house, even as a little girl. "And I'll fix it up and I can sleep in my mother's room and you can sleep in your old room again."

But the upkeep of the house had proven too much even for her uncle. He'd thrown in the towel when rain leaked in, for the hundredth time, after a particularly big storm. That time it got into the electrical system, causing a short circuit and making all the computers in the firm crash.

The house has been empty for five years. But now, for the first time, Gabriella realizes the difference between simply being empty and not being there at all.

"Nini, can you give me the keys?" she asks. "I want to go and look around for one last time."

"Of course, nena," says Nini. She reaches across the table and brushes a stray hair from Gabriella's face. "I know what you mean. I cry every time I go in there and think of what it was."

In the afternoon she walks slowly up the hill, the keys tucked in her jeans pocket. The house is only a few blocks away, but farther up, on a street where stately homes have succumbed to luxury condominiums. The house is not the last one standing, but it looks ready to go. The stone walls, now covered with moss, give it a haunted mansion air it never had in its haughtier days of parties on the terrace staffed by white-clad waiters bearing silver trays. Even the grass on the curb is overrun with weeds. But the house, windowless on its entrance side, seems impervious to the humiliation the years have brought. Gabriella slowly turns the key to the top lock of the huge metal door—her grandfather had insisted on a metal door as a safeguard against savvy thieves with God knows what kind of tools—then to the bottom dead bolt, and eases the door open.

She's momentarily startled, as she is every time, by the sunlight that drenches the main room. It's inescapable, pouring in from the wraparound terrace on the other side of the house and the now blindless, curtainless windows that look out at the park below. Every room has a view—that was such an object of pride and joy for the architect who built the house—but now the tall-paned windows, so avant-garde in their day, look sadly dated; the paint is peeling from the wooden balustrades and the wooden, barren bookcases, struck daily by the relentless, tropical sun. Even the staircase marble has faded under decades of foot traffic and no polish.

Gabriella unlocks the top and bottom hinges of the glass double doors that lead to the terrace and pushes. The door is stuck. How long has it been since anyone has swept the house? She pushes again and again, until the debris stuck underneath gives way and the doors swing back.

She gasps out loud. The garden has practically eaten up the house; the vines have climbed from the garden below to the terrace on the second floor, and the branches from the acacia tree hang over the balustrade, the leaves aggressively poking at the bedroom windows. Down below, the grass looks like it hasn't been cut in more than a year; if she were to go down, it would reach her waist. Mango season has come and gone, and the rotting fruit is barely visible in the green tangle of weeds and unruly plants. Even from upstairs she can smell its sweet, pervasive decay.

In a month, she thinks in wonderment, this will all be gone. Just getting rid of the acacia, which is monstrous and straining against the boundaries of the stone wall, will alone probably cause the house to crumble; its roots have taken over the entire garden, and Gabriella sees them, like knotted arms, extending into the fountain on the other side, lifting the tiles from their foundation.

Even in its current condition, Gabriella loves this house. She's convinced there are ghosts here, although she's never seen one. They are good ghosts, she always tells Nini, because only good people lived here.

One summer, when she was fifteen, Juan Carlos got a Ouija board, and they spent afternoons on end going from room to room, trying to summon her mother. When it didn't work with just the two of them, Juan Carlos brought in his friends; they needed additional energy, he said, and they spent hours locked up in his grandfather's library—her mother's favorite room—asking, "Are there spirits here? If there are any spirits here, please give us a sign!"

But the lights never flickered, a gust of wind never materialized, and their fingers on the Ouija board pointer stayed immobile, even when they went up to Helena's walk-in closet and huddled with the lights off.

"It means she's at peace, Gabby," Juan Carlos told her comfortingly. "It means she's already left the world of the living. Only spirits who have unresolved issues hang out."

Now Gabriella walks around, taking in the view from her grandparents' room—the biggest in the house. Looking for...what? Nothing.

Everything.

"Is there anything left there, Nini?" she'd asked before coming, because she loves to explore, sift through her grandmother's things, take home scarves and purses and old cocktail dresses from the '70s that are way too short for her, but show off her legs like a dream.

She's never seen any clothes in the closets of this house, just boxes of stuff—papers and books and scores of business folders dealing with transactions made decades before she was born.

"Oh, baby. I think I've taken everything out. Everything that was worth anything, you've probably looked through before," Nini said. "Some books and records, I think that's all there is now."

That's all there is now.

Her mother's room is right in front of her grandparents'.

How did she manage to sneak in nights when she came in after curfew? Gabriella wonders.

She swings the bedroom door back and forth. It creaks. How did she close it without making any noise?

Her grandmother never gets into this kind of detail about her mother.

She was beautiful. Artistic. Sensitive. She had so many boyfriends. Sometimes two at a time! This part she always accompanies with laughter.

But Gabriella has never heard about where she went, what she wore, what books she read. When she comes inside her mother's space, she always wonders. Were those boyfriends good-looking? Nerdy? Did they look like her beautiful father? In her mother's arsenal of photographs, she has rarely found pictures of her mother with anyone else.

Helena saw the world through her camera, but she rarely photographed people. Her subjects were places, things. She made a living of giving life to what was lifeless.

And what about her? thought Gabriella. Who was her confidante?

Elisa was her mother's good friend; Gabriella has always regarded her as an aunt, always imagined she and her mother were like sisters.

Imagines because as an only child she cannot fathom what it's like to grow up with someone close to your age in the same house.

Did her mother talk—really talk—with her uncle? He's told her they did. He talks of pranks they played together when they were kids. But then again, he's not a man of many words, much less confidences. Gabriella can't picture him in this room, sitting at the foot of her mother's bed, exchanging secrets.

Gabriella has her father, who is more than a father, who read her to sleep every night of her childhood, who would pack her up and take her on location, paint their trailer pink just for her, allow her to watch any movie she wished until he finished the day's shooting deep into the night. Just as she has no notion of a sibling, she has less so of what a mother's function would have been. She only has Nini.

"My kindred spirit," her grandmother calls her. "God took your mother away, but he made sure she had you first. For that, I will always be grateful."

Gabriella looks around her mother's bedroom and only sees a room that's harshly bare under the midday sun, with peeling yellow paint on the walls and missing linoleum tiles on the floor. Anyone could have once slept here. Everything that belonged to her mother has been neatly transplanted into Gabriella's room in Nini's apartment. Her mother's bed is her bed; her mother's vanity is her vanity. Even the book-shelves have her mother's old Nancy Drew collection.

Gabriella looks inside the bathroom, which is pink and prissy, two things she's never imagined her mother to be. Was she?

She turns toward the closet and tries several keys in its lock before the right one fits and turns. It's a huge walk-in closet, every girl's dream: a dress rack all along the back, and shelves along both sides. It's big enough to comfortably fit furniture, and that's exactly what her mother did, turning it into a darkroom.

It was the only room in the house that sunlight couldn't reach, Nini had told her. So Helena set up shop there when she was only sixteen. This much Nini tells her. That her mother would spend hours—hours—every day, developing film, experimenting with different exposures. The smell of the fluids impregnated her clothes and they had to be taken out and placed in the guest room.

Gabriella never saw this closet as a darkroom, simply as a closet. By the time she came around, all the photography equip-

ment was long gone. She flicks on the light switch and is gratified to see that one lonely lightbulb manages to sputter alive.

There is nothing on the floor, nothing on the shelves. She
opens the drawers and finds them empty as well. When she
pushes them shut, the sound of wood connecting on wood
echoes against the bare walls.

Almost as an afterthought, she looks up and sees the edge
of a box, on the very top shelf, almost touching the ceiling.
She wonders why she hasn't noticed it before. Maybe it wasn't
there, or maybe, like most people, she never looked up above
her head. She gets on her tiptoes, but can't reach the edge of
the box. It's too high, even for her. Gabriella takes a jump,
but only succeeds in pushing the box farther out of reach.
This is silly, she thinks. I'm going to have roaches and spi-
ders raining down on me any second now.

But her curiosity is piqued. She puts her foot on the ledge
underneath the drawers and steps up, reaching for the cardboard box, dragging it toward her, and finding it, to her
surprise, light. It falls, landing on the floor behind her.

"Damn it," she curses quietly under her breath, and steps
down, her hands black with dust. This silly closet is depress-
ing me, she thinks, and kicks the box out of the black hole
and into the bedroom.

It's sealed. Gabriella runs her fingers over the tape, surprised. Nini never seals a thing, she thinks. She hesitates for
a few seconds. The whole thing seems...private. But then
again, nothing too private would be kept in an empty house
for five years, would it?

Gabriella sits on the floor and peels the tape off and opens the cardboard flaps, slowly taking out the blue tissue paper lying on top.

Underneath, there are clothes, neatly folded and pressed. She takes out the shirt—a gauzy red shirt, clean, but ripped in shreds. Gabriella looks at it uncomprehendingly. Is it a costume?

She takes out the next item: jeans. They're worn and also ripped, but wearable. Tiny jeans, she observes, for a tiny person.

She digs further. No shoes. But there's a purse. An over-sized red leather purse, with a long thick strap and a big brass buckle. The kind you hang across your body and can carry all your worldly possessions inside.

Gabriella frowns. So bizarre, she thinks, but gingerly undoes the buckle and opens the purse, reaches inside, and finds what she didn't know she was looking for.

At first, she only sees the wallet. It's red, too, soft, beautifully worn red leather that matches the bag and the shirt and, now she's certain, the shoes that aren't there. She opens it and searches slowly, methodically, for proof that this is hers, and finds it in, of all things, a California driver's license.

Helena Gómez Richard
DOB: 01-10-1960
253 Costa Drive, Santa Monica, CA 90404
Height: 5-01
Sex: F
Eyes: Yellow
Hair: Brown

She reads all this deliberately, one time, two, three times, until the words become a blur, because she needs to catch her breath and still her heart, which she can hear in the still-ness of the house, and stop the tears that are pushing against the eyelids she has now shut very, very tightly. When that doesn't work, she digs her fingernails into her arms, hard, and lets that pain obliterate the tears.

She opens her eyes and looks at the picture. Her mother is smiling at the camera. Her smile is happy and sincere, and her hair is pulled back in a shocking pink bandanna.

She must have left it during one of her trips. Her wallet. Her things. She looks inside again. An American Express card, a Mastercard, a library card, an access card for the country club, a health insurance card, a baby picture. Gabri-ella's baby picture.

Gabriella takes it out very, very slowly, because her fingers are trembling and she's afraid she might drop everything. She holds the little picture carefully between her thumb and her index finger, looking at it curiously, unbelievingly.

Her mother carried her baby picture in her purse. In it, Gabriella's eyes are huge and blueish in a serious face with a determined mouth. She now touches the locket that sits at the hollow of her throat. She knows she also carries the same photo in her locket. She didn't know her mother owned a red wallet and that her photo traveled with her. She fingers the folds of the leather and finds not money, but a thick, folded piece of paper. She takes it out slowly. Duty free. A receipt from duty free.

She still doesn't get it. Not even when she sees what the

receipt is for: whiskey and perfume. Not even when she sees the date: December 21. Not even when she sees the city: Miami.

Her mother went to Miami. Bought a bottle of Johnnie Walker Black Label whiskey for her grandfather and a bottle of Shalimar for her grandmother at the duty-free shop.

And then.

And then, she got on a plane bound for Cali. A plane that crashed. And her mother died. She died. She really died, Gabriella tells herself, panicky, because she's visited her grave.

In the bright sunlight, she grows suddenly cold and looks around nervously. Is her mother's ghost here, after all? Has she done something wrong? This rotting house is empty, except for her and this box full of things that's been left behind for her to find.

She feels nauseated, like she's never felt before. She hears a gasping sound and realizes it's coming from her. Like an old woman. Her heart is beating so quickly her breathing can't keep up. Gabriella claws at her throat anxiously, pulling at her T-shirt, even though it isn't tight, even though it's nowhere near her neck.

It takes her several minutes, holding on to the now-empty box, before she can look inside the purse again.

The notebook is lying at the bottom. A red leather-bound notebook. She runs her hands over it softly, divining what's inside. Like the wallet, it has the worn look of something cherished and much touched. Comfortable.

The binding is stiff, and the sheets of paper, when she opens the notebook, stick together, thick with humidity. She gently separates them, careful not to shred the paper, until she gets to the very first page.

The words jump out at her, cursive letters, written in bold, black ink.

Querida Gabriella:
  You were born today, July 7, at 7:32 a.m. Weight: 8 pounds, 6 ounces. A big girl! A perfect baby girl, the doctor said.

She doesn't know how long she sits there, looking at the first line.

Querida Gabriella.
Querida Gabriella.
Querida Gabriella.

Gabriella. Gabriella. Her name. It's for her.

This time she feels the cold reach deep inside her, like an ice pick that has gotten inside her chest and is literally piercing her heart. Her mother is touching her. She feels it. She is touching the last thing her mother touched.

Gabriella drops the book, as if the jacket were burning her instead of turning her fingers to ice, and sends it clattering across the room. She rocks back and forth on her knees and looks at it, lying half open, the letters simply scratches on a paper, blurry because her eyes are now full of tears, but this time she makes no effort to stop crying. She needs to get up to get it back and read.

She needs to move. But she can't. Is it all for her? Letters to her, lying there, dead, unopened, intact, for all these years? In the emptiness of the house with its cracking floors and escalating vegetation it feels—absurdly, she tells herself, but she can't help it—like she's somehow set a curse in motion. Why did no one find it before?

Her cell phone has been ringing, but all she hears is the rushing in her ears, and she covers them tightly with the palms of her hands. Outside, the light changes, and when Edgar and her grandmother finally come to the house looking for her, the afternoon sun hits the kneeling figure in the middle of the room. The illumination is perfect for a natural light photograph.

That night, she sleeps with the notebook clutched tightly in her arms and the light on.

She hasn't told her father about the notebook, and she's refused to give it to Nini. She doesn't really know why. Maybe because Nini never told her about her mother's possessions, either.

"It was one of those things that wasn't supposed to happen," Nini tells her that evening, stroking Gabriella's hair gently, insistently, as she lies on her bed, her back to her grandmother, looking at the wall.

"When I learned that her things were actually in one piece, well, I just didn't know what to do," Nini continues. "What is the point in having possessions without the person? And so, I put them inside the box. And everything else that had to do with that day, I put away. I locked it out of my memory—as much as I could, that is—and I put it as far away from me physically as I could. I made a conscientious decision to forget.

"I hadn't even remembered where I'd put it until today. I just know that at the time, I wanted it as far away from my mind and my soul as humanly possible. I wanted to remember her alive and triumphant as she always was. Not dead. That was my daughter. Not the person with the dead face whose clothes I put away.

"After your grandfather died, I moved out of the house and into the new apartment. I moved here, I moved your mother's room here, and your father started to send you down. That's when I realized that I, too, had died that night. Because when you started to come down to visit, I started to live again. I started to feel again. You made me laugh again with your earnest stories and your beautiful face.

"And this box, with these clothes and this purse and all these things that I can see mean so much to you, I forgot. I forgot because I couldn't bear to remember.

"Please forgive me, Gabriella," she says, her voice sounding so profoundly, so hopelessly sad that Gabriella finally turns around and brings her hand up to her grandmother's.

"Forgive me, Gabriellita. I did the best I could."

Helena

I shut the garage door behind me, took my shoes off at the foot of the stairs, and slowly, quietly walked up, a practice I'd perfected in my teen years, when Julián and I would routinely violate our curfew. Our frequent inquisitor was my father, an insomniac with a voracious appetite for chocolate ice cream and books, who would raid the refrigerator past midnight. Years of lack of sleep at the hospital had made him comfortable with being awake at night.

I should have known my father would be there tonight as well, but my long absence from Cali made me complacent.

He was on the sofa, reading a book under the light of a single lamp, a lit cigarette poised on the ashtray, the TV on but muted in front of him.

"Why, Papi, what are you doing up?" I automatically asked, feeling as guilty as I had when I was fifteen, caught going barefoot up the stairs at an unconscionable five in the morning.

My father peered at me intently over his reading glasses. "Muñequita," he said with slight emphasis, calling me by my childhood nickname—little doll—and from that tiny edge I could tell how terribly upset he was, this man who never got upset.

"It's late," he finally said calmly, but half questioning, when it's obvious I have nothing to say.

"I'm sorry, I lost track of time," I finally offered, even though I thought that I was way too old to have to give explanations for any behavior I engaged in. "Good night, Papi," I said quickly, resolutely, from across the sitting room, starting to move toward my room.

"Helenita," my father said quietly, stopping my progress. "You shouldn't be out this late. I was worried. And your husband called."

Gabriella. My first thought was Gabriella.

"Did something happen to Gabriella?"

"No," my father answered in that same measured tone. "Marcus just wanted to speak with you. You really shouldn't be out at these hours," he repeated.

I was about to talk back, give him a piece of my mind, but the look in his eyes stopped me. It wasn't anger. It was disappointment, I saw with a pang of regret.

I had disappointed my father.

Damn it, and why couldn't I? A lifetime of doing what appeared to be right, of pleasing everyone, of being the accomplished, brilliant daughter who married the accomplished, brilliant filmmaker.

I was five thousand miles away from Los Angeles. Who was I hurting? Who would know?

Because, if Marcus knew, I couldn't stand it. I couldn't begin to imagine the look on his face. But now, looking at my father's face, I no longer knew if it was him or Marcus that I was worried about.

My friend Elisa and I spoke often about infidelity. The what-ifs.

"What if your husband finds out you're cheating on him?" Elisa queried.

"You deny it," I said flatly, unequivocally.

"What if he finds you in bed with someone else?" asked Elisa triumphantly.

"You deny it," I said again, shrugging. "He's wrong. He's mistaken. It's not what it seems. You always deny it, Elisa," I insisted earnestly. "If they love you, they'll believe you."

I now wanted to ask my father, ask him if he was ever in this place, of wanting but not wanting. But speaking was too daunting. I forced my mind to go blank. I looked sullenly at the rug, a Middle Eastern black and burgundy pattern that curled from one corner into the other and the other and the other, and then started again in an endless repetition. If I looked at it long enough, I could pretend I wasn't here.

"You're an intelligent woman, Helena," my father finally added, when he didn't get a reaction beyond my silence. "Act intelligently."

He paused one more time, looked at me intently, waiting for an answer, an explanation, then pushed his glasses back up on his nose and deliberately resumed his reading.

"Good night, mi amor," he said with finality, not looking up.

"Hasta mañana, Papi," I answered, chastised. I could feel his unspoken censure, and for the first time since I could ever remember, I didn't kiss him good night.

In my room, I slowly took off my clothes, dropping them on the floor, like a child, then went into the bathroom and turned on the shower. I got it to the right temperature, which is almost scalding hot, the way I've always liked it, and I stepped in and let the water and the soap and the shampoo clean off the makeup from my face, the cigarette smell from my hair, his scent that had impregnated every inch of my skin. I stood there for a long time, the water beating down my neck, and when I finished, my back and buttocks were a bright, angry red.

I looked intently at the reflection in the floor-length mirror on the bathroom door as I dried myself, then hung up the towel and removed my wedding band. For the first time since my marriage five years ago, I was completely naked.

I was twenty-nine years old, almost thirty. I had a husband. I had a daughter. Now, I had a lover.

Was I still beautiful? I looked anxiously at myself, closer into the mirror, ran my hands over my breasts, my stomach, my thighs, which startled at my touch. I've long known I have something men crave. It's in the delicacy of my bones, the misleading fragility of my limbs. My breasts were still high and rounded. I knew they were beautiful. I'd been told that. I was told that just tonight. My stomach was still flat, despite the baby. The muscles still defined. I wondered how long it could stay that way. How many more children could it bear before it sagged into middle-aged oblivion. How many more children could I bear before *I* sagged into middle-aged oblivion? Before this body stopped being desirable? Before men stopped asking me to dance?

I looked at my face, still unlined, the skin still taut.

I told myself that this wasn't important. What was important was my husband. My family. My daughter. I had a daughter.

I tried to conjure the feeling of my daughter's breath against my cheek, but all I could feel was his mouth against my breast. Not hers. Not my baby's. His.

Through the open window, I heard the dull beat of salsa music wafting up from one of the homes in the barrio below. This was the soundtrack of my life, this relentless music that never stopped on the weekends.

For the past five years, I've lived in a tree-shaded home in Beverly Hills with a vast front yard and a row of trees that shield me from the world outside. A strict noise ordinance banned any music or loud noise after 11 p.m., and I realized I'd forgotten about the music and the sweat and the anxious imperfections of life here.

Now I could barely remember the quiet of that street anymore. The line between my two lives was stretched so taut, a flicker of my finger could break it and send one end recoiling into itself.

On an impulse, I picked up the phone and dialed Los Angeles, even though it was already 1 a.m. there. But the machine picked up, and I heard my own voice, delivering a friendly California message: "Hi, this is Marcus, Helena, and Gabriella."

"Hi," piped in Gabriella in a baby voice we'd found irresistibly cute when we originally recorded an announcement.

"We can't pick up, but we want to hear from you. Leave a message!"

"Leave a message," Gabriella echoed, then giggled.

"Marcus?" I said urgently. "Marcus, pick up!"

But he didn't, and I remembered that Marcus and Gabriella were spending the weekend with friends up the coast.

I slowly hung up and turned off the lights, leaving the curtains open so I could continue to hear the dull thud of the music and look at a sky heavy with clouds.

In the darkness, I ran my hands over my breasts and brought back his touch, fresh from an hour ago. In the darkness, the only scent I smelled was his as it closed over me.

Gabriella

The diary looks innocuous in the morning light.

She lets it sit on the dresser while she has her coffee and breakfast, while she showers, while she dresses, sneaking furtive looks at it, but forcing herself not to touch it.

When she's ready, she tucks it under her arm, then goes to the kitchen and pours herself another cup of coffee.

She goes to the terrace, where the light is brightest and the hills and the city spread out before her, and the traffic and the shouts from the vendors below remind her that all is well, that things have not come to an end.

Gabriella looks at her mother's handwriting on the first page curiously. She tries to feel a connection with the strokes of the pen, tries to recognize the curve of the words, the cadence of the language.

Helena's entire life has been an anecdote for her, up until this point. Now, she can physically touch her. The last thoughts she placed on paper are now hers.

Helena was nearly thirty-one years old. Not so much older than she is now. She couldn't have imagined that she was writing her last words. Couldn't have imagined things were going to be all over. What would she have done—what would she have written—the next day or the next or the next had she lived?

Gabriella has never believed in fate. Her mother's violent death made her a skeptic. Destinies are carved out by individuals, she always says, and in the middle of everything, accidents simply happen, like thunderstorms.

Now, the pages between her fingers seem to mock everything she's lived by. How many single, independent acts were necessary for this book to end up with her? wonders Gabriella.

She literally holds her mother's life—what's left of it—in her hands. The enormity of the thought stops her for a second.

But just as quickly, she surrenders to the joy of the moment, to the thrill of the possibilities that lie in these words her mother wrote. For her.

Then she slowly, methodically, begins to turn the pages, carefully separating each sheet of paper, smoothing it gently before she reads.

The diary is all written in Spanish. The chronicle of her life. Her baby adventures. Her first steps. Her first haircut. The outfits she wore for Halloween the first four years of her life.

Gabriella turns the pages faster and faster, anxious to read the next word and the next, anxious to go back and make sure she has grasped the significance. How important are these entries? How momentous these daily anecdotes?

The time she had a frighteningly high fever and her parents had to rush her to the emergency room. How her mother slept on a chair at her bedside and looked at her frail self in the bed, attached to tubes and monitors, and how she realized that she was part of her now, as vital as the air she breathed.

The writing vacillates from neat to sloppy, from leisurely to rushed. Where was she when she wrote this? What was she wearing?

Gabriella reads, intent, almost tasting the words, so absorbed, the intrusion inside the narrative initially escapes her.

But then, she goes back, and finds it, again and again, as quickly as cigarette burns forever branding the pages.

Only when she finishes reading the entire diary for the third time does she realize that somewhere along the line the entries have stopped being addressed to her. That her story has become her mother's story, and Gabriella is no longer part of it.

She closes the book firmly on her lap and looks from the terrace at the view before her. It's noon, and the cries of the cicadas in the park across the street are fierce and insistent.

The sun is suddenly piercing bright and she's momentarily blinded. But it doesn't matter. For the first time in months, she has a mental clarity she didn't know she possessed.

When Lucía tells her to pick up the phone, her mind turns as deliberately blank as her eyes that can't see.

"Gabriella," he says, and when she hears her name again, she can almost smell the sound of his voice over the telephone. She no longer considers her father, her grandmother, her cousin, the words that others will inevitably whisper, when she says, "Yes, yes, I want to see you. Yes, I will see you. Yes."

*   *   *

He drives a black Ford Explorer, and he's flanked by a battalion of bodyguards, four in an SUV behind him, four in an SUV in front.

Alone in his car with him, she concentrates on the minutiae of the moment: the way he smells of clean soap, the way the muscles in his arms stretch and contract as he navigates the curves up the mountains, how his hair falls against his eyes.

"So tell me something about you that I don't know, something true," he says, looking straight ahead as he winds up the mountain.

"Like what?" she asks.

"Mmm. Your favorite movie?"

"Oh, God. That's too hard. I've seen every movie ever made, I swear. I can tell you my favorite movies."

"No. One."

Gabriella squeezes her eyes shut. Her world is unraveling and she's talking about movies. She laughs ruefully.

"*The Wizard of Oz*," she finally offers.

"You're joking."

"No, I'm not," she says smiling. "I'm really not. I love *The Wizard of Oz*. Do you know it was the first movie that mixed black-and-white with color? Can you imagine what people must have thought when they walked into those huge theaters from back then and then the screen just exploded in color? I used to watch it every month when I was little. I'd see something new every single time. I still do. And Dorothy was all alone in the world, with Toto. And she had to figure everything out on her own. She had to be so grown-up and so responsible."

Gabriella pictures Dorothy, leaning on the fence, singing "Over the Rainbow."

"She was so pretty," she says musingly.

She feels the tears begin to well behind her sunglasses and she stops, horrified, biting down her tongue.

"So it's your turn," she says, changing the subject. "Tell me something about yourself that I don't know. Something true."

"My favorite movie?" he asks.

"No," she says slowly. "I bet it's *The Godfather: Part II.*"

"How could you possibly know that?" he asks, looking at her incredulously.

"You're a guy," she says simply. "All guys who are serious about movies have one of the *Godfathers* as their favorite. And *The Godfather: Part II* is the best one. Am I right?"

"Well, it's on my top five."

"Okay, so tell me something else," she says. "Like, your favorite ice cream flavor."

"Vanilla," he says without hesitation.

"Oh, I don't believe that. Vanilla is bland! You're not bland."

"*That* is not true," he says. "Vanilla is subtle. It goes with everything. It's adaptable."

"But you don't like everything," Gabriella says, remembering. "You hardly like anything, in fact."

"No," he says calmly, shaking his head. "That's not true, either. I like a lot of things. I just don't like a lot of people. And there's nothing more delicious than vanilla ice cream with hot guava sauce on top. Or vanilla ice cream on a chocolate soufflé."

"Or vanilla ice cream on a hot apple pie," she says slowly.

"Or plain vanilla ice cream, but the homemade kind, where you can taste the cream and the butter, and it's so totally rich, you don't need any other flavor or topping because the purity of the vanilla is enough," he says seriously, in a way that makes her want to taste what he's tasted.

Gabriella looks at him obliquely, trying not to stare as she attempts to divine this otherness he is supposed to have but she can't discern. In the stark light of day, she can see the hint of a beard stubble on his golden skin, the slightest of lines around his eyes—not fine lines from squinting at the sun, but actual creases—though he can't be much older than her, and a very faint white scar that hooks from his jawline and into his face, like a thin, transparent half-moon.

She wonders yet again what it is about him that makes her want to be so physically close, makes her want to reach out and trace the marks that break up his skin. She feels empowered suddenly. If she were to do just that—touch him—nobody would even know. And if they did, how could it hardly matter. Look at her mother, at her sequence of actions, and not a single consequence as a result.

She feels almost detached from herself, ethereal. It's been so long since she's done something, anything, without considering what others will say; she's forgotten how liberating it can feel to just—be.

"Can I see what music you have?" she asks, even as she leans forward and starts to flip through the iPod hooked to the stereo, until she finds Jorge Celedón and Jimmy Zambrano's "Qué Bonita Es Esta Vida," a hymn to positive thoughts, she thinks, and cranks up the volume.

She rolls down her window and leans back on her seat,

feeling the air cool down the higher up they go. When his hand finally reaches out for hers, she closes her eyes for just an instant at the impact of his touch, then remains perfectly still, her eyes ever trained on the scenery below as he runs his fingers proprietarily over her knuckles, her wrist, the veins and tendons that run the length of her hands.

He takes her to the house in the mountains. The house her mother photographed for her book. The house his mother bought.

She doesn't know the destination until they get there, and she recognizes the home, nestled at the foot of a hill as they approach from the road above. He must have thought the gesture over carefully, not anticipating it could be the wrong gesture at the wrong time. She will know this house because her mother wrote about it in her journal, photographed it for her book. But right now, the sight of it takes her breath away, leaves her slightly dizzy.

"Angel," she says, holding him back as he steps out of the car, looking at the mountains that beckon around them. "Is it safe to hike? Can we hike alone here?"

He looks at her, puzzled. No one hikes anymore for fear of running into stray guerrillas.

"If we stay within the perimeter, yes," he says carefully. "But that means we can't go too far. I had lunch prepared, though."

"Can we take it?" she asks excitedly. "Let's take a picnic. With a bottle of wine?"

He considers the proposal, and likes it.

"Okay. Okay," he says, smiling his slow, lazy smile. "Let's have a picnic."

She waits for him outside, her back to the house, as he

gives instructions to the cook, to the drivers, to the guards. He goes to them, one by one, speaks quietly, in a tone of voice others can't pick up. His demeanor is contrary to that of any man in control she's ever met, men who like to be seen and heard issuing orders, establishing their place.

He doesn't need to shout to be heard, and momentarily, he reminds her of her father, so preternaturally cool. Except her father doesn't run the equivalent of a small army, and when she looks down as they climb into the hills, she can see his men, posted around the house, near the road.

"We also have guards outside," he tells her, noticing her slight apprehension. He's walking ahead of her, their picnic packed in a backpack, and as he hoists himself up onto a boulder, she sees the bulge of a gun tucked inside his sock.

"Can't you go out without them?" she asks.

Angel continues to climb farther up to a small plateau before he finally answers.

"No." He extends his hand to help her up the last step. "Not right now, anyway," he adds.

They're at a ledge on the side of the mountain. The air is chilly up here, and below them, the hills spread out in deep, green rolls, peppered with villas of varying sizes, the weekend homes where city dwellers go to escape from the heat, their red-tiled roofs shining between the foliage of the trees.

He lights a cigarette and inhales deeply.

"Man, I haven't been up here in a long time." He sighs.

"What do you do?" Gabriella asks him with no preamble. "I mean, do you have a job?"

Only after the words are out does she wonder if the question is extraordinarily naïve or extraordinarily stupid.

"Of course, I have a job," he says with a snort. "Why wouldn't I?"

Gabriella is momentarily chastised, then regains her nerve. She deserves to know these things, she thinks. And he needs to know that; otherwise, what in the world is she doing up on this mountain with him?

"Well," she says carefully, "people say your dad is very rich, and they say he's in jail, and, I'm sorry, but I . . . I'd like to know if you work for his business or if you even need to work. . . ." Gabriella's voice trails off and is met with silence. She thinks of her mother, pictures her maybe lying beside her father in bed, a trove of secrets between them as she pretended to be someone she wasn't any longer. And her father oblivious. Or perhaps, just pretending he didn't see.

She takes a deep breath.

"I'd like to know who you are," she finally says, quietly. "Everyone talks about your father. But hardly anyone talks about *you*."

"I promote concerts," he says, looking at her speculatively. "Not your kind of concerts," he adds. "Not classical music. Big pop shows. Dances during the fair."

"Oh," she says, surprised. Of all things, she hadn't expected this. "Like, who are you bringing during the fair?"

"You know, Grupo Niche, salsa bands for Christmas, all kinds of music. Oscar D'León," he adds with a smile, and she smiles back in complicity, remembering their dance at his party. "I bring music people want to hear," he says matter-of-factly. "I need to sell tickets. But sometimes, I'll just bring music I really like, groups that are a little obscure, a little off center, and hope enough people will want to open their ears to something new."

Angel stops himself. He's reserved by habit, wary of being measured and used.

"I brought Youssou N'Dour last month to the theater, and it was pretty packed," he says tentatively, testing her, hoping she'll say the right thing but still bracing himself for the inevitable "Who?" he's fielded for weeks.

"I love Youssou N'Dour," she says simply.

"I thought you would," he answers, allowing his half smile to tug at the corner of his mouth.

"How did you know I played classical music?" she asks, suddenly registering his full words.

"People talk about your father, but they also talk about you," he says shortly.

He doesn't know what compels him to continue answering her. He's checked her background—something he does with everyone he gets remotely close to—and there's nothing in her history to trigger any alarms. There is just her. A girl who plays the piano, who is here only fleetingly, once a year. Whose mother died and whose father is known in the realm of film, but whose entire life seems otherwise steeped in normalcy, in comfort, in a cocoon of family and affection utterly removed from the millions of threads that complicate his existence.

Angel lies down on the blanket, legs stuck straight out, his face up to the sky, and slowly brings his cigarette to his mouth, visibly relaxing as he blows the smoke into the clear air.

"I used to go skiing in Switzerland in the winters, and

people used to say they have the bluest sky there," he says pensively. "But it's nothing like this. Or, I don't know. It never seemed to be so blue. Whenever I'm here, I feel like I've been inside this gray place that's suddenly dipped into a can of paint, you know? Like your *Wizard of Oz.*"

Gabriella lies down beside him, her face, too, turned to the sky, and she watches legions of clouds, forming and disintegrating, their bodies plump and white against the shocking blue of the heavens. It's one of those days of extraordinary contrasts. The mountains are etched in sharp relief against the sky, every tree clearly delineated in its upward progress, all the way to the point where their tops meet the permanent fog at the highest portion of the peak. If she looks deeply into the sky, she can see a tiny moon, visible even in the early afternoon.

"Yeah, I know," she says. "I think it's something about the tropics. The colors are just brighter. Even the air smells different here. Not that it's—purer. It's just more real. More raw. I've tried to explain it to people that haven't been here, but I don't think they really understand."

Angel laughs.

"You can't explain the things that go on here to other people," he says. "It's too crazy."

"Angel," she says, still looking at the sky. "I know you need bodyguards, but why so many? Do they want to kidnap you, or do they want to kill you?"

"I'm not sure," he says, truthfully, carefully. "But they definitely want something," he says, looking away from her again.

"Is it because of your dad or because of you?" she asks softly.

No one asks me these things, he wants to tell her. But when he turns around to look at her, all he sees is her profile, deliberately avoiding his eyes as she stares at the sky. There's something in her that makes him want to talk, to say at least some of the things he can never say. To anyone.

Sometimes, he still thinks back to when he was a little boy, when he didn't know he was any different from anyone else. They lived in a smaller house then, and to the best of his knowledge, his father had a job, a job that required him to get up in the mornings in time to see Angel off to school. He would walk down the stairs, smelling of fresh aftershave, his hair still wet from the shower, his tie hanging undone around his neck, and he would kiss him as he ate his cereal at the kitchen table and cuff him lightly on the side of his head. Angel had friends then and birthday parties, and one time he was even allowed to go to a sleepover.

And then, the money started to seriously come in, inexorably transforming everything it touched, as if a flicker of fairy dust had suddenly descended on his existence, making his world bigger, shinier, newer. It began with the cars—no longer the staid, run-of-the-mill Mazdas, but a procession of SUVs and Mercedes-Benzes and a silver Jaguar for his mother that arrived one morning, tied in a gigantic red bow. He stopped taking the bus to the elite British school he had gone to since kindergarten—a luxury his father could barely afford—and was driven instead by a chauffeur in a black Bronco, followed by a jeep with two armed guards.

The new furniture came next—bright and lacquered. Then they moved to the new house and things were never the same. He was only twelve, but he immediately perceived the difference, surrounded by an opulence he had never seen—not even in movies, and certainly, not in the homes of even his wealthiest classmates. They were, finally, the ones who told him one afternoon when he invited a group of them to swim at his house after a heady game of soccer where he actually scored a goal.

They looked at each other, mildly uncomfortable, and Juan Luis, his best friend since the first grade, finally said it: "Man, Angel, you know we're not allowed to go to your house anymore."

"What do you mean?" he asked, genuinely perplexed because he still hadn't noticed the small fissures in their relationship, hadn't sensed the subtle changes in behavior, the slowdown in invitations, the little social niceties that mothers tune in to first, but children seldom grasp.

"You know," said Juan Luis, looking down, kicking softly at the worn grass with his soccer cleats. "Your dad."

"What about my dad?" asked Angel, utterly at a loss.

Everyone looked at Juan Luis expectantly, waiting for him to fix the awkwardness of the moment.

"Well, you know, he's a mafioso," Juan Luis said, finally looking Angel in the eye.

"Liar!" said Angel angrily, instinctively pushing Juan Luis hard enough so he fell to the grass with a thud, hands quickly coming down to break the fall.

"Come on, Angel," someone else said. "Everybody knows. Your dad's a drug dealer."

It was an afternoon of liquid blue sky, like this one, and above the white netting of the goal, Angel could see what looked like hawk—or maybe just a vulture—slowly circling the perimeter, the wings barely moving against the stillness of the air.

He looked down at Juan Luis, still on the ground, gazing up at him expectantly with a glimmer of defiance, but also a touch of fear in his eyes. Angel wondered what he looked like; wondered if his eyes showed his sudden panic, the realization that they could be right, that it all made sense. And then Juan Luis slowly, carefully, extended his hand, and Angel instinctively leaned over and grasped it and helped him up.

"We'll go to my house, okay?" said Juan Luis, and Angel nodded, but he could still see the glimmer of fear that had appeared in Juan Luis's eyes, and it wasn't the same that day, and it was never the same again, not really.

That night, he ate dinner alone, as he usually did, and much later, in the early morning, he heard his father come home, with a cavalcade of cars behind him.

He didn't confront him; you didn't do that with his dad. But by then, he didn't need to. He knew. And save for the time he got sent away to Switzerland to school, everybody in his lifetime has known.

The unspeakable topics, the knowing looks, the business deals that, no matter how legitimate, are always executed quietly. In almost everyone he deals with, he sees an underlying layer of fear.

But in Gabriella, he sees curiosity. No, he corrects himself. He sees interest. She is interested. She truly wants to know.

"My father has a lot of enemies," he says carefully, sitting up and looking closely at the face that doesn't look at him. "He's in jail," he continues. "And I'm his only son. I'm a very easy target. It could be that they're not interested in me at all. I'm not part of his business. But we can't take that risk. So, until he gets out, until he does whatever it is he needs to do to resolve things, I need an army."

"But why don't you go live somewhere else in the meantime," she asks logically.

"I don't want to," he says flatly. "I don't want to be anywhere else. I love it here. And I want to be close to my father."

"But Angel," she says, and finally looks at him directly, her eyes cloudy with concern but clear in their intent. "He..." Gabriella stops herself short.

She wonders how involved he is, wonders how much he really does. She wills herself, for this moment at least, to believe that he indeed stands alone, apart, like her mother stood alone and apart, close to her father but so completely separate he never knew.

"Are you close to your father?" she finally questions, because this much she can handle, this much she could share with him.

Angel considers her. A nice girl. From a nice family. The last time he dated a girl like her, she went to bed with him, but milked him in the process, made him buy her Prada bags and Jimmy Choo shoes. Then her parents sent her to study in Miami and she never returned his calls again.

He knows better now.

He looks at this girl who he wants to make love to so very

badly his stomach hurts. He could have simply insisted his father is in the "import-export" business, the standard line for people like him. He could insist on the other standard line—he's been wrongly jailed.

But she's not stupid, he knows. He does neither.

"Princesa," he finally says, the term of endearment slipping from his lips so easily, so softly she feels she could reach out and capture it in her hand. "My father isn't perfect. He's had to do what he's had to do, and a lot of it hasn't been that pretty. But he had a horrible life. Everything he has, everything I have, he worked for. I don't always agree with him, and I definitely do things differently, but he's my father. He's the only father I have, and I love him, even when I know he's not right. And now, he wants me to do well.

"And I've done well. I have my own business; I make my money. And it's legit. But he's in jail, and I'll support him as long as I have to. And that's the package, princesa," he says, slightly defiant.

She is silent for a long time, looking at the sky, deliberately thinking of nothing again, because she can't think of anything today; the weight of it all would crush her.

"Okay," she finally says. "Okay."

He stubs out his cigarette, and when he leans over, she can smell tobacco on his breath, and for the second time in her strict, antismoking life, she wants more of that smell, and when he leans down to kiss her, she reaches up and pulls him closer, to taste the cigarette he's been smoking.

She has no makeup on, and her skin is very white and tinted with a high, feverish blush, and her hair is very black underneath the many streaks of color, and her eyes have the same hue as the rain-filled clouds that now sit on top of the mountain ridge in front of them, and he thinks that she doesn't look like anyone else he knows and that each of her contrasts fits into this landscape and that every dip and curve and joint in her body fits underneath his hands.

Helena

I told Marcus once that if he ever were unfaithful to me, I didn't want to know.

"Don't come to me with one of your American guilt trips, pouring your heart out over your infidelities to get it off your chest," I said. And I meant it, too.

Ojos que no ven, corazón que no siente, they say. Out of sight, out of mind.

If I don't know about it, it hasn't happened. But if I did find out, well. Well, frankly, I didn't know what I'd do.

I asked him what he'd do if he ever found out I was unfaithful.

"I would put your stuff out on the street and kick you out of the house," he said calmly.

"You can't do that!" I laughed. "This is the twentieth century! You don't kick someone out of the house because they slept with someone else. Anyway, it's my house, too!"

"I don't care," said Marcus. "You'd be out. You broke the vows."

I couldn't believe this was my Marcus talking. The man who made love to me in the teacher's lounge.

"Marcus, that's unreasonable," I said, and I was serious

now, because I could see he wasn't joking. "What if you're the unfaithful one?"

"I would never do that," he said.

"How can you know that?" I countered.

"I wouldn't," he said again.

"But how can you know that?" I insisted.

"Because I made a decision," he said and took my hand. "I married you. Forever. Because I love you. Because I don't love anyone else. Because I didn't love anyone else. And I won't break this marriage. And I won't be unfaithful."

With Marcus there are never ambiguities. He listens, he analyzes, he weighs. But in the end, things are black and white for him; right or wrong.

I'm a waffler. My decisions change with circumstances; plans with me—as my friends well know—are like air. That's why I love Marcus. My anchor.

My transparent Marcus.

Or maybe not so transparent. If you say something long enough, you come to believe it, even if it isn't true. And if you believe it, then I guess it becomes true. Maybe that's all I need—to be a little more like him. I need to believe.

Gabriella

Gabriella's room is a replica of her mother's room. Gabriella's bed is her mother's bed.

The bookshelves are her mother's, and so are many of the books, although Gabriella has added her own over the years.

Even the closet harks back to her mother. Gabriella's clothes fill the hangers and the shelves, but way on top, Nini has stored Helena's stuff: dresses that stretch tightly across her back and T-shirts and scarves and old, tiny bikinis.

There is a picture of her mother on the nightstand. It was taken at her college graduation in Los Angeles. Her hair is very, very short, and she looks like a little pixie with that ridiculous cap on. It occurs to Gabriella that it was taken when she was her same age, twenty-one years old, all grown-up but still intrinsically linked to her parents.

Her father phoned today and yesterday and the day before, but she hasn't had the energy to return his call and say . . . what? I know you were made a fool of? I know we both were? She has never been unavailable to her father before. Never. But the mere thought of speaking with him fills her with the most profound shame, for him, for herself.

Gabriella looks at Helena's picture closely now, trying, as she often does, to see herself in her mother's face.

But this time, she sees nothing. She sees nothing at all.

She picks up the picture and turns it over, facedown on the nightstand, and when her cell phone starts ringing, she answers it automatically and braces herself to speak with Marcus.

But it's Angel, and she feels a pang of guilt at her relief.

"I'm sending someone to pick you up in an hour," he says shortly.

"To do what?" she asks, uncomfortable with simply taking orders from a person she's just started to date.

"It's a surprise," he says, his voice softening. "It'll be worth it."

"But," she protests, confused. "How long will it be? What should I wear?"

"Wear whatever, it's not formal," he says. "It won't take long. I'll see you," he says and hangs up before she can argue further.

Gabriella looks at the phone, now silent in her hand, and considers. She's just agreed to go somewhere, with someone, for God knows how long. If Nini knew about this, she'd have a fit.

But Nini isn't home.

Gabriella slowly picks up her mother's picture again and stands in front of the mirror, holding the frame next to her own face. She leans forward, until both their faces are almost touching the glass, trying to read her mother's eyes next to hers. Her mother, who always did what she pleased, and yet, those last years, was so sporadically happy.

Gabriella, instead, has been a good girl.

"And so, what?" she says out loud to her reflection. "What do you have to show for it?"

Gabriella sighs and tosses her mother's picture on the bed, not looking at it this time. She runs her fingers through her hair and looks at herself dispassionately in the mirror, at the features she knows are arresting, at the eyes everybody says are her best trait, at the white skin that burns so easily, at her hands, her hands that she loves, which remind her of sculptures by Rodin. She remembers her mother's words. She won't look like this forever.

She looks at herself and sprays perfume on the insides of her wrists, on the crooks of her arms, behind her cheeks, and on her temples and grabs her bag and her cell phone and walks out of her room.

"Lucía, I'll be back in a bit," she calls from the front door, and before poor, anxious Lucía can ask, "But where will you go, niña Gabriella? What will I tell your grandmother?" she is gone.

She waits outside, by the entrance of the building, so no one has to call her and no one has to see or wonder who she's going with when the black SUV slides to a stop beside her and the armed guard opens the door for her to get in. She sits alone in the back, the driver and a bodyguard in front. No one speaks. Chitchat, Gabriella has quickly learned, is just not the thing with Angel's staff.

They drive north toward the opposite end of the city, where the structures begin to intersperse with empty lots, until they reach a hangar surrounded by a makeshift metal fence that opens slowly to let them through.

As she gets out of the car, Gabriella hears the strains of the music, the thump of the bass making the floor vibrate, even where she stands.

"Don Angel wants you to go inside," says the bodyguard, motioning her toward a flimsy-looking side door that looks prefabricated, like this entire structure, which she now recognizes as one of the ballrooms that is built only for the holiday season dances. One of Angel's shows, she suddenly realizes.

Gabriella pushes the door open and is greeted by a wall of sound and the ripples of accordions echoing throughout the vast room, where the space seems even more immense, with the chairs and tables that will later accommodate six or seven thousand people still stacked against the walls. There is no one here, except a handful of people milling at the front and the band on the stage, Jorge Celedón and Jimmy Zambrano.

"Oh my," says Gabriella, bringing both her hands up to her face, and laughs out loud in sheer pleasure, her first, genuine, spontaneous peal of laughter in days.

She lets the music wash over her, such pretty, happy music, all for her. She's so absorbed she doesn't notice him until he's already standing beside her.

"Do you like it?" he shouts eagerly in her ear. "They're playing tonight, but I thought you'd enjoy them better during the sound check with no one around!"

"Oh, Angel, I love it," she says in wonderment, and impulsively, turns around and holds his face between her hands and, with infinite tenderness, kisses him gently, lovingly, on the lips. For a moment he's shocked into immobility, taken aback by the purity of the gesture, and then he brings his hands to cover hers as they cup his face and he smiles back. An open, unguarded smile of unadulterated joy. And for a moment, he is just a boy, and she is just a girl, and they are happy.

Helena

The first woman Juan José had sex with was a prostitute.

His father took him to see her. He was seventeen years old, a swaggering boaster, the coolest guy, the one who smoked cigarettes during the week but who'd never gone beyond fondling his girlfriend's breasts.

He grew tall that summer and girls were constantly calling. One Sunday with no preamble, after a long horseback ride, his father, slightly drunk, announced it was high time his boy became a man. They were in the car—his dad's silver Mercedes-Benz—and he felt sticky and filthy in his dusty riding breeches and grass-stained shirt. His hair, matted with sweat from four hours of riding in the sun, stuck to his skull like glue.

His father took him to a nondescript home in a quiet middle-class neighborhood, a part of town rich boys might drive by but never stop at.

Her name was Ingrid. Or so she said. She was a skinny girl with very sleek olive skin and a tight, generous ass, the kind so many mulatto Cali girls are famous for. When she drew him to her, her hands were cool and slightly sweaty and she smelled of patchouli oil and rose water. He was terrified, but he didn't protest. Defying his father wasn't really an option. Besides, how could he say no to an afternoon of sex? What kind of man would that make him?

She sat him in a chair covered with a white cotton sheet and knelt before him, taking off his riding boots and his socks. His feet stank and he felt acutely embarrassed and ill at ease and completely at a loss as to what he was supposed to do.

"Relax, papito," she said, bringing a wide pan with warm, sudsy water. She stripped him of his pants and underwear, placed his fetid feet in the water, and again knelt before him and took him in her mouth.

He'd read about blow jobs, but didn't know anyone who'd actually gotten one, and certainly no girls who gave them. The simple touch of her lips against him sent him over the edge and he came in seconds.

He was mortified. When she started to laugh, he felt tears welling up in his eyes, as the shame swept over him in waves.

He reached down for his clothes, but she stopped him, firmly but not unkindly, and pulled him up instead, leading him toward the bed even though he felt ridiculous and exposed, walking naked except for his stained shirt.

"I mustn't cry," he told himself. "Only babies and maricones cry."

So he let Ingrid take him to her bed and take off his shirt and walk him with infinite care through the fine details of making love.

Two hours later, when he was shown the door, his father was waiting in the car, smoking a cigarette.

To this day, he doesn't know if he went for a drive or if he went to another room in the house. He never asked.

"Todo bien?" he asked.

"Todo bien," he answered. His father laughed and slapped him on the back.

Juan José didn't mention the embarrassment, the tears that almost engulfed him. How lost he felt on that bed, how awkwardly he had moved inside her, like a child with no rhythm.

But afterward, he felt like a man. A real man. Spent but powerful.

He didn't say anything to his mother that evening. When she kissed him good night, he hugged her tightly but saw her in a different light.

She was una mujer bien, from a fine family. He was sure there were things his father never did with her.

The next day, he bragged to his friends in school, leaving out all the parts where he'd acted like a boy.

He went back to Ingrid over the years, when he felt overwhelmed or disappointed. When Ingrid was no longer there, he found someone else, and then someone else. The only name he can still remember is Ingrid's.

Whores, he found out, never demanded more than he was prepared to give. They didn't want a long-term commitment, and they didn't want his money beyond the evening at hand. With whores, he always knew where he stood. With other girls, he could always see the calculation in their eyes when they recognized the family name, when someone told them where he came from. Even if they themselves were rich, his money beckoned.

He could be a blob, and those girls would still let him fuck them.

His head was cradled against my bare stomach as he spoke. He smoked and I gently ran my fingers through his hair as the sun trickled in lazily through the blue shutters of the farmhouse. It was two in the afternoon and so stiflingly hot that all you could possibly want to do was lie there like that, with the fan slowly twirling overhead and a pitcher of ice-cold lulo juice sitting by the bedside. Juan José should have been working, but he owned his business and I owned my time, and right then, I also seemed to own him.

"Y tú? Tú que quieres, Helena? What do you want from me?"

There was an antique porcelain water pitcher on its basin placed on a wooden table in the corner. It was white with pink flowers, and the handle was chipped. The wall was bright yellow, the floor dark oak, and the irregular swaths of light that peeked in through the half-closed shutter made the pitcher look like it was lit up inside. I gently lifted his head from me and got up to reach the camera I had left on the armchair. I came back to the bed, to the exact position I was in before, adjusted the lens, and snapped the shot.

That's the way it is when you work with natural light. The moments are only seconds long. If you miss them, they're gone forever.

I took a whole roll, and only then did I finally answer him.

"I don't want anything, Juan José. I don't want anything at all."

Gabriella

What's this? The inquisition?"

When she gets off the elevator that opens onto her grand-mother's apartment, she finds Nini and Juan Carlos sitting in the living room. Waiting for her. Obviously.

Gabriella is annoyed and guilty and angry and defensive, even before the speech starts, because she knows what the speech will be about.

"Gabriellita, no one wants to put you on the spot, but we want to make sure you know what you're getting into," says Nini firmly, but her voice is trembling with barely sup-pressed outrage. "This boy you've been going out with, he's Luis Silva's son. We're talking about a very dangerous man. You should have told me who he was."

"Nini, Luis Silva is in jail, and anyway, Angel is not in his father's business," says Gabriella, not sitting down, retain-ing the advantage of height and stance over her diminutive grandmother.

"Gabriella, don't pretend to be silly. It doesn't suit you. Of course, he's involved," says Nini impatiently. "And even if he weren't, what do you suppose he's going to do if you no longer want to go out with him? If you meet someone else? Gabriellita, this is just not advisable—"

"Do you remember the story of the girl a couple of years ago?" interrupts Juan Carlos. "She was dating some little mafioso, and he whacked her new boyfriend! This is no joke. Gabriella, this isn't a good thing."

"I . . ." Gabriella's voice trails off. How to explain when they don't know him. "If you spoke with him, you wouldn't say what you're saying," she says helplessly. "Maybe you should get to know him. Invite him to dinner or something," she adds with a shrug, ignoring Juan Carlos and looking at her grandmother instead.

Her grandmother looks at her stone-faced, and for a ridiculous moment, Gabriella stifles a giggle.

"I can't believe this!" shouts Juan Carlos, affronted at Gabriella's lack of respect. "What are you, deaf or just plain stupid?"

"Juan," says Nini warningly.

"Oh, please. All you care about is what people will say about you, Juan Carlos," interrupts Gabriella, folding her arms angrily in front of her.

"Okay, I do," Juan Carlos answers, pounding the sofa with his fist, nodding vehemently. "I do care what people say about me. I live here. This is my city. And I care. And you should be considerate of that, because in a few weeks, you'll be gone again, and you can pretend this didn't happen, while we have to live with the consequences of your little fling."

Juan Carlos stops to catch his breath. Gabriella has never seen him like this, and she feels just a twinge of guilt. Just a little.

"I honestly think you're overstating this," she says. "Nini," she says, turning again toward her grandmother, her palms turned up in entreaty. "Angel is not that way. I'm not embarrassing you. I'm not going to embarrass you. I don't do that, Nini."

"But this is more than that," says Nini. "At this point, I'm worried about your safety, and frankly, about my safety and the family's safety."

Gabriella pauses. She hadn't considered that her family could possibly be in any danger. But, she rationalizes, the only one who's a target is Angel, and he is too zealously guarded to instill real fear into her. And the idea of Angel himself being dangerous simply doesn't factor into her equation. For a brief instant, she sees his face above hers, feels his hand stroking her stomach, and involuntarily she closes her eyes.

"He is not going to hurt me. Or you," Gabriella says, decision imparting firmness to her voice. They are trying to make her feel like an obtuse teenager, which she isn't, and she wants them to understand that, despite everything they may think, they're simply mistaken. "I know where he comes from. I know who he is. But, he's not in that life. He's—he's normal! He can't help who his father is. But he's not his father!"

It doesn't sound right, she knows.

"I like him. I like him, Nini," she says earnestly. "And why, why can't I be with someone I like? I'm not married. It's my right."

Nini stares, the skin around her mouth pinched and tight.

"It's your right," she says finally. "But not in my house. I'm going to have a talk with your father tonight. And I'm going to have to tell him about this. It's my responsibility."

Gabriella feels a hole opening in the pit of her stomach. Her father, whose calls she's ignored, who she can't bring herself to speak to. He will come personally and get her, she's sure. He is not going to let this one go by.

"You tell him," Gabriella says carefully, "and I'll tell him that you knew about this Juan José character and my mother. I'll tell him how she had an affair while staying in your house, and you let it happen. And *that*, you didn't have a problem with."

The words spill out before she can stop them, and she's appalled at how awful they are.

She wants to grab them back, but now they hover in the hushed room and she can see them poisoning the air, physically attacking her grandmother, who suddenly and for the first time looks to Gabriella like an old woman.

"What the hell?" says Juan Carlos, confused.

But it's Nini whom she sees looking at her with an expression of bafflement and profound hurt. Nini so taken by surprise she doesn't even scold Juan Carlos for the language.

All these years she has kept silent, thinks Gabriella. She knew all this time. But I couldn't. It's been only three days of secrets, and yet, it was killing me.

"Tell him," Nini finally says in a tiny whisper. "Go ahead and wreck his life, and wreck what's left of mine. Will that make you feel better?"

Gabriella can't bring herself to speak.

She shakes her head no, looking beyond Nini, because she can't bear to look at her face now, she feels so ashamed.

"Who told you?" Nini asks.

"No one," she answers, almost under her breath. "I read it. I read it in her diary."

For a few seconds, no one speaks, and Nini resists the urge to stand up and put her arms around her granddaughter.

"Ay, mamita," says Nini finally, shaking her head with sad disdain. "It was nothing. It wasn't important."

"That's not what she wrote, Nini," says Gabriella quickly, wanting to give details but profoundly ashamed of repeating the intimacy of her mother's words.

Nini pauses and sighs heavily.

"I am telling you, Gabriella," she says finally, recovering a sense of decorum. "That it was not important. That it might have seemed important to her at the time—and that was a shame—but it wasn't. And the last thing I would have done was to tell your father about it," she says, looking Gabriella in the eye, the warning tacit between them.

"You don't ruin good marriages over a little"—Nini will not use the word "affair," so she goes for a mild alternative—"flirtation. And you don't spread rumors, either. Gossip is the worst enemy of relationships."

No one says anything for a few moments, not even Juan Carlos, who's found himself in deeply uncharted territory.

Gabriella wants to leave but doesn't dare make the move now.

Nini is afraid to ask, but she feels compelled. Helena was part of her, too. "Can I read it?" she says, and there is pleading in her voice.

"Nini," says Gabriella, uncomfortable. "I...I can't. She wrote it to me. I can't dishonor that."

The air in the breezy room is suddenly heavy. No one speaks. No one moves. The ticking of an antique clock is all that can be heard.

"She was infatuated, not in love," Nini says after a long silence. "Just like you are now with this Angel. And I think that if she hadn't died, she would have ripped those pages out. If she hadn't died, she would have written a very different book."

Juan Carlos is in the room, but she is speaking only to Gabriella now, all her energy zeroed in on her, on making her see what she sees, what she would like to be true.

But now Gabriella shakes her head no.

No.

"No, Nini," she says, and there's a sad bitterness in her voice. "I think she would have written the same book. I think," she continues, looking straight at Nini, because she feels that somehow she can reach her, "I think she had a chance. And she took it. And now I have my chance. And I'm going to write my own book. And you have to let me, Nini. I think you owe me that."

Helena

I could tell him not to place the palm of his hand flat against my back when we dance, not to close his eyes and bring me close, so close to him, his mouth periodically brushes against my hair where my head rests beneath his chin. I could ask him not to allow his hand to linger at my waist longer than a few seconds when he escorts me into a room. I could ask him not to be my date for every art function, pretending instead to run into him, as if he were a casual acquaintance, but not so obviously my lover.

At dinner with his friends last night, he leaned into me to say something softly, his hand underneath the tablecloth sitting high on my thigh, and I couldn't help but lean into him in turn, pressing my other thigh into his hand, shivering in quick anticipation before I glanced up to see the frank stares of curiosity from the other side of the table.

I felt myself blush as I tried not to look guilty and casually put distance between us, as if the closeness had been nothing more than just an errant moment, not the constant state of affairs.

"So how old is your daughter now, Helena?" asked Lilian. She is Juan José's cousin and her question is deliberate, a reminder to the table of who I am and what I'm doing.

"She's four," I answer with my brightest smile.

"Wow, that's young! And you left her alone for . . . what's it been, over a month?"

It's more an accusation than a question, and I feel the warmth reach my cheeks all over again.

"Well, she's not alone," I say, far less pleasantly. "She's with her father and she's having a ball. I don't think children need to be attached to their mothers every second of the day, unless, of course, their mothers have nothing else to do," I add pointedly, because there are several nonworking mothers here.

"It must be nice to have a husband who doesn't mind staying alone for a month, much less with the children in tow," rejoins Lilian, all pretense of niceties apparently forgotten. "That is, if you're married. You *are* still married, right?"

I seriously consider hurling my glass of wine at her.

Everybody has affairs, don't they? I want to shout. Why then are you trying to make me feel like the town harlot?

But Juan José intercedes smoothly.

"Lily, you're such a little snoop," he says with a laugh, draping his arm around my shoulder. "I always told Lilian she should become a journalist," he says to the table at large. "You would not believe the things this girl used to ask us when we were kids!"

We laugh, but now the shrimp appetizer feels like lead in my mouth.

Later, as I head back to the table from the bathroom, I

pass a half-open bedroom door and the words buffet me once again.

"That was harsh, Lily," I overhear one of her friends say.

"Someone has to say it," I hear Lilian answer impatiently. "She's married; she has a kid, for Christ's sake. She has a little girl! And she's here happily screwing around with my cousin. What kind of mother would do that? Not to mention poor JJ."

"Come on, Lily. I don't hear Juan José complaining," her friend answers with a laugh.

"Maybe not, but it isn't fair to him, either," says Lilian, sounding angry. "I think he's falling in love with her. He's smitten. Really. And it's just a game to her. She thinks her husband is an idiot and she thinks my cousin is an idiot."

"Lily, Juan José is right. You overthink things. He's a guy, she's pretty, he's just having a good time. And God knows what her husband is like. He probably doesn't even care what she does."

I hear their footsteps coming toward the door and I quickly move to the other room. From where I stand, I see Juan José sitting on the terrace, a glass of whiskey in one hand, a cigarette in the other, talking animatedly, then bursting out in loud laughter.

Marcus would be nursing a Groth cabernet, he would never smoke a cigarette, and his voice would never carry across the room.

But he would care. He would care a lot.

Gabriella

As much as she hates to admit it, the conversation with Nini has rattled her.

That night, while Angel works, while her grandmother sleeps, she lies awake in the dark, her thoughts punctuated by bursts of music or an occasional trail of laughter left behind by a car as it speeds by on the street below.

She can still stop it, she reasons. She could call him tomorrow and put an end to it, and continue her life as if nothing had happened. In a few days, the world—her very small world that cares about this—would have forgotten it, rendering the moment nothing more than a small parentheses in her life.

"But why?" she asks out loud softly, overwhelmed by the blatant unfairness of her predicament. There is nothing sinister about him or what he does. So he travels with a small army. That is hardly unusual in a country fraught with kidnappings and uncertainty. His father is in jail. She admits to herself that it is hardly the ideal situation, and yet, she parries in her mind, it's not uncommon, either, what with the wave of white-collar prosecutions.

But a father who's a drug dealer, a major drug dealer, a

drug dealer so powerful his net worth is estimated at nearly that of the country's gross national product?

Gabriella presses the palms of her hands against her eyes, rubbing them until she sees stars. But he is not his father, Gabriella tells herself. I don't care what anyone says. He is not his father.

She'd slept with two men before him. One was her high school boyfriend, a football player who was gloriously tall and well built, a boy she couldn't quite believe had fallen for her. He had discovered her in her senior year, when she went from gawky to beautiful, when her legs seemed to grow and she joined the track team, her quickening speed seemingly leaving her shyness behind. She ran around and around the track while he practiced tackling in the field, distracted by her legs and her unwavering gray eyes. It took him a month to get her into bed with him—a rushed and totally unsatisfying affair, for her, at least, that took place on a sagging couch in his basement. The sex never improved and that was all they ever did together.

She surprised all her friends by dumping him first. But he surprised her by taking it in stride; a gracious loser who never quite got over her and who left the door open for her to continue basking in the glow of his popularity in her last months of high school. She never stopped feeling grateful to him for that, and even now, when they meet at an odd party or restaurant, their hugs linger.

"My backup romance," she would say, not unkindly, when she talked about him.

She poured her affections far more generously on her second lover, a tortured film student named Seth Girard, who had a brilliant mind and an unshakable sense of self-importance.

Her father disapproved. He knew the type. And he could tell she was simply infatuated with the idea of the man rather than in love with the man himself.

But she liked the intellectual challenge and charged on, convinced she could somehow teach him an iota of consideration.

For a long time, she couldn't figure out why their love-making didn't work, when their minds were so finely in tune. But he never quite understood the rhythm of her body, the kind of touching she needed him to do. For a while, she actually thought it would always be like that: relentless foreplay that led her nowhere. If she moaned hard enough, she thought, she could will herself to feel something more. For a while, she thought good sex was a myth. But when Seth broke up with her, he blamed what he called her "repressive persona" and recommended she see a sex therapist.

Her friends put him in his place.

"Bad sex is always the guy's fault," they said categorically.

And then, she met Angel and realized they were right.

She just hadn't known.

Except that with Angel it isn't just the sex.

Gabriella closes her eyes and sees him. Sees the genuine spark of pleasure that reaches the clear depths of his green eyes when he makes her laugh, like he did yesterday in the dance hall. With him, she has nothing to prove, and she feels the ease of the time spent together roll over her in waves, like a sailboat that finally catches just the right amount of wind to reach the perfect speed. When they're together in his car, he steers with his left hand, and with his right, he seeks her out, touching her hair, her arm, her hand, which he holds as he drives, sometimes releasing it for just seconds at a time to shift gears, then firmly claiming it again, never taking his eyes off the road but periodically running his thumb over her wrist, joining her pulse to his.

And yet, the next morning, when he calls and invites her to work out at his sports club, she caves just a little to her grandmother's wishes.

"I'll meet you there," she tells him over the phone, rebuffing his offer to send a driver over, her mind made up to go with Edgar, forgo the showiness of the bodyguards and draw the least attention possible on herself and her family.

The short silence on the other end registers his surprise.

"I'll pick you up if you want," he says resolutely, and she feels a surge of guilt, because she knows it's dangerous for him to drive around unnecessarily, and yet, he's willing to do that for her.

"No, you know you shouldn't," she responds, saying the right thing, but almost choking on her duplicity, angry now at having allowed herself to entertain any doubts.

And yet, as Edgar drives her, each passing mile reassures her that this indeed makes sense; that she can be with him, but still stand apart if she wishes.

"Luis Silva's son? That's pretty big leagues, Miss Gabriella." Edgar interrupts her thoughts with the bluntness earned by years of service that make him more a family member than an employee.

"He has his own business, Edgar," replies Gabriella curtly, prepared to cut the conversation short. But she can't help herself.

"How did you know he's Luis Silva's son?" she finally asks.

"People talk," says Edgar, looking straight ahead. "The other drivers in the building. The guards. I'm very sorry, Miss Gabriella. They say he's a decent guy, but I still had to tell your grandmother."

"Oh, Edgar," says Gabriella softly, understanding where yesterday's scene came from, yet feeling strangely relieved. No matter how furtive she and Angel have been, it was only a matter of time before the truth came out. At least now she no longer has to scurry around in a sea of half lies, like her mother did, and the thought gives her fresh impetus as they pull up to the health club.

Already, his three cars are parked outside, making an immediate statement, his bodyguards leaning nonchalantly against the SUV doors, semiautomatics held loosely at their chests. They don't look anything like the Armani-clad security detail they show in films. They simply look dangerous and on edge.

For a fraction of a second, Gabriella hesitates, then walks in, coming face-to-face with an immaculate receptionist in tiny white shorts and a midriff-baring halter top, who holds court at a chrome-and-white desk at the entrance. Her breasts are huge, her biceps incredibly toned, and her very straight black hair is caught back in a tight ponytail, revealing a perfectly made-up face of fine little features and manicured eyebrows that she now raises with a touch of insolence.

For a moment, Gabriella pictures Angel's house. The blatant flashiness of it, the elevator, the long marble halls and winding staircases, the lawn that stretches forever, and the cars, the endless line of cars. In all fairness, some of it could be right at home back in Los Angeles, but here his reality assaults her senses.

Gabriella is much too sensitive to be rigid, but she's always been righteous, like her father, her world an easily discernible division of right and wrong, truth or lies. Everything is fuzzy now, she thinks, and then she sees him, walking toward her, wearing baggy shorts and a loose mesh T-shirt, looking like any other guy would look in a gym.

"She's with me," he tells the receptionist quietly, authoritatively, and gives Gabriella his half smile, his eyes and his hand reaching for hers. In that moment, all Gabriella's thoughts come sharply into focus, and everything makes the clearest of sense.

He assigns her a trainer, and in the beginning, he comes by her station occasionally, but it flusters her to have him see her doing leg lifts and lunges.

"Go away!" she finally says, exasperated, swatting him with her towel. "I can't concentrate when you're looming over me."

"Okay, okay," he says, raising his arms in surrender. "Just be careful with her hands and wrists," he admonishes the trainer. "She can't do heavy wrist work. She's a pianist."

"Please, Angel, you sound like my dad," says Gabriella, acutely embarrassed, although she's noticed from the onset that her trainer—like everyone else here—is more interested in Angel than in her, tuned to her needs only as a function of Angel's wishes.

Gabriella smiles wryly to herself. She grew up on movie

sets full of sycophants, fawning over the actors, the direc-
tors, her father, even her. "Don't believe any of them,
Gabriella," her father would tell her, sometimes laughing,
sometimes dead serious. "They're about as real as what you
see on the movie screen."

She looks surreptitiously at Angel, watching the easy
grace of his movements, appreciating the fact that he's not
one of those obnoxious types that swaggers and shows off in
the weight room. He's focused, or perhaps deliberately aloof,
studiously avoiding eye contact with the few people that are
here at this time of the morning. Gabriella wonders if Angel
knows this isn't real, either; wonders if he knows how handsome he is, how alluring. Wonders if he wonders what it
would have been like to be just Angel, not Angel Silva, Luis
Silva's son.

"When do I get to meet your friends?" she asks him later,
as they sit in the sauna.

"You already did. At the party," he says lazily, eyes closed,
head leaning back against the white tile.

"No, I didn't," she says with a laugh. "You didn't intro-
duce me to anyone at all!"

"I was busy dancing with this beautiful girl," he answers
smiling, eyes still closed.

"Angel, really," she insists, because this is suddenly important to her. "Don't you have any close friends you hang out
with?"

Angel sighs, finally opens his eyes. He looks at her appraisingly for a moment, measuring what he's going to say. "No,"
he finally says with a small shrug of his shoulders. "I don't
have any close friends right now. Quite honestly, I'm going

through a phase where I really am not close to anyone at all. And for the time being, I'd like to keep it that way."

"What about me?" Gabriella asks.

"You're different," he answers, smiling gently. "You..." His voice trails off, then picks up again. "You don't judge. You have an open mind. No one here has an open mind."

"Why did you throw that huge bash then?" she asks, perplexed.

Angel shrugs again, and for a fleeting moment, he doesn't look like a self-assured, powerful man, but like a sullen, slightly hurt little boy.

"They're acquaintances," he says slowly. "They all expect me to throw parties, so I do it from time to time. But no one there was really my friend. Well, there's a few people that I've known for a long time, but I don't really have good friends here anymore."

"Why?" she prods.

"Why?" rejoins Angel, his voice edgy. "Now, why do you think?" he says sarcastically.

"Look," says Gabriella firmly, emboldened by her relaxed state of mind and chafing at his patronizing tone. "Don't get mad at me, but you are intimidating, you know? Your house is intimidating. Your gun is intimidating. Everything about your dad is intimidating. And that army you have out there doesn't help, either."

Angel looks frankly startled, his eyes completely open now. The people around him usually skirt this topic, or leave altogether. He can't remember a single time when he's had this conversation with a girl he's dated.

"Wow," he finally says, running his fingers through his

wet hair, then leaning toward her with his elbows on his knees. "You think I don't know that?" he asks seriously. "You think I don't see it? It'd be nice if my father were a rich, I don't know, a rich banker! But I can't change who I am or where I come from, Gabriella," he says softly, looking at her earnestly.

"Couldn't you go somewhere else?" she asks plaintively. "Sons of rich bankers go live in other places. You could go to your Switzerland that you liked so much. No one knows you there, Angel. You wouldn't have to explain yourself at every turn. Do you realize how liberating that would be?" she presses urgently.

Angel smiles at her, a touch of regret in his eyes, and reaches up and strokes her cheek with the back of his hand.

"You can't let it go, can you, princesa?" he asks ruefully. "Remember what I told you? I have to be here for my father. But afterwards, maybe I'll go. Maybe you'll come with me," he adds, and this time he smiles, really smiles, the smile she loves.

That afternoon, he's the one who takes her back home.

Helena

Many people live by the book. They grow up, study, get married, have children. They live happily ever after. Comfortable lives of complacency.

We don't all have to do that. Some of us follow our hearts. It's not just a right. It's a duty. Never live a life of quiet acceptance. That's what losers do. We aren't losers.

In the beginning, when we began dating, Marcus loved the idea of Colombia.

He loved the idea of a Colombian girlfriend, the exoticness it awarded him in a city where the only Latinos his friends came into contact with were busboys and gardeners.

I didn't mean to be exotic, either. I simply was what I was.

But the moment it dawned on me that there was a race card I could play, I started to use it, subtly but decidedly.

I surprised him with a mariachi for his birthday, a quintet I picked up at Mariachi Plaza in Boyle Heights.

It stunned the hell out of his parents, who fidgeted nervously when I joined in the chorus of "El Rey," belting it out with my roommate Carolina, the only other Colombian I knew in Los Angeles.

I gave Marcus a leather-bound collection of Gabriel García Márquez's works as a gift, with a dedication in each one of the books. In the last one, *Love in the Time of Cholera*, I wrote: "Beyond countries, beyond time, some things are meant to be. Te adoro, Helena." I meant it, too.

I never pretended to be anything I wasn't.

I thought implicitly, from the photographs I showed him of my parents and my brother, from the education I had, and the English I spoke, that he understood exactly where I came from.

One day, during a luncheon at Marcus's parents' house, I overheard his mother, Kitty—a thin, elegant-looking blonde with a permanent tan—talking about me to her friends.

"She's Latin American," I heard her say. "From Colombia. She's very exotic looking, don't you think?" They were sitting at a corner table on the balcony, and I could see only the tops of their heads from the open window in the studio.

"Colombia! Isn't that where all the drugs come from?" asked a woman, slightly horrified.

"Well, yes, but of course, I'm certain the entire country isn't dealing drugs, sweetie," Kitty replied calmly. "At any rate, I find Helena a very simple, down-to-earth girl. Marcus tells me she lives in a little apartment near USC. I can't imagine she's involved in anything remotely like that."

"She must be so grateful to Marcus," said another of Kitty's friends. "Imagine"—I saw only the suntanned hand, glistening with gold rings, gesturing grandly toward the garden, the pool, the tennis court—"she's probably never been to a house like this in her life."

"Of course, she's grateful," Kitty said with assurance. "I mean, Marcus says her family is very decent. Her father is a physician, I believe. But she does come from a little country in South America! This must all be very exciting for her."

I felt my cheeks grow warm. That someone would even question my place in life was just completely alien to me. But worse still was the outright condescension. I had been dating Marcus now for five months and had felt comfortable in his parents' company. I had no inkling that I was regarded as an extension of the hired help. The lack of understanding, and more than that, my failure in conveying who I was, infuriated me.

"Is Marcus very serious about her, Kitty?" asked the voice belonging to the woman with the gestures and the golden rings. "She's quite darling, actually, but I wouldn't have thought she was his type."

Kitty had laughed, the proud laugh of a mother who knows her son can get any girl he chooses to.

"Oh, you know Marcus," she cooed. "He doesn't like to stay anywhere for too long. But in the meantime, she's a nice girl. And to be quite honest with you, at least she's not Hindu or Muslim or something like that. "

Sometimes, you need a serious jolt to get started. I didn't know for certain if I was just a pastime for Marcus. What I did know was that he wasn't a pastime for me. I made up my mind then. What Kitty never knew is that she lost her son to me that day.

We'd been planning a spring break getaway. The next

morning, I booked two plane tickets, and that evening, after we made love, I placed them on his bare chest.

"This is your bonus birthday present, my gringuito," I said. "We're going to Colombia for a week."

He couldn't say no.

Gabriella

The length of the city is connected by La Quinta, a road anchored by huge, shady trees side to side and alive with commerce and chaotic traffic—where each sector is defined by its storefronts. In the north it's the tire dealerships and hardware stores. In the south it's cafeterias and nightclubs and bars and restaurants. Scores of them, each one distinctly different from the one next door.

They drive in the uneasy silence of uncertainty.

They went to the club today. Her club, because in her search for normalcy, she insisted on going there instead of holing up at one of his hangouts. They played tennis, something they both do competently. And it should have been fun. It should have been inconsequential.

Except she took him not to the main clubhouse but to the back courts, rationalizing he'd like the privacy, but now admitting to herself that she chickened out at the last minute, uncertain of what her cousin's friends would say if they saw her with him.

And all that for what? she wonders now bitterly. No sooner had they started to play, all the way on court 18, than a group of Nini's friends descended en masse for their weekly ladies round-robin. It was inevitable that between games, they would eventually coincide at the benches between the courts.

"You're Cristina's granddaughter, aren't you?" one of the women asks, her smile bright and friendly.

"Yes," says Gabriella weakly. In the best of circumstances, these encounters were uncomfortable. Today, her IQ seemed reduced by half, because she couldn't string together a coherent response.

"You are so tall and so beautiful!" the woman continues, looking at Gabriella with open admiration. "Tell your grandmother Monica Garces said hello. And who's your friend?" she asked curiously.

"Oh, this is Angel," says Gabriella, looking at him with a sense of trepidation.

"Angel Silva," says Angel, adding his last name deliberately, getting up to shake the woman's hand, looking everything like a handsome, suave young man, and nothing like a drug dealer's son.

He is beautiful, thinks Gabriella looking up with regret at his wiry frame, because in that instant, she can unerringly anticipate what the next question will be.

"It's so nice to meet you, Angel," says the woman, oblivious to Gabriella's unease. "And who are your parents?" she asks, just as Gabriella knew she would.

Gabriella can see Angel pause, clearly weighing the answer. She can hear Edgar's voice in her mind—"Luis Silva's son? That's pretty big leagues"—and before Angel gets his bearings she interrupts smoothly.

"Angel just moved back from Europe," she says. "His

family has been living there for a while." And then, before anyone can intercede anymore, she gestures Angel toward the tennis court.

"Shall we finish the game?" she asks brightly.

"You just can't wait to lose, can you?" Angel says with a little laugh, but Gabriella can sense his irritation, if not his outright anger, even as he politely shakes everybody's hand and walks nonchalantly to his side of the court.

They finished their game in silence and left immediately, not even stopping for lunch or to relax by the pool.

Angel said he needed to work, but Gabriella knows better. She senses his acute discomfort at being out of his element and out of control, at a place where he knows he's not welcome, at a club where his dubious family ties will forever bar him from becoming a member. And somehow, instead of making it easier for him, she's managed to compound everything that was wrong.

On the way home they've stopped at a light and a band of children are doing their merry tricks for petty cash. To the right, a group is juggling oranges. Good juggling, with oranges going under legs, over arms, under the legs again. To the left, they're doing pirouettes, one skinny black kid balancing himself on the shoulders of two equally scrawny kids who flip him over, so he lands in front of their car.

Before he can stop her, Gabriella opens the window and hands over five thousand pesos to the jugglers on the right, then reaches over and hands five thousand to the acrobats on the left.

They can't believe their luck.

"Gracias! Gracias, señorita," they cry, their white smiles lighting up their dark faces, hands touching hers for an instant before they dash to the divider to share news of the unexpectedly large bounty with their buddies.

Gabriella loves this. Five thousand pesos is two dollars, but here, for kids like this, it's a small fortune.

"You know, I'm trying to talk my dad into shooting something here," she says, feeling warmly benevolent and desperate to break the tension.

Angel doesn't say anything, and for a second, she thinks he hasn't heard her.

"I'm telling you," she adds, getting animated at the prospect, "I'm going to convince my dad to shoot a movie here. I've been working on a script. If he gets the right partner, I think we can do it."

"Yeah, yeah," says Angel. "Just what we need. Another gringa telling us what we're all about."

At first, she thinks he's joking.

"I'm not a gringa, Angel," she says, not even looking at him.

"Oh, yes, you are," he says, and this time she hears the hardness in his voice and now she does look at him. "Coming here once a year doesn't mean you're from here."

"Oh, and what about you, Mr. Swiss Private School?" she asks. "You were even farther away than me!"

"No, no," he says, shaking his head. "You see, the difference is you think like a gringa. It doesn't matter that you speak like a Colombian. You think like a gringa. You're like one of these..." He pauses, searching for a word he's read but never used. "What do you call them, Oreos? Isn't that what blacks say? People who are black on the outside, white on the inside. That's you."

"How can you say something like that?" she asks, anger rising from the pit that has formed in her stomach. "Weren't you the one telling me I had an 'open mind'? Now, something doesn't go your way, and I'm suddenly an execrable character?"

"Something doesn't go my way? Are you joking? You just showed your true colors, and how!" he says with a snort. "Come on, tell the truth. You think my dad's a shitty drug dealer, and you think I'm one, too. You think I go around offing people in my free time! You believe every cliché you've ever seen in those little Hollywood movies your daddy makes."

Gabriella feels her face get red. Last year, after a dismal fall recital at St. Stephen's, her teacher had approached and whispered furiously in her ear. "That's not the way we play the piano at USC," he said angrily, and she felt the same embarrassed futility now, of having tried to do the right thing, of having failed, and at a loss as to how to correct it.

"I've never thought anything like that about you," she says quietly, wishing she could somehow hit a rewind button and take back the morning, do it all over again. "I don't know enough about your father. But I do know about you."

"And what *do* you know about me?" he asks evenly.

Gabriella shrugs. She struggles with the words.

"You're kind," she says finally. "And that when I'm with you, I don't want to be with anyone else," she adds with a smile, attempting to make light of the matter, putting her hand on his arm tentatively, wishing for this gentleness even though she feels the muscles tensing and relaxing as he grips the steering wheel.

"And this is why you hid me out in the back courts, where you thought no one else was playing? So you wouldn't have to be with anyone else? Is that why you were freaking out with your grandmother's friend? You actually think I go around and brag about my father? You are such a lying little hypocritical bitch. Like all the other ones like you."

Gabriella takes her hand from his arm. She feels like she's been slapped, which has never happened to her in her life. She stares straight ahead until he slams the brakes at the next traffic light, and then, without any preamble, she opens the car door and gets out.

She walks in the direction they came from, toward the children, stepping onto the grassy median where the children and their parents and the hawkers converge, looking at her curiously, as she tries to get as far away from him as she can.

She sees two of his bodyguards looking uncertainly in her direction. Angel's SUV is parked in the middle of the street, obstructing traffic, and other cars are honking furiously. The honking doesn't faze the guards in the least, she knows, and for a second, their eyes meet hers—or seem to—from where she stands, and she imagines that they start moving toward her. But they halt abruptly, and instead, they both get into Angel's car, one claiming the front seat, the door of which she's left open.

Gabriella looks at the bus lane that separates her vulnerable median from the opposite sidewalk and makes a dash for it, weaving her way in and out of traffic and vending carts, until she reaches the other side of the street.

When she looks back again, their cars are gone.

For a second Gabriella panics. She thinks they might go around the block and come back to pick her up. So she dashes into one of the many cafeterias that line the road and takes the seat farthest away from the door, the chair's metal hard and cold against her bare legs.

She has enough money for a Coke, enough money for a hot pandebono. She doesn't have enough money for a cab.

She sighs, defeated. How is she supposed to explain this? she wonders. Stranded in the cafeteria. It dawns on her that there isn't a single person who can empathize with her predicament. Juan Carlos and Nini will give her "I told you so" speeches. Her father is oblivious to all this. She doesn't have close enough friends here, and her friends at home couldn't begin to grasp the situation—him, her, the guards, the guns, this moment.

For the first time she feels a wave of sympathy for her mother. Who could she have possibly confided in? she thinks. Who would have understood? Perhaps, if she had had someone, it wouldn't have gone as far.

She fidgets with her cell phone, delaying the inevitable, then finally calls Nini's house, gives a lame excuse about car breakdowns and emergencies, and waits for Edgar to come pick her up.

When her phone begins to ring, she doesn't answer it.

When it rings again and again and again, insistently, she turns it off.

The metal chair in the cafeteria is cold against her bare legs, and overhead the speakers are playing "Te Mando Flores." She sings along, never missing a word: "Te mando flores, que recojo en el camino. Yo te las mando entre mis sueños, porque no puedo hablar contigo."

She knows the songs, she thinks. She belongs.

Gabriella

Her father's call on her cell phone woke her up this morning, at seven sharp her time, 4 a.m. L.A. time, his way of not taking no for an answer, because after all, what excuse can she possibly give for not picking up at the crack of dawn?

"Where the hell have you been?" he asked irritably and with no preamble.

"Here," she said nonchalantly, and immediately regretted the unintended insolence of her words. "What's wrong?" she added carefully, fully aware that he's had to either wake up at four, or stay up to call her. Both options are dramatic.

"You're unreachable, that's what's wrong," he answered curtly.

"I've been really busy, Dad," she answered, sounding uncharacteristically formal. "You know it's hard to call with the time difference. I've spent weeks in Europe without calling you."

"But you're not in Europe, are you?" he snapped back.

"No," she agreed testily. "I'm in Colombia."

"Precisely," he said curtly.

"Precisely, what?" she countered, egging him on, although she knew full well what he was about to say.

"It's dangerous," he replied slowly. "Colombia is dangerous. You cannot, ever, be incommunicado, and you have to return my calls in a timely manner."

"It's dangerous?" she asked with a laugh, thinking, If you only knew. If you only knew that I've been sleeping with someone who has the ability to have anyone he wants killed.

Gabriella takes a deep breath and lashes out at her father. "It's not Iraq, you know? And if you would ever take the trouble to look into it, or to come here, you would realize that," she adds.

She could hear the meanness in her voice, but the distance between them emboldened her.

"Gabriella, do I need to cut this trip short?" he asked tersely, but underneath the terseness, she heard the defensiveness—no, the impotence in his voice.

He doesn't know that if he were to call Nini right now, she'd ship Gabriella right back to him in a heartbeat. All he knows is she's an ocean's distance away. She is an adult. If he were to close the purse strings, she could still do as she pleases. Just like her mother could, all those years ago.

Left out once, left out twice. Her father's grasp on her is unraveling, just as it did with her mother. Everything in his world has changed since then, but here, all remained the same, time crouched still, waiting for her to resume her mother's footsteps.

Did he know? she wonders. Did he feel something had shifted against him in the same way he now does, the empty seconds ticking away—one, two, three, four—at the rate of two dollars and fifty cents per minute?

"Gabriella, I know something is wrong. Tell me what's

going on," she heard her father say, his tone changed from chastising to entreating, and she felt the urge to reassure him that it was okay, that, despite everything, she was still his. But immediately, she rebelled against her own thoughts.

She was the one who needed comfort now. She was the one who needed someone who could listen, just listen, not say a word. Or maybe, say just a word or two. Perhaps, all those years ago, her father wasn't as attentive with her mother as he is now with Gabriella. Maybe he missed all the cues that could have allowed him to discern a change and force his hand. Or maybe he didn't want to see, blinded by the unwitting arrogance of someone who is so certain of himself he cannot fathom that those he holds dear could simply let go.

"You chart your own waters, Gabriella," her father has often told her. "There is no destiny. Only volition."

"Gabriella?" he repeated, cutting through her thoughts, but she interrupted him.

"Daddy. Please. Daddy, listen to me," she said. Demanded. "I am fine. I am safe. Nothing is happening to me. Nothing will happen to me. It's just that . . . You have to give me a little space right now, okay? Because I'm sorting through things, and I need you to let me breathe, and do what I need to do, okay? Isn't that what you always taught me to do? To take control over my life? Well, I'm doing just that."

The silence this time was even longer than before.

"Perhaps it would help if you spoke to me," he told her, resigned.

Gabriella looked around her room. Saw her mother's portrait, facedown on the nightstand, picked it up, and once again, looked at it curiously, divining her intentions. Perhaps it would help. But she couldn't.

"When I have something to say, Daddy, I will," she finally said.

Gabriella laid back on her bed, exhausted, and turned on her iPod, clicking until she found it, Arthur Hanlon, then turned up the volume and let the spiraling lines of the piano wash over her and inside her. No words, just music. The soundtrack to her roller coaster. She closed her eyes and pictured Angel's face the last time she saw him, blank, rigid, showing his true self, perhaps. How easy to read people wrong, to make mistakes, she thought, and impulsively looked at her mother again. What did he look like? she wondered.

Juan José.

Juan José who should have never been reduced to a banal JJ.

He still lived here, Nini told her. It was likely they had crossed paths, at some point, in a city as small as this. She tried desperately to remember the name of his company, fleetingly mentioned the day she fought with Nini.

Juan José Solano.

It comes to her in a flash, and she yanks the headphones from her ears, runs to the kitchen, and thumbs through the phone book.

Before she can lose her nerve, she places the call.

"El señor Solano," she asks softly.

"He arrives at nine," the voice on the other side answers. "Would you care to leave a message?"

"No, no," Gabriella says quickly. "I'll call back."

In her room, she sorts through her clothes, sweeping everything out of the closet and dumping it on the bed.

She wants to look anything but ordinary to him. She wants to look dignified, refined, hard to get. She wants his respect.

She settles on khaki pants, red halter top, and low, strappy sandals. She ties her hair back loosely and carefully applies makeup, even though it's not even noon.

Living in Los Angeles, Gabriella long ago stopped wasting her time on false modesty. Now, she looks at herself in the mirror dispassionately and sees in her reflection a strikingly beautiful girl, the kind of girl people will turn to look at, will wonder what her story is. This is the kind of girl she wants to be today.

Her hand shakes as she brings her lipstick up to her mouth, and she stops, takes a big breath.

"Relax, relax," she tells herself. Because for the first time all week, she knows exactly what she needs to do.

Gabriella brings her lipstick up to her mouth again and carefully paints her lips a delicate pink.

From time to time, Juan José's secretary looks up at her, but she doesn't smile. Her eyes hold the deliberate, offended blankness of forced servitude. She would like to send Gabriella packing, but she can't because she looks rich, because she acts rich, because she is rich.

"Please let him know I'm here," Gabriella had quietly but firmly demanded when it was reasonably pointed out to her that she had no appointment.

"He's busy," the secretary countered rudely.

"Please tell him I'm here," she repeated with the somber dignity learned from her grandmother. "I'll wait."

It's a large room with leather couches and a massive Obregón painting hanging on the main wall. A model of his latest project stands ensconced under glass in the center. It's the shopping center Juan Carlos has been saying will revitalize the southern portion of the city. When she gets up to look at it more closely, she sees fountains and wide-open spaces. Her uncle Julián likes the project because it will lie within a one-mile radius of the two housing subdivisions he's now building. She wonders if he, too, knew about her mother and Juan José. If he tacitly encouraged the relationship, thinking of future business deals.

But the thought is too poisonous to bear, and she returns quietly to her seat and waits.

Gabriella adjusts her sandals, reties her hair. This morning's overpowering urge to throw up has given way to sheer hunger. It is past two o'clock, and she hasn't eaten a thing all day and her thoughts and emotions are starting to simmer.

She's about to ask for a coffee, a glass of water, anything, but the phone rings and Juan José's secretary listens for a second, then looks at her again.

"You can go ahead," she says dryly, motioning.

Gabriella sits quietly for a moment, taking deep breaths, like she does before a concert, but her legs still shake slightly when she walks into his office.

He stands up from behind his desk, and for a long time, they simply look at each other from across the room.

She's not sure what she had expected. A handsome man

certainly. A man more handsome than her father, or at least comparable. She had imagined his darker skin, his black, black hair, the firmness of his hands.

But his body is now bulky, softer, his face slightly puffy, its angles folded by time. His widow's peak has receded high above his brow, and the graying hair lightens up his skin.

He is like a faded painting.

Unremarkable.

Only in the eyes, the assured, slightly sardonic eyes of a man who knows what he wants, does Gabriella find a flicker of justification for her mother's actions.

He looks at her steadily. Then he reaches for the pack of cigarettes on his desk, offers her one, and when she declines, lights his own, without bothering to ask whether she minds his smoking or not. His hands, she sees, are manicured.

He motions her to take a seat and she finally comes forward, aware of his eyes following her movement across the room.

"You look nothing like your mother," he finally says, leaning back against his desk.

"You don't look the way I expected, either," she replies.

He snorts.

"Time," he says, turning his head to flick the ashes into a silver ashtray, "doesn't pass in vain."

They consider each other warily, the air heavy with mistrust. She can't even begin to pretend she's here on a cordial mission, and he's utterly unprepared for her visit. Had she been the daughter of a friend, maybe there could be easy rapport. But she's Helena's daughter, and everything is complicated.

On the shelf behind his desk, she catches a glimpse of a family picture: He's sitting on a couch next to a woman and two children, faces bright with laughter. She looks young—much younger than him, much younger than her mother would be today—and has long blonde hair. The girl she hugs to her right side has hair like hers, tied back in a red bow. The boy is younger, and he, too, has sandy-colored hair, slicked back to expose a widow's peak.

He's married. Her father never married again, but he did.

"My mother was married when you had your affair," she says suddenly, taking him by surprise. "Didn't you care?"

He looks away from her. Pueblo pequeño, infierno grande, he thinks, wondering who told her about them. He is fifty-two years old and has never been questioned about his relationships in his entire life, much less this relationship. The girl has balls. There is something about her mother in her after all, he thinks dryly.

He considers asking her to leave but instead looks at her intently again. Her eyes are slate gray. They're nothing like Helena's yellow, slanted eyes. But in their depths he recognizes something he's been looking to see for the past seventeen years.

"Why are you here?" he counters.

"I found her diary," says Gabriella quietly.

"What?" he asks, puzzled.

"I found her diary," Gabriella repeats, louder now. Juan José shakes his head. He's had a diary inside his head for all these years, a diary whose pages have been fading. Only flickers remain, as the details he so carefully guarded have been slipping with time, with his marriage, with his two children. Helena's face has been replaced by another face. Only rarely does he think of her anymore.

"A diary of what?" he asks again, uncomprehending.

He didn't know, Gabriella realizes. He didn't know, either.

"Of everything," she says evenly. She stops and looks away uncomfortably. Like a flash, she imagines his mouth on her mother's breast and covers her eyes with her hands, then uncovers them and looks up at him again. "She wrote everything down. She wrote about you."

For the first time in a long time, Juan José is at a loss. His hands actually start to shake, and he stubs out the cigarette in the ashtray. He doesn't know what upsets him more: the notion that she had a diary and that he didn't know about it, or the fact that what he did with her is public knowledge. He tries to remember what he and Helena talked about. What they did. How would she have described their time together? He can't bring himself to ask for details from this young girl with the morose, accusing eyes.

"Has your grandmother seen it?" he asks, trying to sound nonchalant.

"No! No," she repeats emphatically, shaking her head quickly, nervously. "No one saw it. No one will see it. Not even my father. Just me."

"What do you want from me?" he asks after a brief silence. He wants her gone. He's sorry he ever agreed to see her.

"Nothing," she says, shaking her head, confused. She really doesn't know what she wants. "I mean. I— I just wanted to see you. I didn't know you existed."

The words were coming out in a torrent now.

"I didn't know you existed until I read her diary. No one told me. I was— so little. I hardly remember her. I remember we were happy. I thought we were happy. I mean, I don't remember any sadness. But she wrote that she fell in love with you. I wanted to know why she would do that, when she had us."

It doesn't come out the way she wants it to, and even to her ears, she sounds naïve, pathetic.

Juan José never considered that he was doing anything wrong with Helena. Her family, barely mentioned, was a continent away. Gabriella was a tiny inconvenience. Too tiny to protest. Too tiny to realize what happened or didn't.

He makes a genuine effort to remember their clandestine conversations. Helena had told him she'd discussed leaving Marcus with her friend Elisa, whose father had left when she was twelve.

"She says it's better when they're young," Helena had told him earnestly during one of so many nights of endless plans that seemed to go nowhere. "Their lives aren't disrupted. It becomes normal."

And until now, he reflects, it was normal.

Normal. He repeats the word in his mind, like a mantra, wondering how much she can take and how much he can give.

"She didn't do anything wrong," he finally says slowly, not because he believes that anymore, but because it's much too late to have regrets. "People fall in and out of love. People make mistakes, they have affairs, sometimes they get divorced and they remarry and that's normal."

"No!" she says, shaking her head. "No."

"Yes," he counters firmly. "Many couples get divorced. It is normal," he repeats, spacing out each word.

"It's not normal to want to leave your child!" she spits out. "Did you think she was going to do that? Did you *ask* her to do that?"

He feels like telling her it's none of her business, but when he looks at her, he sees how young she is. A child. A child who looks at him expectantly, as if he holds all the answers to the secrets of the universe.

Juan José's mother is still alive. He has lunch at her house every Wednesday. He tries to imagine growing up without her, and can't. He wonders what he'd think if he ever found out she'd been unfaithful to his father. He wonders if she ever felt for his father what he once felt for Helena. What the years have muted now comes back to him in waves, and he's unable to lie to her daughter or send her away or trivialize it, as he's forced himself to do for all these years.

He looks at his polished wooden floor, then stands.

"Would you like some water?" he asks quietly, walking toward the minibar at the end of his office.

Gabriella nods quickly.

He gets two bottles and motions her toward the leather couch in the corner, opens one bottle for her, one for him. Sitting on the edge of the couch, his elbows propped on his knees, he looks suddenly younger. A stray lock of hair—the hair that he still combs straight back—falls over his forehead, and for a second, Gabriella catches a glimmer of the man her mother fell in love with.

"I had known your mother for years, but I had never *seen* her. I wouldn't be able to tell you why. It just wasn't meant to be at the time, I suppose. And then, I saw her at this party."

He stops and she can almost see her, reflected in the memory in his eyes.

"She was…a vision. She was wearing a lilac dress. It looked a little bit like a flapper dress, but she was so wonderfully small and slim she could wear it. She looked like a figurine. And she had this…this long"—his fingers go up to his neck as he describes it—"this very long scarf that she'd tied so it fell down her back. I'd never seen anyone dress like that.

"I hate to say it was love at first sight, because it sounds so corny and because it wasn't love at first sight. I'd practically grown up with her. But that night, I saw her, and I knew, like I'd never known about anyone before. Can you understand that?"

Gabriella pictures her mother, the photographs that practically speak to her. Although she doesn't say so to Juan José, she can understand. Oblivious to her thoughts, he continues.

"I once read, long after Helena died, that you're extremely fortunate if you find true love once in your lifetime. Twice is practically impossible. I didn't know that when I saw her that day. All I knew is, there was…something. I've never really figured it out. Her perfume? Her dress?

"I had to talk to her. I had to dance with her. I couldn't let her go and risk not seeing her again." Juan José pauses to take a small sip from his water bottle. When he speaks again, Gabriella hears the strain in his voice.

"Of course, she told me she was married. And of course, she spoke about you. Constantly. About how you learned how to walk when you were only nine months old. She told me she only spoke to you in Spanish, because she wanted you to be fluent, never forget where you were from. She said you played the piano. That you were picking out melodies at four years old.

"Do you still play?" he asks, his voice wistful.

"Yes," she says softly. "That's what I do. I'm a pianist."

Juan José smiles, a wan, sad smile. "I'm glad," he says. "She would have liked that."

There's a small, restless silence, punctuated by the hum of the air-conditioning.

"So, yes," he finally continues. "I knew about you. I knew all about you. But I still fell in love with your mother."

Juan José takes a long swig of water from his bottle.

Talking about personal issues is alien to him. After Helena died, he dropped the subject, and his best friends did, too. Those close to him were unsure how to react. Give their condolences for someone else's wife? His future with Helena had been formalized only between the two of them. Taking it beyond that—insisting to the world that they had planned on getting married—was not only absurd, but futile.

In the beginning, he resented the silence, even though he himself was unable to break it. He felt cheated out of mourning her, a stranger at her funeral, standing to one side as Marcus shook hand after hand, finally coming to his. When he looked him in the eye, there was no recognition of who he was. Just one more of Helena's friends, now forever relegated to anonymity, not even a snapshot in some lost photo album.

Only one night, many months later, did he acknowledge the finality of the situation.

His father was away on business, and his mother invited him out to the movies in an effort to lure him out of his funk.

It was a weeknight, and they sat in the half-empty theater, watching *Amadeus*. Later, they walked to the ice cream parlor, where he sipped a Coke as his mother daintily ate a scoop of tangerine sorbet and made small talk.

Only when they got into the car, alone again in half darkness, did his mother stretch her hand over his on the steering wheel and finally ask, "Are you okay, m'ijo?"

Juan José, who had long ago ceased to be a boy, let himself be one for the last time in his life.

"Helena always had tangerine sorbet after the movies," he said simply, looking at her with lost bafflement. "She used to say that they didn't make it in the States. Isn't it funny that she had the same tastes you did?"

"Ay, m'ijo," his mother said softly, reaching over across the car seat to smooth his hair from his forehead, like she did when he was a little boy.

He tried not to cry, but he couldn't hold it, and his mother brought his head to her shoulder, gently rocking him as he sobbed helplessly, a month of tears for what he'd lost and what could have been and what he now would never know.

It's all coming back to him. So many years. Such a long time. Until you begin to think about things, and then they come back in a rush.

"I took her to a lot of the haciendas she photographed in the book," he tells Gabriella now. "I even took her to places she hadn't planned on including. That was the wonderful thing about her. I know this valley so well. I know every place worth knowing in it. But with your mother, I rediscovered everything.

"She made me see things I didn't know existed," he says, and there's wonderment in his voice, a wonderment Gabriella has never heard in anyone's voice when they speak to her.

She looks at him carefully and sees that, even now, his eyes sparkle with the thought of her mother, his face grows animated as he recounts things never said before.

"One day, we were driving back from Palmira and we ran into a circus, of all things," he says, shaking his head. "They were setting up the tents. She made me stop, and we bought cotton candy and she convinced the circus manager, or the circus director—I don't know what the title is—to give us a private tour. We got to see the lions, the tigers, the elephants. They even let her try out a trapeze. It was unbelievable.

"That was the kind of person she was. She could convince people to do anything for her. Before we left, she took pictures of everyone. These great black-and-white pictures, Richard Avedon style, where you could see every crease on a person's face. She developed them, and we took them back a week later. Gave them out to everyone. I never understood why she didn't do more portraits. She was a master at bringing out people's true expressions."

He stops and rolls the water bottle between his two hands.

"I asked her to marry me after the first month," he finally says and looks directly into Gabriella's eyes. "I know that's not what you want to hear, but that's what happened."

An image of her father flashes through Gabriella's mind. All the girlfriends. All those beautiful girlfriends. A different one every year, every second year. Aspiring actresses, writers. None of them Latina. An entertainment attorney once, who bought her a PlayStation for Christmas. Silvia, a grant writer, who's been his companion for the last three years. A reserved, practical woman who likes to work while Gabriella practices her piano. In her steady presence, she's almost found a friend.

In all their eyes, Gabriella has recognized, even as a child, that longing look she now sees in Juan José's. She always thought her father hadn't remarried because he had never found anyone else to love. Now, she wonders if it was because he was afraid of losing someone all over again, or if he simply lost faith in women, because he knew he'd been betrayed and couldn't stand the thought of it happening again. Her father's perceptiveness is a gift that makes him a great director of photography. He must have sensed things were different when Helena returned from her two-month tryst. He must have seen it in her eyes as well.

Perhaps he did know, after all, she thinks, and she's filled with sudden pity, a feeling she has never associated with her father.

"What did she say?" Gabriella finally asks.

"What did she say about what?" he asks.

"When you asked her to marry you. Did she say yes?" she presses.

"What good is this doing you?" he replies, frowning, shaking his head in impatience. He looks at Gabriella with something close to disgust. "You love your mother, don't you? Why do you want to dredge up what's over and done with?"

"I didn't dredge up anything," Gabriella says. "She left the diary for me to find. You know, I've never believed in fate, but now I'm starting to. If I found it, I was meant to find it. I was meant to know what happened."

Gabriella's voice quickens and rises with her heartbeat. "You know what? I *deserve* to know what happened. I'm her daughter. Her only daughter. It's my right. So tell me. What did she say when you asked her to marry you?"

Juan José sighs. A big, heavy, tired sigh.

"At first she said no," he says, shaking his head. "She thought it was a big joke, or a fling; I don't know what she was thinking. So I let some time go by, and I made sure she knew how serious I was. And I asked her again. And the second time, she said yes."

I should be stunned, Gabriella thinks to herself. I should be crying. I should be protesting.

Gabriella opens her mouth to speak, but he silences her with a wave of his hand.

"She said yes," he continues, "and we settled on a date. January. And then she left. And then, something changed. I'm sure it had to do with you and your father and being together as a family again, and I expected that. She had to sort things out. Figure out how to bring you here. I kept asking her to come, even for the weekend. And she finally called and said she would be here before Christmas, but only for a couple of days. She said she needed to see me, and then she had to spend Christmas in Los Angeles.

"It was a ridiculous time of the year to come, for only two days, but I was dying to see her. I should have talked her out of it, because what was one more month? But I didn't."

Juan José leans back, closes his eyes briefly.

"And she took that flight. You don't know how many years I spent thinking how I could have changed the outcome of things. If I had insisted she come a day late or a day early. Or if I had insisted that she tell me whatever it was she was going to tell me over the phone. If she had missed the connecting flight to Cali from Miami."

He had spoken to her the night before, one of so many evenings when he took advantage of the three-hour time difference with the West Coast, calling her right before Marcus came home for the night.

"The nights here," Helena had told him, "they're so still. Like a painting. I miss the cacophony of home. Here, I have to turn the lights on, play the music really loud, so I can pretend that I'm not alone."

"What about Gabriella?" he had asked her stupidly.

"What about Gabriella?" she'd said testily. "She's four. I can't exactly have enlightened conversations with her just yet."

He tried to reach out to her across the continent and the ocean, tried to feel her hair, soft against the palm of his hand.

"You'll sleep in a really loud place tomorrow night," he said gently.

"That's right," she said. "I sure will."

Only later, when he replayed the conversation in his head, did he hear the gentle sadness in her voice.

He rubs his temples, the memory making his head hurt.

For years afterward, he had pictured that last scene of her life. Helena running with her bag and her red purse flying behind her—running because she was chronically late and in the short time he'd spent with her, she had been late for every single meeting they ever had—cursing, because she would most certainly be cursing (*carajo, carajo, carajo, damn, damn, damn*), yet somehow managing to make it to the gate, to dash into the plane, hot and bothered and disheveled and alive.

She would have taken a book.

"*Madame Bovary,*" she had told him wryly over the phone. "To get in the mood."

He's pictured her with the book in her hand, because she would have read it until the last possible minute, and he's wondered what she thought about at the end, when she must have realized that they were going to crash, because he knows, he's convinced, that Helena, in her brilliance, would have figured it out.

"You know what the chances are of dying in a plane crash?" he asks Gabriella, and there's wonder and regret in the question. "I looked it up. One in eleven million. One in eleven million," he repeats. "And she was the one."

Gabriella doesn't say anything to this, because she, too, has looked up statistics. And because she's thinking of what he said before.

"You don't know why she needed to see you?" she asks.

He smiles a little.

"Yes, I thought that, too," he answers. "That she was coming to tell me no to my face. It sounds like something she would do. I never met a more up-front person in my life."

He shakes his head ruefully. "Yes, I thought that. And I also thought she may have wanted to see me before the holidays."

He hears himself speak as if from a great distance, hears how callous he sounds. Cruel. But he can't help himself now.

Helena's daughter, he thinks, looking at Gabriella critically. A girl who looks like a woman, with the classic, symmetrical features of a beauty who will age well.

Her face looks crumpled now, dissolved into childish helplessness.

Should he have lied? At least a little?

"Have you ever been in love? Really been in love?" he asks suddenly, earnestly. Because in the end that's what it was about between him and Helena. It wasn't about family or obligations or money or provenance, and certainly, it wasn't about children. It was two people who fell in love, and for one of them, perhaps, the timing wasn't right, but the love was strong enough to win in the end.

She thinks momentarily of Angel. Of his hands, his breath, his mouth, of everything that happened to her when she was with him.

She looks at Juan José, lumpy and middle-aged, and cannot imagine him with Helena, forever youthful in her mind.

Gabriella shrugs, feeling uncomfortable. She wants to leave.

"When it happens to you, you'll know and you'll understand," he says urgently, as much for Gabriella as for himself and for Helena, because he can clearly see how they both must look in this young woman's eyes.

Eyes that Gabriella closes briefly. Opens them again.

She has seen what he thinks she would see: A selfish man,

who fell in love with a selfish woman. A woman who was up-front with everyone except those that mattered. She didn't even have the guts to write the marriage proposal into the journal. The sex stayed in, the marriage proposal went out.

For most of my life, thinks Gabriella, I've been living on lies.

"Thank you for your time," she says formally, getting up and walking toward the door. Her finality catches him by surprise. He can't let it end on this note.

"Wait!" he calls beseechingly. "There's something you should see before you go."

He goes quickly to his desk and unlocks the bottom drawer, takes out folder after folder, until he finds the one folder he only very rarely looks at now: a simple, military green file folder that is bound with string and fading at the edges. Juan José smooths it out with his hands, even though there's nothing to be smoothed.

"I kept the photos from that shoot," he says, and there's a quiet softness in his look now. Pride, Gabriella suddenly recognizes. He is proud of the photos. He was proud of her mother.

He extends the folder toward her, and she hesitates, then reaches out for it.

The first photo is that of a young woman, her black hair slicked tightly back in a lacquered chignon, her mouth pulled back in a smile, but it's a smile that doesn't reach the grimness of her eyes. She's wearing tights underneath dark sweatpants, and one hand is extended over her stomach, each finger wrapped in tight bandages. You can see the calluses on her hands.

The trapeze artist.

Gabriella goes through them all. The lion trainer. The juggler. The horseback rider. They're beautiful pictures, but each face is filled with quiet, resigned despair.

But her mother's and Juan José's aren't.

His face is framed by the window of the car. He's smoking as he drives and his widow's peak accentuates the haughty nose, the chiseled profile. Tendrils of smoke surround the angles of his face.

This is what he looked like when she fell in love with him, Gabriella thinks. So...Latin. So from here. So different from the people that surrounded her in Los Angeles. The antithesis of her father.

At the very bottom is her mother's picture. Whoever took it caught her unawares. She's eating cotton candy, facing slightly away from the camera, and from the lens' vantage point, you can't see what she's looking at. She's just—looking.

But she's smiling, a wide, delicious smile that appreciates the cotton candy and delights in her surroundings and pops out even in this vague, nearly twenty-year-old black-and-white photo.

"I will be happy, despite it all!" it seems to say.

Even now, Gabriella can't help herself. She would have liked to know this woman. This woman whose style would have certainly been cramped by a little girl.

Gabriella quietly hands the photographs back, and thinks that, after all, it's not his fault.

"Thank you," she says again, looking at him intently for a long moment. And this time she leaves.

*   *   *

The sun outside the building blinds her, and Gabriella senses, rather than sees, the hand striking past her face, halting for the briefest of instances on her neck, tugging hard at her locket until it snaps from around her neck.

She instinctively takes off after him, weaving in and out of the crowded sidewalk, her long runner's legs gaining on the kid—because she sees now that he is just a kid, skinny and barefoot—screaming all the way. "Stop him, stop him, thief, thief, ladrón, ladrón!"

Someone trips the boy, and before he can scramble up, Gabriella kicks him, hard on the back of his legs. She feels his flesh and bones against the thud of her foot. She's never kicked a real person before, not since she was a child, and even then, never hard enough to cause harm. It feels good; she's able to think in the middle of her muddled frenzy. It felt good, so good, to be able to finally hurt someone who was hurting her.

"Give it back, give it back!" she screams with each kick, vaguely aware of the crowd gathering around her, egging her on. It is hot, and the hotness of the air fills her with an almost dreamlike torpidity. As if from a distance, she sees herself, awkward and menacing, kicking the boy methodically in slow motion, and around her, the growing crowd of people takes on a red, amorphous shape that eggs her on, prods her to kick him harder, harder, harder.

"Eso, monita, go blondie, kill the punk, kick his ass, fucking rat."

"Let's settle this right now," whispered one woman furiously, tugging at Gabriella's sleeve. "No cops. Just beat the shit out of him."

The woman smells of soil and cooking food; the smell of poverty. It shakes Gabriella out of her daze.

"Take it, take it," she hears the boy whimpering and realizes he's been doing so for a while now, his cries swallowed by the din. He tosses the locket angrily at her feet, bravado still remaining despite the beating and because, after all, she kicks like an amateur. "It's just a shit piece of tin anyway," he mumbles under his breath, but she hears him.

"It was my mother's," she cries, snatching the little heart up and kicking him again, this time aiming hard for his stomach, again setting off the crowd that had quieted down with curiosity. "My mother's. My mother's! How dare you!" Her voice is getting shriller with each kick; she sounds, even to her ears, deranged.

The boy rolls up in a ball, covering his head.

"I'm sorry," he shouts, and this time she hears him sobbing. "I'm sorry. Please, stop. Please, no more."

Gabriella stops. She is dizzy with heat and her red halter top clings to her chest. She looks at the crowd; their faces are angry and sweaty and indifferently amused. One more piece of scum to wipe out in a city full of scum. Tonight they might not even mention it over dinner, because it will have been so run-of-the-mill.

The street is dirty, full of litter and God knows what from the sewers. She looks at the boy—a boy who probably has nothing, no home, no parents. No mother, like her. No father. Her father would be so ashamed. She feels so ashamed of herself. The crowd looks at her expectantly as she kneels there beside the boy.

"Hey," she says, shaking his shoulder. He doesn't look up. "You can't have my locket," she says.

She opens up her bag, takes out the money from her wallet—100,000 pesos. A little more than forty bucks. A small fortune for someone like him.

"Take this," she says, nudging his hand with the money. He uncovers his head slowly and looks at her uncomprehendingly. He doesn't say anything.

"Take it," she says again, opening up his fist enough to push the wad of money inside. "It's okay," she adds, tired and impatient now. "I'm not going to call the cops. I'm not going to do anything. Just take it and go."

Gabriella stands up and looks at the now-silent crowd. Far away a siren wails, and she feels an impossible sadness.

"Leave him alone," she says simply. "No pasó nada. Nothing's happened."

She waits for a moment, until the crowd begins to disperse, until the kid stands up, wobbly, and starts walking away, his hand clutched tightly around the money. He stops, stoops down, places it inside his shoe, looks back at her once, then walks off quickly, breaking into a run, never turning around.

She starts walking, too, even though Nini's building is far and she should never, ever (that's what Nini always said, never, *ever*) walk alone. She really should take a cab or call someone to come and get her. But she has just given away her money. And there is no one she wants to see.

She goes the long way home, along the river, past downtown with the locket held tightly in her hand, afraid of letting go to wipe the sweaty palm on her jeans. It had been a dry summer and the riverbed below looks as brown and wilted as the surrounding grass, which up close reveals little piles of litter never visible from her usual vantage point inside her air-conditioned car.

Someone calls out to her and she turns to face an old beggar with a hideous stump for a hand. She shakes her head no, no money, and hears him curse her as she steps up her pace. "Malparida, whore," he hisses, and for the first time that day, she is afraid.

He could touch her, she realizes. And hit her and rob her and kill her, and no one would know for days. Her body would be thrown down the river, and it would reappear weeks later. That, she'd heard, was what was happening with the mafiosos that were getting their due of late. Men like Angel's father. Shot and dumped in a river that took the bodies to inhospitable regions. They could be lost forever.

The factory owners that operated on the river's edge, farther north, had voiced their protests.

"We refuse to continue fishing bodies out of the water," a manager had said on the news. "That's the police's job. We won't do it anymore."

Since then the bodies piled up at a fork in the river, snagged by the bend and the vegetation. Every Thursday, the army would come and drag the corpses out, most of them unidentifiable John Does whose bodies were later sent to the morgue of the university hospital, for the medical students to practice on.

If the victims were missed, few people ventured to say so. Being quiet wasn't only a virtue; it was a survival skill.

What could I possibly have found pretty about this? she

wonders, taking in, really taking in, the dirt and the trash and the unrepentant chaos.

Juan José had said her mother had given him energy, made him see things he had never seen before.

And all that time Gabriella had been a continent away. Her cries soothed by someone else. Her food cooked by someone else. Someone else's voice reading Dr. Seuss to her at night.

While her mother made him see things he'd never seen before.

When she gets to the contemporary art museum, she stops and climbs up the steps to the outdoor fountain. She feels safe here, surrounded by people that come in and out of the gift shop and a new, trendy café that serves fruit shakes and salads. She looks longingly toward the entrance, but the thought of people repels her. Instead, she sits at the water's edge, feeling the noon sun hit her in waves timed to the steady chirping of the cicadas.

She's hot and thirsty and needs to pee and needs to cry.

She could call Edgar, but the thought of going back to Nini's right now is unbearable, having to give explanations surrounded by her mother's things.

Her mother, who's been dead for seventeen years, yet remains inextricably linked to everyone and everything that Gabriella knows in this place, down to this museum whose gift shop still sells her book and whose permanent collection still includes some of her photographs.

Maybe her mother had gone back to Los Angeles, saw her, carried her, heard her read, and heard her play "Aura Lee" on the piano, and maybe she fell in love with her all over again. Maybe she really had decided to stay with them.

Or maybe Gabriella wasn't good enough for her, not good enough to keep her home.

This is what wives must feel when their husbands leave them for someone younger, more beautiful, more accomplished.

Not saddened. Ashamed.

The secret she can't tell is literally making her dizzy. She'd like to lie down alone for a week, empty herself of all this.

Gabriella looks at the river across the street, and from this short distance, it looks beautiful again.

When she picks up the phone to call him, she doesn't think about the horrible incident in the car last week or the roses he's sent every day since or her grandmother's vocal disapproval or what her father would say about her choice of friends.

She wants to hear his voice, and when he speaks her name—"Gabriella?"—softly and tentatively and happily, she starts to cry.

"Gabriella!" he repeats, alarmed now, but she can't stop.

"Where are you?" he asks urgently. "Just tell me where you are, I'll come get you." She stammers the words out, holding tightly to her phone, not moving at all until he pulls up twenty minutes later, alone, without the guards—or at least, none that she can see—and takes her hand and gently guides her to his car.

Inside, he holds her fingers with one hand and drives with the other.

"Did someone hurt you?" he says calmly.

She shakes her head.

"Can you talk?" he asks.

She shakes her head again. Tears are pouring down her face.

He reaches back for a box of Kleenex and hands it to her, watches her take five at a time.

"Should I take you home?" he finally asks.

This time she shakes her head vigorously. No.

"Okay, Gabriella," he says again, steadily, reasonably. "I'm going to take you to my house. We can talk. And you can stay there as long as you want. Okay? Is that okay?"

She nods.

She leans back into the leather seat, tears still streaming down her face. He looks at her hand, clenched in a fist on the black leather upholstery, and every so often, his fingers tighten around hers.

The apartment is big and airy, with a panoramic view of the city. It's on the west side of town, up in the hills where, as in her grandmother's neighborhood, stately homes have been torn down to make way for high-rise, luxury buildings.

She's surprised that his place is cozy, that the floor is wooden, that the decoration is subdued: leather couches and beige linen curtains. She expected the glitz and shining armor of his father's house; the wide, open slabs of marble. He's right, she thinks, ruefully. She sees him as a cliché, and he's not.

The biggest surprise is the baby grand piano, sitting in the corner of the living room.

She walks toward it automatically, runs her hands gently over the keys, plays an arpeggio to test the action.

He's always been proud of his piano, even though he'd originally gotten it as a prop. If he was going to promote concerts, wouldn't it be nice if he had a piano in his living room? his decorator had asked. He'd agreed.

In Cali, not exactly a bastion of piano stores, they'd had a hard time finding a brown piano to match the furniture, and he categorically refused to buy a used instrument. In the end, they had to order it from Baldwin's catalog and have it shipped through a dealer in Medellín.

Moving the piano had been a hassle, and word had even leaked to his father in prison, who'd confronted him in his next visit.

"What's this fag bullshit I hear about taking piano lessons?" he had demanded. "Don't you have anything better to do with your time and my money?"

"No one is more respectable than a patron of the arts," Angel had replied wryly, a comment that managed to coax a laugh out of his father.

"A patron of the arts," he said, shaking his head. "I must say, Angel, I didn't know you had it in you. It's a good line," he said with grudging admiration in his voice. "Although, I wouldn't exactly call presenting salsa shows patronage of the arts. You're going to have to do a little better than that to be Mr. Respectable," he added, laughing again, looking around at the cadre of bribed prison guards and personal employees that hung out in his private jail wing.

"It's just the beginning," said Angel calmly. "I'll pay your money back. I'll give it back to you nice and clean, as a matter of fact."

"Nice and clean," his father had repeated, nodding, serious now, leaning forward in his chair and placing his hand on his son's knee.

"You do that, m'ijo. Otherwise, I'm wasting my time here eating shit. You let Julito run my numbers. Never mind what I say, never mind what I do. Whatever you do, keep it fucking clean. I'm going to be the last one in my family to sit in a shithole like this one. Don't forget that."

The business was clean in a year. And it began to become profitable as he expanded his reach. Being his father's son and having an army of men at his disposal gave him an edge over the competition: he could always offer artists security as part of the package. The first time government officials investigated his finances, they found nothing out of line in his books. The second time, only six months later, they didn't, either. Angel was by nature meticulous, but the years of business school in Switzerland and France had made him more so.

Angel kept a low profile. His shows could be over the top, but he was never part of the press. The word out in the street now was that if they were to nail Luis Silva's son, they had to look at something other than the concert promotion business.

He also kept the piano. He found it gave him a certain cachet to invite the stars he booked for a drink at his apartment and have a grand piano to show.

Impulsively, he hired a piano teacher, who for a while came to his home every single morning at seven. Angel paid well for the service, but after a year, he had to recognize it was an exercise in futility. Much as he felt the music, his brain refused to convey the message to his hands, which felt like lumps of coal on the keys. Worse still, he found practicing tedious and meaningless. He fired the teacher, but as a consolation prize, he hired him regularly to play at his parties.

Now Gabriella runs her fingers over the keys of his piano. No woman had ever played—really played—his piano. How many planets had to have aligned themselves to bring this particular girl to this particular house? he wondered. Angel didn't believe in coincidences. His life was too precarious for coincidences. He believed in plans. But he believed in fate.

A door had opened here, and doors only opened briefly, he knew. This one he had almost shut. And now, he was getting a second chance.

"Will you play?"

Gabriella shakes her head, but smiles a little, her first smile in hours. She has an arsenal of melancholia at her fingertips, but she never plays it in front of anyone, not unless it's a performance.

Angel walks toward her slowly, and through the sunglasses she won't take off, she again takes in how very beautiful he is, how tall and lithe, how his smooth golden skin contrasts against those strange green eyes. How odd his circumstance, she thinks, that such outward perfection could result from the chaos of a father who now sits in jail and a mother who abandoned him.

Gabriella lifts her hand to his cheek and leaves it there, feeling herself steadied by the warm, new planes of his face.

He lifts both hands and gently removes her sunglasses.

The gray eyes that so beguile him are swollen almost beyond recognition, and her pale skin is splotchy.

"Qué quieres?" he asks her. "What do you want?"

Gabriella shakes her head. "I want to be with you," she says, her voice hoarse, speaking very slowly in the beginning, then rushing the words. "I want to be with you, and stand next to you, and I don't want to hide or lie or pretend you're anyone else..." Gabriella's voice rises and breaks off.

"I just want to be with you," she repeats, quietly now.

Gabriella lifts her other hand to his face and brings it close to hers, so close she can smell the sweat of his skin and the clean smell of shampoo that clings to his hair. When he kisses her, she tastes beer and cigarettes and an almost unbearable sweetness that she doesn't want to let go of. He's the one who pulls away, who leads her to the bedroom, who undresses himself first, then slowly takes all her clothes off and covers her with his body so he touches every inch of her, his legs against her legs, his thighs against her thighs, his stomach against her stomach, so he obliterates everything else but his skin on her skin, his mouth on her mouth.

"I remember very few things about my mother," she tells him later. "Very few *real* things, I mean. You know how, when you look at a picture so many times, you come to believe you've actually seen what's in the picture? I think that's what happened to me. I remember a birthday party where my parents got me a pony and a petting zoo, and I remember my mother kneeling beside me, taking my hand, and helping me pet the baby sheep. But that's also in my photo album, you know what I mean? I don't know if I remember her, or just the picture."

She's lying with her head on his chest, not looking at him as she speaks. Overhead, the fan whirls, and the long white gauzy curtains billow gently as the Cali afternoon breeze pushes through the open balcony doors. In the stillness of the room, she can hear the rhythmic in and out of the curtains sweeping up and down, accompanying the kitchen clock, which ticks loudly and steadily a room away.

"I went through a phase where I wanted to find out the"—she lowers her voice to a dramatic level—"the long-term effects of growing up without a mother. I even joined a support group. We'd sit around and talk about the emotional void and how it's so important to have a substitute mother figure to provide the tenderness and comfort that a woman gives. Blah, blah, blah.

"But you see, the thing is, I never really felt a void. I mean, yes, I missed having a mother. Terribly. But my dad was so, so extraordinary. He would even go to the Mother's Day breakfasts. He would take me with him when he went away for a long time. He would go shopping with me. When I got my period, he sat me down and gave me this long talk about the meaning of being a woman.

"So it's not that I was unloved. I was so loved. By everyone. But by him especially. And he would always tell me how very much my mother had loved me, too. How I was the light of her life. Have you heard that song by La Oreja de Van Gogh? It's a waltz, a kind of children's waltz, very whimsical. It sounds like a windup toy. And the mother—I always think it's the mother anyway—sings about how she has to visit her child when she's asleep, in the world of dreams. And when her daughter wakes up, she'll think she dreamt of her, but really, it was a visit. That's what I held on to for all these years. That my dreams were visits. And in my dreams, she was always the way I remembered her. The way she looked in the pictures. So beautiful. And so happy. It kills me to think that she was unhappy with me. That in the last days of her life, I was a burden to her, an obligation that kept her from her happiness."

Angel doesn't say anything for a few moments, then offers simply, "She would have come back, you know."

"I don't know that."

"Maybe she didn't say it. But she would have. That guy Juan José is right. People do fall in and out of love. They have affairs. They think they're in love with someone else, and then they realize they're not, and sometimes it's too late."

Angel looks at the fan. It's hypnotic.

"It had nothing to do with you," he says matter-of-factly.

Gabriella is quiet now. The fact that she lost her mother tragically, that her father never remarried, and she was raised only by a man has been a defining ingredient of who she is.

It's been fodder for pity and attention and curiosity, a void she can't truly fill, but a crutch she's used, sometimes shamelessly, to get her way. She doesn't remember the Mother's Day celebration of her kindergarten year, but she vividly recalls the first-grade breakfast, where each child in the class had to write a note to their mom and read it aloud.

She had mulled over the note for hours in her seven-year-old head. She prayed to her mother every night, like Nini had taught her to do. But no one had ever told her she could actually write to her, mail her a letter, a letter that could be opened and read. It was even better than writing to Santa Claus, she decided.

She finally wrote:

Dear Mommy,

Happy Mother's Day! I didn't know you celebrated it in heaven, too. Does it ever get lonely up there? I don't get lonely too much, but sometimes I wish you could take me shopping and that you could wear the gifts I make you for Mother's Day. This year I made you a pin. It's made out of newspaper, but we call it papier-mâché. It's red because Daddy says it's your favorite color.

I'm sending it to heaven with this letter. If you can, let me know if you like it. Maybe you can visit me in a dream, like an angel. I know you're probably angry because I got a C in math. But I've been practicing a lot, and now I'm getting A's. Daddy says everyone in heaven gets A's or B's. So, can I get a puppy now?

Happy Mother's Day. I hope you like your pin. Don't lose it!

I love you very much, Mommy.

Love, Gabriella

Her father was in the classroom, as he always was for these events, and he'd listened attentively, ignoring the hush in the room, the mothers discreetly dabbing at the tears in their eyes, the other kids staring at Gabriella in awe. She had a mother in heaven. How cool was that?

A week later, she got her puppy. But Marcus, who definitely didn't want to foster some notion about wish-granting ghosts, went through a lengthy explanation of how the puppy was a gift for her good grades.

Gabriella didn't believe him.

She continued to write her mother. Past the age when she knew there was no Santa Claus, and past the age when she knew, in her heart of hearts, that there was no possible way to send a letter to heaven. One Sunday, when she was ten years old and Marcus was out jogging, she rummaged through his desk drawers looking for a stapler for her school project. Inside a brown envelope box, at the very bottom, she found her letters, neatly tied up, the stamps—the dozens of stamps needed to send something to heaven—still pasted on each envelope. They were still sealed, intact. Never sent, never opened. Her father hadn't had the stomach to read her letters to her mother.

Only then did it sink in that her mother was someone that could only be seen in her dreams. She never wrote her again, and Marcus never questioned the abrupt halt in the correspondence. For him, imagination was the product of having your feet planted firmly in the ground. While he was all for preserving Helena's memory, the letters to the dead made him decidedly uneasy.

Gabriella continued to talk to her mother at night, every night before she went to bed. She continued to invoke her name when she really wanted something; the words "my mother would have..." were an effective button pusher. She continued to think of her mother as an ethereal guiding light, not manifest, invisible, but somehow there.

"A mother," Angel now says, and his voice is convinced. "She's important, but she's not indispensable, Gabriella, remember that.

"All the memories I have of my mom when I was a child are beautiful," he adds, slowly stroking her head again, looking up at nothing. "Like little postcards. She was gorgeous, she always smelled so good—she used something called Diorissimo. It smelled like jasmine."

His hand pauses, and she can sense, not see, that his mind is somewhere else, that his fingers are touching someone else's skin.

"She always looked like she was going to go to a party or something like that. Her hair would always be perfect, her hands were manicured, she wore these gold bracelets that tinkled when she walked. But she didn't really take care of me. She didn't see that as her role. She was more concerned with looking good for my father, being a beautiful wife to him. So I learned how to do things on my own. You don't know what kind of mother yours would have been, either.

"Look at all you've done without her," he continues, reaching down and lifting her face to his.

"You did it without her. You're a wonderful pianist," he says. "A composer of beautiful music. And you're not a fucked-up mess of a person. Whatever she did had nothing to do with you. It still doesn't. Okay?"

He kisses her carefully on her upturned face.

"And what happened between you and me the other day, it had nothing to do with you, either," he adds very carefully, in what she recognizes is the closest Angel Silva can come to proffering an apology. "Sometimes," he continues, uncertain at first, then slowly emboldened, "people need to take a step back, they need to reassess, and it can happen over the smallest of things. What's important is being able to regroup and return. And sometimes, it's not possible. But many times, it is.

"Okay?" he asks again, and for the first time that day, she nods.

Helena

We hide. I hate to hide. But we do.

He took me home one day, out of necessity because he had left some papers at the house and, really, making me wait in the car would have been a bit much.

But, as luck would have it, his mother was there. In a way, I was perversely happy to finally meet her face-to-face, to force Juan José's hand.

I could see all the questions in her expression, all the questions she would later ask Juan José: Isn't this Cristina's daughter who married the American film director? Didn't she have a little girl? Why are you bringing her home then?

But to me, she was just polite.

"Ah, I'm so delighted to see you!" she said, smiling brightly. "You look exactly like your mother; it's the most incredible thing. Don't you think so, m'ijo?"

And Juan José, looking uncomfortable, looking guilty, as if such behavior weren't cliché in this city where everybody has a backstory.

Even in Los Angeles it isn't like this, or if it is, I don't hear about it. Perhaps I don't because I've never been an insider, just an appendix to Marcus's social sphere.

Here, I'm part of it, and people talk. I see it in their eyes, in my mother's surreptitious comments—"You're going out with JJ? Again?" Resigned. Hurt.

She always wanted me to marry someone like Juan José. A boy from Cali. From a nice family. A known family—una familia conocida. Someone familiar. Predictable. And I would continue my life like hers: raise my children, prepare lovely dinners, and on the weekends, play tennis at the club.

But now all that seemed frightfully provincial alongside Marcus and his blond, stately good looks and his money and his fame and his mansion in Beverly Hills, for Christ's sake, not in Cali, Colombia.

I saw this in her reproachful glance when I went out at night, again, to hide with him.

In the morning, she asked me about it directly, the one and only time that she did.

"I don't understand, Helenita," she said as she sipped her tea, looking away from me. "You never liked JJ, or did you?" A small frown furrowed her creamy brow.

I looked at nothing, blanking out, as I did more and more often those days.

"You never liked boys from Cali," my mother plowed on, relentless. "What does this one have?"

I was momentarily stumped.

What did this one have?

"I don't know," I said, not realizing I'd spoken out loud and startled by the matter-of-fact loudness of my voice.

"I don't know," I said more quietly, more to myself than to her, and I shrugged. We both finished our breakfast in silence.

Gabriella

Gabriella has made no more references about Angel to Nini since their argument, and the air has been charged with unsaid recriminations, an enormous elephant in the living room that both of them steadfastly refuse to acknowledge. Nini hasn't told Gabriella's father anything, either, simply because she's uncertain how to proceed with this. She wants to believe Gabriella would never be so cruel with Marcus as to reveal what she knows. But she doesn't want Marcus to take her away from her if he finds out who she's dating.

It's selfish, Nini knows, but she can't help herself.

Bad things happen, but to other people, she tells herself at night, as part of her prayers. And as the days pass, she really starts to believe it.

"Call me if you need me," are her only words, religiously repeated every day, every moment that Gabriella goes to be with him, which seems to be every moment of the day.

She has yet to bring Angel to her grandmother's house. And he has yet to take her to any house at all that isn't his own. His father is in jail. His mother simply isn't here; he's never offered an explanation. There are grandparents that he visits, but she hasn't been invited.

Neither of them is ready to venture out of this delicate balance again. With him, Gabriella often feels like an orphan, ensconced in a world of their making. All her friends who are Angel's age are fresh out of college, living with their parents or in little untidy apartments. At best they hold jobs on Wall Street or in film, and even when they make six figures, they are just boys, really; boys who depend on other people, not just for money, but for love and comfort.

Angel, as far as she can tell, doesn't depend on anyone. She has yet to see him ask for advice, has yet to hear him chat on the phone about something that isn't business.

He lives with Chelita, his childhood nanny, and in his same building, he's bought a studio for Julio, his head bodyguard, a man who used to work for his father and whose mission in life now is to make sure nothing happens to Angel. "Nada, pero nada," Chelita tells her one rare afternoon when Gabriella wakes up and finds Angel gone.

For the past three days, since her fight with Nini, Gabriella has spent the early afternoons here, playing the piano alone in the living room while he listens from his bed, taking the music in with his eyes closed, allowing Bach to align his thoughts. Gabriella prefers his listening from afar; his presence makes her self-conscious. But sometimes, he'll stand silently at the doorway, watching her play, oblivious to him as she hums, slightly out of tune, along with the melody. Singing out loud helps her make the piano sing, too, she explains to him when he asks. He doesn't quite get the concept, but he hears what she means; under her hands, his piano does sing.

After he goes to work, Gabriella likes to feel his home without him, touching the edges of the tables and the textures of his clothes, meticulously folded in the walk-in closet.

The phone doesn't ring here like it does constantly at Nini's, and the first time she sat down to play the piano after he left, the quietness reminded her of the practice rooms of her conservatory days. She automatically started playing her warm-up exercises, hands extended over an octave-long chord, each finger pressing a black key on the inside. The trick, her teacher had taught her, was to isolate each finger in this excruciating position, to enable it to be relaxed even in the most uncomfortable situation. Then, she launches into scales— C major, C minor, C sharp major, C sharp minor—going up the scale with the metronome ticking in her head, the rote of it all soothing in its monotony.

She thinks of other things when she does this—of him, of the way he made love to her today, bunching her skirt around her waist but not taking it off ("so you can smell of me when you're alone," he whispered in her ear), of what her father will say when he finds out what's going on—and she doesn't hear Chelita quietly placing the tray with coffee and pandebono behind her.

Only the smell of the coffee alerts her to turn around, and she's surprised and delighted at the offering, because Chelita hasn't said a word to her since she's been sleeping in his sheets in the afternoons.

Later, when Angel comes to pick her up, she takes the tray back herself to the kitchen, where she knows Chelita watches TV in the afternoons.

"Gracias," she says simply. "Estaba delicioso."

"Con gusto," Chelita says dryly, barely mustering a nod, but an agreement has been reached. Two days later when she brings the coffee, she sticks around long enough for Gabriella to notice her.

"Can't you play a real song?" Chelita finally says, frowning.

"You mean something that's not classical?" answers Gabriella, who had been playing Bach.

"I don't know," says Chelita, shrugging. She's a heavy-set woman with a quiet air of injured dignity who is always reading the newspaper with the TV on, tuned to an endless succession of afternoon soap operas. "I mean, like a normal song," she finally says helplessly.

Gabriella begins to play "Sabor a Mí," but midstride switches to Arthur Hanlon, whose piano music she knows Chelita hears on TV, the soaring melody lines flowing easily from her fingers.

"Eso sí," says Chelita, smiling for the first time since Gabriella has met her and nodding emphatically.

"He's a gringo, like me," Gabriella says, with a smile, because she loves this music too, the blend of her two worlds. "That's why our Latin music sounds special."

Chelita nods politely not fully understanding the parallel or the humor but sticks around until the end of the song, the melancholy lines bringing a sad smile to her face.

"Play another of that Arthur," she asks her when she's done. "Please," she adds, then retreats again to the kitchen. Gabriella hates to be hovered over when she practices, and Chelita has tacitly acknowledged this. Because she has,

Gabriella plays songs especially for her, every afternoon
before she goes back to Nini's after Angel goes to work.

When she takes her breaks, they talk, small fragments of
conversation that tell Gabriella the essentials: Her son, Giosvanny, who is now in the States, sent to study there with
Angel's father's money. He has since married and stayed
there, a legal resident who regularly sends money to his
mother.

"He and Angelito were very close," she tells her days later.
"Like brothers."

Her other son had died, killed by the guerrillas along
with her husband when he was only eight years old. That
was when she went to work for Luis Silva, who heard about
her through the grapevine of paramilitaries he employed to
guard his coca fields.

They spoke about a Doña Chelita, a tough Indian woman
who'd managed to shoot five guerrillas before the paras came
to the rescue on the day her husband was branded a traitor
and shot to death in the fields.

They took her to Luis Silva's house in Pance, and he hired
her as a general helper around the house. She took it upon
herself to do two things: cook and jealously guard her own
son and Angel. "That poor little boy that no one looked
after," she now says, shaking her head.

"But I thought he was so close to his dad," Gabriella says,
confused.

Chelita snorts derisively.

"That boy," she says. "That poor little boy," she repeats.
"His father would get drunk, and if Angelito got in the way,
he would punish him by sending him to sleep with the dogs

in the kennels outside. We would slip him a blanket so he wouldn't have to sleep on the floor."

Gabriella is stunned into silence. She's never met people who these things happen to. A little boy in a dog kennel. She cannot fathom the thought, so removed from her reality and from the hardness of the man she made love to earlier today that she can't reconcile the two.

"But . . . but how old was he?" Indignation, and just a touch of embarrassment—she doesn't think Angel will appreciate her knowing this—making her stutter.

"I don't know exactly. Seven, eight?"

"Are you serious? Why did you let it happen? Why couldn't you take him to your room or something?"

"Ay, señorita Gabriella," Chelita begins to say, then stops herself, realizing she's long overstepped her bounds.

"What, Chelita? What happened?" Gabriella asks urgently.

"You just didn't mess with Don Luis's orders," Chelita finally mutters defensively. "Giosvanny went once, even though we all told him not to butt in. He took Angelito to his room and had him sleep in the bed with him. The next day, Don Luis found them and beat them both with his belt. For disobeying his orders, he said, and for behaving like a pair of maricones, sleeping together in the same bed."

Chelita shakes her head. "Giosvanny tried one more time, but Angelito wouldn't let him, he was so scared for him. He just took to getting really quiet when his father was in one of those moods, so he wouldn't notice him. And then one day, when he was about twelve—he grew really tall all of a sudden—he fought back. He said there was no way he was going to sleep with some damn dogs and punched his father in the face. Well, Don Luis was so surprised, he took it. We were hiding in the kitchen, thinking he was really going to beat Angelito up this time. But he didn't. He laughed. And laughed. He said he had finally turned him into a real man. He said he'd finally learned to stand up for himself. And Don Luis never messed with him again. At least, he never lifted a hand against him anymore."

Gabriella closes her eyes and tries to see Angel, because there were no family pictures in this house, so different from her own, where frames litter the piano.

Angel, twelve years old, thin—because the way he looks now, he had to have been thin—squinting his eyes like he does when he hits the punching bag that hangs in his room, and swinging at his father's jaw. A little boy that no one took care of, until he could take care of himself.

"And his mother?" Gabriella asks.

Chelita waves the notion of the mother away dismissively.

"The mother," she grunts. "The mother was hardly ever there. And she was more scared of Don Luis than we were. That's what we thought anyway."

"Why? Did he hit her?" Gabriella asks.

Chelita looks pained. "Ay, niña, don't ask me these things. It's hard to know what people do behind closed doors." She looks away momentarily, at nothing. "Don Luis was good to me. I owe my life to him, so whatever he did, it couldn't be too bad. Anyway, she had a choice. She could have walked away if she had wanted. And she chose not to, until they sent him to jail.

"Maybe she loved Angel," Chelita adds, shaking her head

sadly. "She just didn't know how to take care of him. He was like a little pet to her. She would show him off when he looked good, and then when he wasn't there, or he had a problem, she would simply forget about him. She couldn't be bothered."

Chelita abruptly changes the subject. "Anyway, the only time his father really seemed worried about Angelito was when he got sent to jail," she says. "He was so worried about his only son. Or at least, the only one he knows of." She chuckles forgivingly. "So he gave him Julio. It's Julio's job to make sure nothing happens to Angel. Nada, pero nada. That's what Don Luis said. That's why Julio lives here in the building. Julio does it because it's his duty," she adds, looking directly at Gabriella. "But I do it because I love him." Chelita holds Gabriella's eyes for a moment longer. "Do you know that Angelito never brought a girl to sleep here before?"

Gabriella feels herself blushing as mortification sinks in. She hasn't been herself, she knows, and she's forgotten the rules of the game. She's not spending nights here, not yet, probably never. Here, that wouldn't be an act of defiance but of spite, and her simmering resentment with Nini can never become that. But she's treading dangerously close to the rules of propriety. No matter the time of day, you simply don't screw in someone else's house when there's an adult inside, even a maid, because maids talk. Now she learns that the maid is some kind of surrogate mother.

"I'm sorry," she says finally. "I'm sorry if I've done anything to offend you. I didn't mean to."

Chelita looks at her blankly, then her expression changes to surprise as Gabriella's words sink in.

"No, no, señorita," she says, her eyes widening in alarm, and for the first time since she's met her, Gabriella hears servitude in her voice. "You haven't done anything wrong," she says, looking down at her hands. "It's just that you're the first he brings. I just meant, you must be special to him."

The nanny, Gabriella thinks to herself, getting a grip on who she is and who she should be apologizing to. She is speaking with the nanny. The nanny who loves the man Gabriella loves as if he were her son, who did things for him with a mother's selflessness. But a nanny, an employee, just the same, who is now babbling apologies for overstepping her bounds.

He's never allowed anyone to sleep here before. The thought, the specialness of it, makes her smile. But looking at Chelita, she knows that the words weren't about her. They were about him.

Julio's job is to make sure nothing happens to Angel, but that, too, is Chelita's calling. Her words are not a congratulations, but a request.

"Tranquila, Chelita," she says, gazing at the flat, black eyes steadily. "He's special to me, too. Conmigo no le pasa nada. Nada, pero nada."

Chelita smiles her small, tight smile and she picks up the now-empty tray. "Ande pues, play me one more of those Arthur songs I like, and I'll let you work."

*   *   *

She's always watched the cabalgata. But she's never ridden in it.

"Eight hours on a horse!" Nini reminded her tersely, when she announced her intentions of riding.

The cabalgata is the kickoff to Cali's annual fair, seven days of drunken revelry, punctuated by daily bullfights and relentless partying.

If you want to fully experience this fair, you buy season tickets to the bullfights, you dance to the beat of salsa orchestras that play long after the sun is up, and you go to the cabalgata.

You are part of it—one of the nearly seven thousand riders who will trot down this city, from the northern tip to the bullring in the south, the sun beating on your wide-brimmed hat for five hours—or you watch it: one of hundreds of thousands who line the streets to see the horses, to see the riders, to drink, to let loose, because in this brief week, there are few rules or scripts or parameters.

She's always watched this ride from the sidelines, from the outside looking in. She had been part of Juan Carlos's posse when they were younger, and they would ride on a flatbed truck, stopping in strategic locations to cheer, chat, and drink with their riding buddies, identifying every rider and every mount along the ten kilometers of this path that neatly crosses the city.

But today, she's sitting on a horse. Her name is Grace Kelly, but the trainers call her Greiskeli, all one word. She doubts they know for whom she's named. She is elegant,

Gabriella will grant Greiskeli that, a gray Paso Fino horse with a haughty head.

Angel has been giving her instructions on what to do with Greiskeli since the moment she said yes, she would go to the cabalgata with him, and now he reiterates all of the horse's fine points.

Gabriella shouldn't, can't make Greiskeli canter because that will ruin her step, he cautions, for the hundredth time. Greiskeli is a Paso Fino horse; her small, even, quick steps can't be broken. She can't try and ride her like a normal horse; she'll look ridiculous. She must be absolutely relaxed, or the step will kill her back. Gabriella can't use her crop. She can't pull on the bit too hard; Greiskeli is very, very sensitive to the bit.

"Angel, why are you letting me ride her if you're so afraid I'll damage her, for Christ's sakes?" she finally asks, exasperated.

"Because she's my best and most beautiful horse, and I want everyone to look at you on her," he says matter-of-factly.

"Ah, you want to show me off," she says smugly, smiling.

"As a matter of fact, I do," he answers, bringing his horse close enough to touch hers, taking one of her hands away from the reins, bringing it up to his mouth and kissing it, palm up, before returning it to her again.

Gabriella smiles, but almost automatically looks around for her cousin. Juan Carlos can't be bothered to go anywhere this year; he watches from a single vantage point—either the club downtown or some friend's house.

She hasn't seen him today, but then again, from the inside

looking out, she feels like she's part of a massive blob, and in the sidelines she sees a blur that has only twice been interrupted by calls of "Gabriella!"

When she hears the shouts, she looks inquisitively from under her broad-brimmed black hat, trying to discern the faces of her friends, until finally she locates them on balconies or on the ground.

But calls to her are far more sporadic than calls to Angel, and it takes her by surprise, his undeniable popularity.

During their time together, they have rarely left his apartment, save for occasional trips to the farm, which he knows she loves. But mostly he works nights and sleeps days, and his few undisturbed hours are for her and her alone. Sharing has never been part of the equation, and for the first time, she sullenly begins to resent all this implies.

She wonders if this will be the pattern for the remainder of the feria, for the nightly parties, the bullfights where he holds prime seats. She, it sinks in, is his girl; his girl to show off to the world, but on his terms.

He's been showing her off already.

"This is Gabriella," he says simply, never adding "mi novia," my girlfriend, and she's not sure yet if she would have liked the label or not. In the end, it's understood, and she takes in the appraising, frank stares, from the guys and the girls, who look her over carefully, who take in her not-yet-siliconed boobs and her curly hair, which she has tied loosely with a red ribbon that matches the red bandanna around her neck.

She isn't his type at all, they seem to be thinking. A part of her worries that they're right, that if she didn't have the appeal of her piano playing to offer him, he might have cut things off already.

But here she is, in the most public of public displays, and she feels gladly defiant when, in a brief stop, he leans over and, with an air of proprietorship, kisses her long and hard, letting the strong anise taste of the aguardiente he's been drinking trickle down into her mouth.

The crowd is cheering by the time he lets her go, and all of a sudden, she sees everything around her more clearly: the polished black riding boots, the blinding white of the crisp shirts accented by bright red bandannas, the black hats with orange trim, the leather drinking canteens with their red caps, the blue and pink and green polo shirts and tight jeans and cans of beer tossed over beautiful heads of beautiful people while streamers rise into the incandescent blue sky.

That newfound clarity, she would later tell him, might have saved her from falling, because she saw the man—a teenager, really—step from the crowd into the path of the horses, and she took up the reins left slack during her kiss to turn Greiskeli away from him, when he threw the firecrackers at her feet.

The mare reared high on her hind legs, and with the sun shining directly into her upraised face, Gabriella felt as if she were being dropped, weightless, from an infinite height. She clung to the reins even as she felt her feet slipping from her stirrups, her hips sliding from the saddle.

Angel's hands came down hard on the reins, snatching them from her hands with such force, she had to wear bandages for two days to cover the welts. But his voice, when he spoke to the horse, was gentle, an incantation that calmed her down as quickly as Gabriella had lost control.

She was too stunned to be angry, it had all happened so fast.

Later, when Juan Carlos pressed her for details, she told him honestly that she didn't know what finally happened. But she couldn't bring herself to tell him what she did see. That, before giving her back the horse, before even asking how she was, Angel was calling Julio on the walkie-talkie, speaking in that low, measured tone he used to give orders. "Enséñenle a ese hijueputa que no se mete ni con mis caballos ni con mi hembra."

Tell that son of a bitch he's not to mess with my horses or my woman, she heard him say tersely, and to her surprise, she felt a small rush of adrenaline. He could indeed teach a lesson, and the notion thrilled her and soothed her sense of impotence.

"Come on," Angel says now, pressing her to keep moving away from this spot. He doesn't turn back, but she does, in time to see two of Angel's bodyguards elbow their way to where her prankster is now obliviously talking with his friends.

"But I didn't do anything," she hears him protest in a loud drunken voice.

"Come *on*, Gabriella!" says Angel, harshly now, when he sees her strain to get a better look, and this time, Gabriella urges Greiskeli on. When she turns back again to look, just a few moments later, the man and Angel's bodyguards have been swallowed by the crowd. For a second, her eyes lock with those of someone else standing at the edge of the street, a young man who looks confusedly after her, then frantically calls out to someone inside the crowd, pointing at her, at Angel, before someone else pulls him also out of sight.

In the early evening, Angel hosts a party at his father's house, the house where she first met him. If anything, the terrace upstairs is even more crowded than that first day, as stragglers from the cabalgata arrive in a steady stream throughout the late afternoon and into the night. She knows the faces, but she doesn't really know the people. In this city that she's so familiar with, she's never been deeply involved beyond the close-knit group commandeered by her cousin, and for the first time ever, she feels like a foreigner.

Instead of wandering through the house, this time she finds a corner on the rooftop from where she can watch, undisturbed, the lawn below. The grooms are removing the saddles and stirrups from the arriving horses and loading the animals into boarded-up trucks, which will take them back to the stables tonight. Along the side street, a line of Humvees and SUVs, flanked by bodyguards and drivers, stretches all the way out into the main drag, forcing incoming traffic to slow down and ogle this towering house, lit with tiki torches and strobe lights. Behind her, the valley is dark, save for a smattering of far-flung homes, sprinkled aimlessly into the countryside, because this side of the city is yet to be fully developed. There's little to see here at night, except the darkness that gradually lightens up until it meets the boundaries of the main highway, almost a mile out in the distance.

She sees again, like a flicker in her mind, the face of the boy who spooked Greiskeli, his friend's look of confused bewilderment as he was pulled away. If anything were to happen to her, who could Nini turn to? She could lose herself in the darkness tonight, and no one would even blink.

She remembers her first night here, how she danced with Angel.

But no one's dancing tonight, and she tries to act nonchalant when she finally leaves her spot and wanders aimlessly through the crowd, looking for his company.

"Hey, Gabriella!" a voice calls to her, and Gabriella feels a wave of gratitude sweep over her as one of Angel's friends—Antonio, or is it Daniel—motions her to join a group sitting around a low table.

"Belleza!" he says good-naturedly, slurring the words, putting his arm around her. "Come, let's have a toast!"

She sits on the floor beside him, and gamely takes the shot of aguardiente he offers her, downing it in one gulp.

"Bravo!" he cheers loudly. "Bravo!" "Salud!" the others echo, tiny glasses clinking all around.

"One more," says Daniel/Antonio, serving another round of shots.

"No, no," says Gabriella, who's beginning to feel woozy, and worried that she can't find Angel. "I'll wait for the next one," she says placatingly, but really there's nothing to placate.

Around her, the conversation is meaningless: the horses, the drinks, who wore what, who passed out. She isn't a part of this group and has nothing to contribute.

When Antonio/Daniel takes out the packet of white powder, pours it directly on the table, and begins to break it down in thin little lines with his American Express Platinum Card, she's almost relieved at the change of pace, the shift in attention.

Coke has never been her thing. It gets her strung out but somehow dampens her senses, like drinking coffee after twenty-four hours without sleep.

Daniel/Antonio elegantly rolls up a ten thousand peso bill and almost daintily snorts the first line, then a second, before offering the others a pass.

The girls go first, flipping their long, straight hair back as they lean over into the table, the rolled-up bill incongruous in their perfect, surgically enhanced noses, all upturned tips.

When it's her turn, Gabriella shakes her head no, smiling faintly.

"Come on, belleza," urges Antonio, because by now, she's decided that must be his name. "Don't be such a party pooper!"

Everyone is looking at her expectantly, their expressions tainted with mild amusement and a touch of scorn. They haven't been altogether friendly to her, but she hasn't exactly opened up to them, either, and through their eyes she can see what they're seeing now: a prissy gringa who won't even do a little line to get on the good foot.

Gabriella takes Antonio's rolled-up bill and places it against the last line on the plate, and sniffs hard and quickly.

When she lifts her head, she sees Angel looking at her steadily from across the table, his eyes perfectly blank as he takes a cigarette up to his mouth and inhales, then finally smiles slightly, his half-crooked smile, only this time it's very small.

She almost beckons to him, but he turns around and walks toward the side door beyond the elevator, the door she knows leads to the bedrooms below.

Gabriella is left stupidly holding the rolled-up bill in her hand, the bitter taste of cocaine dripping into her throat.

"And Angel?" she asks Antonio, at a loss as to why he hasn't joined in.

"Belleza," he replies with a laugh and exaggerated wink. "You know what they say. You don't get high on your own supply!"

"Oh," she says quietly, as the implication sinks in. "Well. I'll be right back," she says amiably enough, feeling their eyes on her as she makes her way after him.

She remembers how to get to the library. Their mutual room, she thinks clearly in the middle of her rising panic. If he wants to see her, he'll be there.

He's sitting on the couch, his legs spread out before him, a newly lit cigarette in his hand, and for a few moments, she simply stands at the foot of the stairwell, holding on to the balustrade, because she needs something to balance her thoughts on.

"Hi," she finally says uncertainly, because he's looking at her appraisingly and she can feel the touch of his disdain reaching her from across the room.

"You know, I don't do coke?" she says, ending her statement in a question mark—a habit she despises—and running her hand over the books on the shelves. "I— I really hate it as a matter of fact," she adds, laughing self-deprecatingly. "I always think I'm going to sneeze, like in that Woody Allen movie?"

Angel inhales from his cigarette deeply, then exhales off the side of his mouth as he always does, so the smoke doesn't touch his face.

"If you hate it so much, why were you doing lines?" he asks in a lazy tone, devoid of emotion.

Gabriella shrugs helplessly. She preferred his outburst in the car, when he screamed at her, to this restrained anger that she's unwittingly provoked.

"They were your friends; they— they were really insistent," she says. "It was your house. I was just trying to be nice. I couldn't find you anywhere!" She is babbling now, she knows, and part of her also knows that there is no reason to apologize, but the mix of coke and alcohol always makes her a bit stupid.

She looks at him with mounting apprehension. She wills him to say something, to acknowledge that she's there, that just a few hours before she was important and precious and relevant.

"You know," he says finally, stubbing his cigarette out. "I never thought you were the kind of woman who did what others thought you should do. I thought you were a different sort of person."

To her horror, Gabriella feels tears welling up in her eyes, feels her lower lip start to tremble. "But I am!" she says anxiously, not yet fully believing the turn the conversation is taking.

"I just did it for you. I did it to please you! Because I thought it would make you happy!"

He stays seated, doesn't even stand up to acknowledge her.

"You did it to make me happy?" he asks incredulously, looking up at her. "And why would you possibly think that would make me happy?"

Gabriella opens her mouth to answer, then closes it quickly before she can say what she wants to say. He says it instead, speaking the words she's left unspoken for the past ten days.

"You think because my father is a drug dealer, I would want you to do drugs?" he asks her, very slowly.

"You've been inside my house. In my bed! What was it? Were there drugs lying around for you to use? To make me happy?"

Gabriella shakes her head miserably. In her mind she sees his scrupulously neat room, the flowers on the nightstand placed just so, and changed every day.

In his medicine cabinet, all he has is aspirin and Alka-Seltzer.

"I'm running a business here, Gabriella. This isn't *Scarface* we're talking about," says Angel, who still hasn't moved an inch. "I need to move around with ten fucking bodyguards. I can't afford to be high. No one who works for me can. If you're going to be the exception, I need to know right now."

She shakes her head. She's being given the opportunity to end things, to return to her grandmother and her father and the girl she used to be, but it's the last thing she wants to happen now. He has become indispensable to her, everything she's never had and she never knew she needed.

"I'm sorry," she says, and kneels down between his legs and puts her arm around his calf and her head on his knee. "I'm sorry," she says it again. "I'm sorry. I'm sorry. I'm sorry."

He doesn't say anything to her. Doesn't touch her, but doesn't push her away either.

Gabriella presses her head against his legs, breathing in the smell of horses and sweat on his blue jeans.

"My mother did all kinds of things to make my father happy," he says almost absentmindedly. "She changed her hair, and did her boobs, and I don't know how many other surgeries. I lost count of all the time she spent at the hospital and the beautician and the beauty salon. And that was always her explanation: 'I'm doing this to make your father happy.' And you know what? He was *never* happy. He despised her. That's why he fucked everything that moved. Because he despised her insecurities. And I despise that, too, Gabriella. I don't need anyone to 'make me happy.'" He mimics her words unkindly, his voice rising to match her little plea.

"At least your mother had the guts to go beyond what was expected of her, have you ever thought of that, Gabriella? Maybe she got tired of 'making people happy,' and I respect that. It takes balls to do that."

Gabriella doesn't say anything for a long time. Her ballsy mother. Even Angel admires her, after what he knows.

"It also takes balls to do the right thing, have you ever thought of that?" she finally answers, her voice muffled against his thigh. "Simply gratifying yourself is not ballsy. It's selfish. Maybe your mother's problem wasn't that she was too busy trying to make your father happy, but that she was too busy to be a good mother to you."

She looks up at Angel, and in his tightly shut mouth she can see the comment displeases him.

"Okay. Fine," he says curtly, and surprises her by adding, "you could actually be right, but I don't give a flying fuck.

All I care about at this point is, I don't want anyone doing shit around me. It's *not* my work. And it's *not* a lifestyle."

"Your friend said you didn't get high on your own supply," Gabriella says automatically.

Angel grunts; she's not sure if it's laughter or ire.

"It's not his comment to make," he says dryly, then leans over her, careful not to touch her, and picks up the walkie-talkie he's left on the table.

"Julio," he calls.

"Copy," she hears the crackled response.

"Get everybody out of here," Angel says in his quiet command voice. "The party's over."

"Copy that," Julio answers evenly. "Should I get the car ready?"

"No," says Angel, finally looking down at her. "We're staying awhile."

Gabriella suddenly lifts her head.

"Angel, Nini will be waiting for me," she says uncertainly. "You know she doesn't like me to be out too late."

Angel looks at her clinically, as if she were Greiskeli at an exhibit.

"If you need to go," he says evenly, "I'll arrange for someone to take you. It's your choice." He adds, spacing each word, "And, believe me, it's not about making me happy."

Gabriella measures the space between them, one moment so close, one moment so far. She's still not sure why certain things—things she would have thought were inconsequential—make him explode, but his maddening extremes drive her, ever the conciliatory one, to bridge the gaps. It confounds her that his largesse with her goes hand in hand with the unexpected wrath of his judgment. He's not prone to apologizing, she knows; his little concession of a few moments ago is a grand gesture for him.

Gabriella vacillates. She could leave and placate Nini. She could stay and placate him. Always placating. But she looks at Angel, and underneath his stony exterior sees just the hint of expectation, of—could it be?—yearning.

She silently takes the cell phone out of the pocket of her jeans and dials her grandmother's house.

"Nini, I'll be in later, don't wait up for me," she says as gently as she can.

Helena

I sometimes wonder what has made me feel whole again. If it is your absence, or his presence. Neither of the options is the right option, I know.

It's simply the result. Something I had forgotten I could feel.

Almost right away, Marcus knew something was wrong.

He didn't notice it in my absence; I'm a good liar, always was, and distance made me better. I was supposed to be out, after all. I was supposed to be working. I was even supposed to be distracted about my daughter, about my husband. I think he missed all the early signs, the daily phone calls that began to come once every two, three, four days, the lack of reference to my friends, my absences at night.

And then, I came back. He couldn't put his finger on it, I could tell. He just knew I wasn't the person I had been before I left.

It was little things, in the beginning. Things that didn't bother me suddenly started driving me nuts. Everything was so rigid. The schedules, the ban on smoking, the stupid bank teller who refused to let me withdraw cash the day my ATM card didn't work because I had no picture ID with me, even though I'd been banking in the same branch for six years.

I tried to apply "the glass is always half full" theory, but I couldn't. Nothing worked as it should.

"I was someone there!" I cried in frustration one evening over drinks in the kitchen, after a particularly unproductive day of making my gallery rounds. "Here, I'm meaningless. I don't know the right people, I don't have the right accent, my photographs are too 'Colombian,' they told me today."

"Helena, you know me," Marcus said reasonably. "I carry some clout in some places. Tell me who you're targeting, maybe I can help you with some of them. But you have to tell me!"

"Marcus," I said, rubbing my eyes, because he just didn't get it. Why didn't he get it, after all this time? "I can't use your name forever. Everything I've done is tied to you. Do you have any idea how...*humiliating* it is to always be referred to as Marcus Richard's wife?"

Marcus twirled the stem of his wineglass and sighed.

"No," he said. "Frankly, I don't see what's 'humiliating' about it. My family name helped me get in the door here. And if it weren't for your family name, you wouldn't have been asked to do this book of yours for the governor. It's all in who you know in our fields, and you know that."

He stared at me, trying to read my mind.

"What are we really talking about here? What's pissing

you off? Because you've gotten work rejected before, and you've always turned around and come up with something else. So what's going on, Helena?"

What was I supposed to say. There's someone else? I didn't even know that anymore. Was there someone else?

I looked around me, my beautiful kitchen that I didn't use, my beautiful garden that I hardly ever set foot in, the swimming pool that was too cold most of the year. The one thing I truly, truly enjoyed was the red Mercedes-Benz convertible parked in my driveway, my dream car and an indulgence, because getting Gabriella's car seat in and out of that backseat was a nightmare. I could drive it in peace here like I never would have in Colombia. Here, I wouldn't be kidnapped or carjacked.

"I don't know, Marcus," I said defeated. "I was there almost two months photographing, and everything felt right. My work was right, I was inspired. I took my best shots. My photographs were treated with respect. *I* was treated with respect."

"I don't get it," he said tersely now. "Am I supposed to feel sorry for you because you got written up in the local Cali newspaper and the *L.A. Times* isn't writing a Sunday piece on you? Maybe, if you were as serious about your work here as you apparently were there, we wouldn't be having this discussion."

"And just what do you mean by being serious?" I asked defensively.

"I mean exactly that," said Marcus, setting his glass down. "You don't finish your projects. You don't even present your proposals properly. You've fought with your two past agents. You act like you're in Cali and all you need to do is waltz in and give out your name and voilà! You'll get an exhibit. Or a book. Or a fashion shoot. Whatever. Do you have any idea how many people from all over the world are here, busting their chops, trying to do what you do, while you're taking yoga classes?"

I felt assaulted.

And furious at him because I knew he was right, but right there, right then, I wasn't going to give him the satisfaction of agreeing, even as I saw my dreams drifting from my fingertips as I led the life of a Hollywood wife.

"I have a little girl," I said angrily, my voice low, spitting out every syllable. "You have no idea how hard it is to be inspired when you have to be on top of her every move and take her to classes and take her to the park and try to be a decent mother that doesn't dump her kid in day care or leave her with the nanny all day because I have no family to give me a hand. You took care of her for a little over a month. I've taken care of her for four years! All this time, I've left everything else aside, and I've lived for her. And now, for the first time since she was born, I was able to live for me. Just for me. I was able to have a day to myself, to my things, to my thoughts, without having to worry about someone else's well-being. I could breathe, Marcus!"

I could see the disappointment in his eyes. Like the disappointment in my father's eyes.

I had fulfilled no one's expectations. Never gone on to do the grandiose things everyone always thought I would do.

Things I could accomplish, things I had the talent for, forgotten. Why hadn't Marcus pushed me? Why hadn't he seen what was happening to me?

"I'm not a cretin, Helena," he said tiredly. "Of course, it's hard to work and raise a kid. Of course, you need room to breath. So come up with a plan. We have the money to work things out, so take your time. But don't give me this guilt trip. You chose to be a parent. Unfortunately, parenting is part of the package."

Just then, Gabriella ran into the room.

She had been in the garden and her little white Laura Ashley dress was a muddy mess and her long, curly hair was tangled with flowers and dirt and grass.

"I'm gardening!" she announced loudly and with propriety, and in that moment, she was so amazingly alive and beautiful that I couldn't help but laugh, and I went to her and picked her up and buried my face in that hair, which smelled of soil mixed up with shampoo.

"Come, Mami. I'll show you how to do it!" she said confidently, scrambling to be put down. Gabriella grabbed my hand to lead me out to the garden, and I quickly snatched the straw hat I kept hanging from the back of the door, the one I automatically put on every time I went out into the sun.

The late afternoon sun was low as it hit the bed of roses, and when I crouched down to examine the plants, I had to laugh, because Gabriella had actually planted new seeds that stuck out from under sparsely placed soil.

"Say cheese!" I heard Marcus shout out, and when I

turned around on my heels to look up at the camera he held, I brought my hand up to my head, to keep my hat from falling, and the smile was still on my face, for the moment at least, erasing the discussion that took place only five minutes before.

Gabriella

They make love in his parents' room, in a bed that, he says, hasn't been slept in in over three years, the time his father has been in prison.

His father is due to be released in ten months, he tells her now. In ten months, he repeats, with awe at the proximity. They convicted him on money laundering—the drug charges never stuck—when Angel was barely twenty-two, fresh out of college in Paris. He came back after five years to find himself in the eye of an incomprehensible storm that featured his father on the cover of every newspaper, as the headline of every nightly newscast.

Gabriella remembers that time, but doesn't say anything now; he has never spoken to her about these most intimate, yet most public of happenings, his family travails exposed daily with a level of detail that, back then, was risible and embarrassing.

The house, she now recalls, infamous for its architecture—a replica of the old-money Club Colombia, where her mother belonged, but where his father was denied membership due to his dubious background. He chose to build his own club instead, and proceeded to host the most scandalous and outlandish parties; parties where he would fly in on a private plane, for one night only, the top orchestras in the world; birthday celebrations where party favors were Piaget watches and Gucci ties.

In one particularly scandalous round of testimony, a famous pop musician relayed how he was asked to play the same hit song, over and over and over again, just for Luis Silva and his wife, from midnight until three in the morning. The musician got paid, $200,000 in laundered cash for his efforts, and avoided prosecution for himself by testifying. His words effectively killed his income, however. In an international private party circuit dominated by dubious funds, he became a rat, not to be trusted with discretion.

Gabriella racks her brain now, trying to bring up references to Angel during this time. She remembers the mother ("very elegant," Nini had conceded one day, making reference to a steady supply of Chanel suits), but not the son.

"For the record, Antonio was wrong when he said I don't get high on my own supply," he tells her, out of the blue. "Mi papá, all the stuff he did . . . But from the beginning, he told me I couldn't be like he was. He told me nothing of his business. That's why I was sent to Switzerland to boarding school. It wasn't a security problem. He just wanted me as far away as possible. And that's why I don't get high, on *any* supply," he adds with a small, humorless laugh.

"He wanted to make sure I got the message," he says dully. "So one night, when I was fifteen—when I didn't want to leave Cali because I was hot shit here—he took me to see this friend of his, he said.

"Only they weren't friends anymore. The guy—he'd

worked for my father, doing odd stuff, you know? Collecting bills, making sure the properties were fine, that kind of crap."

Angel stops to look at her, then pushes his hair back, a gesture she knows him to do only when something troubles him.

"And this guy." He swallows. "He started doing heroin. He was one of these people, they start using, and they can't handle it. They literally can't stop. It just takes on a life of its own."

Gabriella is listening intently now, because Angel's measured voice has a touch of agitation she's never heard in it before.

"So apparently, he'd been fucking up. You know, we're driving over there with Julio, and my dad is saying this guy has been fucking up, he's taking drugs instead of collecting my dad's money, he's become a liability.

"And you know, my father never spoke to me about any of his affairs. I knew, but I couldn't know. It was a completely taboo subject with everyone around us. So I'm sitting in the car, and I'm thinking why the fuck am I here?"

He is talking to her almost like a teenager, and when he looks at her, she sees in his face the questions he had that night, almost ten years ago, his puzzlement, and his apprehension at being part of this unlikely scenario, all mixed up with the trust he had for his father and Julio.

"And we got to this guy's house, in the middle of the night, and it was an okay house. I mean, it wasn't like this, but it was a decent house in a decent little neighborhood. And he was up. He was up watching TV and drinking whiskey, and you could tell he was on something. And he was not happy to see my father. He was—" Angel shakes his head at the memory. "He was completely taken aback at seeing the three of us there.

"And my dad walks in and sits down on the couch in front of this guy, and he introduces me," Angel nods now, puts out his hand in a silent handshake. "He introduces me, tells him I'm his son and how proud he is of me.

"And this sap is smiling, but I can tell he's shitting his pants, he doesn't know what's going on. You see, I knew the power my father had over people, but I'd never seen it this close, this directly, at least not like this."

Angel stops now and leans over to the bedside table to reach his pack of cigarettes. When he lights up, she sees his fingers trembling ever so slightly, and she doesn't say a word, afraid to break the unexpected reverie, and waits silently until he inhales deeply and she feels his heart slow down again under his naked skin, under her hand sitting motionless over his chest.

"So anyway. My dad takes out this little plastic package of stuff, and he says that this is heroin. He looks at me and tells me that this is the best heroin that money can buy. That in the States, this tiny little packet, this packet that costs him fifty bucks, sells in the streets for a thousand. And then, he gives the package to this guy, and he tells him very nicely, very politely, because my dad could be very polite when he wanted to, 'I want you to try this out for me, my friend.'" Angel picks up his pack of cigarettes and extends them toward his imaginary antihero.

"He tells him, 'I want you to show my son what great stuff this is.'

"And the guy, he says no!" Angel says, surprise still tinting his voice at the thought of somebody refusing his father.

"He was terrified. He thought the shit was spiked or bad or who knows what. So my dad talks to him, swears it's all clean, swears he just wants him to have a good time and to show me what a good time there is to be had."

Angel licks his lips slowly.

"And he reminds him of how *good* this stuff is. The best in the world, he said. 'Angel, it doesn't get any better than this,' he told me.

"So the guy finally takes it, because as scared as he is, he can't resist it. That was part of the lesson, you see? And he's drooling by now, he's dying to get his hands on it, and it's been taking him every ounce of self-control not to jump on it. So finally, he opens a drawer and takes out his little paraphernalia—the plastic tube, and the needle and the spoon—and he mixes the stuff up, warms it underneath a lighter, and he rolls up his sleeve and he shoots himself up."

Angel grimaces at the thought.

"Have you ever seen anyone shoot up, *princesa*?" he asks pensively.

Gabriella shakes her head no, because she hasn't, except in films, and her Hollywood life is starting to look really meaningless in this context.

"It's really disgusting, to watch that needle penetrate the skin and—*push* stuff into you. Especially if you don't like needles, which I don't. But I watch, because my father is watching and making sure that I'm watching, and I don't flinch and I don't close my eyes and I try not to grimace because I don't want him to slap me or something. I just stand there and watch this guy shoot up, and when he's done, he completely relaxes, and he—you could just see the relief, the intense relief in his face. Like he'd just had the best orgasm of his life.

"And I'm thinking, okay, this wasn't so bad, and now I get to go and watch some TV and forget this weird little evening.

"And the guy smiles very peacefully, and then my father tells him very softly, 'Do it again.' And the guy says, 'No, thank you, Don Luis,' like he had a choice." Angel's voice rises slightly.

"So my dad repeats what he just said: 'Do it again,' and he sounds pissed now, so the guy does his whole routine all over, and shoots up in his other arm, and this time, he doesn't look so happy anymore. And then my dad says, 'Do it again,' and this guy, this grown man, he starts to cry."

Angel stops for a moment, takes another drag from his cigarette.

"I think that was worse than the injecting," says Angel. "It wasn't just tears rolling down his face. He was bawling. It was the most pitiful thing. He was begging my father to let him stop, and I couldn't understand what was going on. I started to go to him, because I wanted to make him stop, too, but Julio grabbed me and pushed me against the wall. And the guy, he did it all over again, but this time his hands were trembling really badly, he couldn't mix it right, he couldn't tie the damn tourniquet. He couldn't find a vein in his arm, either. So my dad did it for him. He was really gentle, and really good at it. He found a vein in his foot, and he put the guy's hand on the needle, and he said, 'All you have to do is push it in.'

"And he did. He sat there looking at my father, and he pushed that shot of heroin into his foot—and he leaned back again and sat there very quietly, with the needle still in his foot—he didn't even take it out."

Angel crushes the cigarette and lies down with his head against the pillow, pulling her toward him.

"At first, he just licked his lips, and my father just sat there—we all waited—everybody was really quiet. All you could hear was the television. It was funny. They were showing *Law & Order* in Spanish.

"When the guy started convulsing, my father stood up and walked away. I tried to go toward the guy, and then I tried to turn away, because it was horrible, Gabriella. It was horrible. Even though he wasn't screaming or struggling. But he was like a different person. Like he had already left himself.

"And my dad came and stood behind me and held my head and forced me to watch, I don't know for how long. Maybe it was a few minutes, maybe it was an hour. I lost track of time. Finally, Julio went and took this guy's pulse, to make sure he was dead, and then we left."

In the silence of the room, Gabriella hears the soft thudding of Angel's heart. She is horrified, and she knows she's meant to be horrified. She wonders who she can tell a story like this.

"In the car, my father gave me a plastic bag so I could throw up." Angel grunts ruefully. "He even planned that.

"And then he told me that's what happened to junkies, and that if he ever heard I was one, I was on my own. He said, 'It's a business, not a lifestyle. And it's my business.'

That's what he said. It's *my* business, not yours. And that was it. He sent me away to school, and he told me to think about what I was going to study after I graduated and what I was going to do with myself, because this wasn't going to be it."

Neither of them says anything for a long time. Gabriella, hazy still from alcohol and traces of cocaine, feels as though she's stepped into a looking glass, a place that's hers but not hers. She wants to take him out of here, once and for all, but the task suddenly feels gargantuan.

"Is this a shocking story for you, princesa?" he asks her, his voice even and in control again.

This time Gabriella lifts her head up, lifts her whole body up and kneels on the bed, looking into his eyes rather than up at him.

"Yes," she says, not knowing what else she wants to say.

"Does it change what you feel for me?" he prods her, gently, and in his eyes she sees not concern, but the dark veil that he wears when he wants to be inscrutable; the veil he probably learned to borrow from his father after all these years.

Impulsively, Gabriella leans forward and runs her hands across his eyes.

"What are you doing?" he asks, laughing, and when he laughs, the veil lifts and she sees flecks of light underneath the crystal green of his eyes.

"No, it doesn't change what I feel for you," she says, not offering any explanation.

And now, his eyes are limpid and grateful and warm, and she holds his face between her hands and kisses them gently, then kisses his mouth, and he brings her close to him and lays her down over him so she covers him like the sheets they can't seem to find, and in these times, at least, she feels he is completely hers, like no one really has ever been hers.

They make love quietly and urgently, as if there were parents listening in the rooms next door, private love-making although they've never known the boundaries of supervision.

Afterward, in the shower, he cleans her gently, shampooing the grit from the ride out of her hair, rubbing soap down her back, behind her ears, in the crevices behind her knees and between her toes and her fingers, careful not to touch the welts left behind when he pulled the reins from her hands.

He manipulates her body almost with clinical industriousness, enjoying the smooth feel of her soapy skin, the indentation of the muscles on her back—a strong back for a girl—the product of a lifetime of windsurfing and swimming. There are freckles on her shoulders and a gentle half-moon of a scar on her lower belly, the remnant of appendicitis; otherwise, her surfaces are clean and unspoiled.

In an hour, he will be working, supervising the hangar he rents for the Christmas season only, a broad space with high ceilings that's allowed to fit seven thousand people. He permits nine thousand inside because no one dares tell him not to and because he makes more money and because he thinks it's right, and that really is what dictates everything he does.

Tomorrow he will have Daddy Yankee and Oscar D'León and Grupo Niche there, and by the time 5 a.m. rolls around and the crowd starts to trickle out, his hair and his clothes and his being will be impregnated with foreign sweat and cigarette smoke and spilled aguardiente and purchased laughter and his hand will have been shaken by hundreds of strangers. They're all eager to curry favor with him, to receive a tiny crumb of the money they say he has, money that—according to local lore—at one point Luis Silva kept stashed in suitcases under his bed, because he was so afraid of stepping inside a bank.

Angel was taught to be anonymous, a frank contrast with his father's penchant for ostentation. Luis Silva learned too late that while Colombia's ruling classes were willing to look the other way as long as he shared his bounty, flaunting it so brazenly was a no-no.

The day he was denied admission into Club Colombia, he pondered his miscalculation long and hard. Much to his surprise, some things truly could not be bought.

"My son," he told his wife the next day, "will be a classy guy."

Angel would be educated in Europe. What did he care that the United States wouldn't give him a visa? Weren't England and France and Switzerland better? Weren't they old money? He would run a legitimate business. He would date nice girls, girls who went to the country club and had apartments in Miami. He would never be turned away because his last name wasn't right.

And it all could have worked nicely, too. Angel Silva was sent to a private boarding school in Switzerland and to college near Paris. He was young, handsome, smart, and rich. Abroad, where all foreigners are judged by the cash they carry, their educational pedigree, and the color of their skin, the name, unknown across the Atlantic, was inconsequential.

Here, however, it placed him on ambivalent ground. He

looked and sounded like the upper crust, but almost perversely, he allowed his father's tarnish to touch upon so many things he did.

He touches her now, and sees an unsullied slate, a chance to get it right. Impulsively, he grabs her shoulders tightly and presses his open mouth against the nape of her neck, hard.

"What?" she says softly.

"Nothing." He shakes his wet head against her. "I want to make you happy. That's all."

"Take me to dinner," she says suddenly.

"Take you to dinner?" he repeats stupidly.

"Yes. Take me to dinner. That will make me happy."

"I don't know," he says, laughing. "Wouldn't a Hermès bag or something like that make you happier?"

Gabriella shakes her head emphatically, delighted at the break in his intensity. "A Hermès bag will make me happy. But a dinner date with you—a date where we can sit, just the two of us, in a beautiful restaurant and wear beautiful clothes and be served beautiful food by beautiful people—that will make me happier than anything else."

Inside the shower, the steam and flow of the water make her words hazy, almost unreal. The simplicity of the request touches him, but the simple things have eluded him for a long time.

"I want to do all the things I do, but with you," she says with a touch of wonderment, because she's not sure when she shed her apprehension at being seen with him; perhaps it was today, just hours ago, when he kissed her while she was on her horse with the proprietary air of a man who is proud of what he owns, and she reveled in it.

"I don't want to hide," she continues urgently, because she needs to say this now, with her back to him, with his hands against her shoulders, and now against the small of her back and on her breasts and down to her stomach as her only gauge of a reaction, and the words pour out of her, the words she thought today, when a sea of people watched them but still didn't see his hand on her thigh, grazing her with his thumb as he pulled her against him from his horse.

"I want people to see us and know that we're together and know, from the way you put your hand around my waist, that we make love three times a day, and I can't get enough of you and you can't get enough of me. I want them to be jealous. To wonder what it is we do together. I want those stupid girls you've gone to bed with before me to look at us and know that I'm better than them. That I do things to you that they never dreamed of."

She stops abruptly, shocked at herself because she's never said things like this, much less done them. But he is hard behind her, and now his hands go up her neck and cup her face and turn her toward him and he pushes her against the shower wall and presses against her and whispers hoarsely into her ear: "I'll take you anywhere you want go."

Helena

He was cold and tense the night before.

Everything about her sudden trip is askew, he said. As askew as I've been for the past five months. He knows he's misplaced a piece of me, but no matter how hard he looks, he can't find it. I'm shut down. I haven't even called my parents since I returned, even though I used to phone them religiously, every two days at the very least. Marcus could call my mother, of course, have a chat with her, ask her what it is that happened to change me like this. But he's much too proud to resort to that. He'll never admit to anyone there's something wrong between us.

I'm sure it's crossed his mind that I'm sleeping with someone else, although he has never come out and asked me outright. I certainly have been careful to obliterate any trace of deceit—not a phone call or a gift or a slip of the tongue or even resistance in bed.

But I can't help myself. Everything he does is reproachable to me. Things that I found endearing before upset me now. He doesn't dress properly. He looks sloppy in flip-flops and shorts. That hat he wears in the garden—what guy wears a hat to go gardening? Most important of all, he doesn't appreciate who I am or what I do or where I come from.

"You wouldn't understand," I dismissed him disparagingly, when he asked why I needed to physically go and revise the book.

"What is it that you need to do that you can't achieve by FedExing the proofs back to them?" he insisted.

"It's all about personal relationships, Marcus," I said curtly, appalled that he still didn't get this, even though I knew it was just a fake reason I was giving to go back. "It's not like here, where you can simply pick up the phone and send things back and forth. It's about knowing who you deal with and talking to them and asking how their families are. If you ever took the trouble to go there, you would get it," I added, convincing myself of the importance of my mission in the process.

Marcus always stays quiet when I say things like that, I think, because he knows that at some level, my anger is justified.

But tonight, I feel the sadness of his reproach, and a surge of tenderness for him suddenly overpowers me.

"Helena," he whispered, as if sensing my sudden change of heart. "Just go do what you need to do. I'll pick you up on Saturday," he says, not waiting for my acknowledgment. He knows me so well, he can always tell if I'm awake. "I'll pick you up, and we'll go out and celebrate your book. Okay?"

I don't say anything for a few seconds. I think of so many nights on this bed, of lying here with Gabriella between us, both of us embracing over her tiny figure. My throat tightens up, and if I speak, I know I'll burst into tears. But I gulp it down, and in the darkness, I let my hand search for his under the covers. "That sounds like a plan," I countered quietly and turned around and put my other hand against his cheek and kissed him very, very lightly on the lips, then turned back again, and after a few minutes, I fell asleep.

Gabriella

Her mother's best friend's name is Elisa. She lives in a down-town building that was once grand, but has now fallen into that state of sad disrepair associated with older buildings that simply can't muster the energy to compete with their newer, more dazzling counterparts.

The lobby here is long and dark. A single guard sits behind a lonely desk whose one stab at high technology is the buzzer that allows people inside. It's a stark contrast with Nini's foyer of white marble ampleness, stretching toward the mountains and the pool and the sky with one gesture.

But upstairs, in Elisa's seventeenth-floor apartment, the views are as grand as Nini's, the light as bright, the easel in the dining room optimally placed to receive it from both windows all through the day.

Elisa is a divorced painter. In her heyday as one of the city's reigning doyennes, she could entertain here with aplomb. Now that her moment has gone by and her ex-husband has remarried, her monthly allotment hasn't allowed her to move to different living quarters. But her status as an artist frees her somewhat from societal expectations; she is eccentric, unique. She can live where she pleases.

The elevator may be dinky, but the maid who opens the door for Gabriella is uniformed, and the tea set that awaits her is antique, sterling silver.

"Gabriellita!" cries Elisa, walking toward her, arms outstretched, wearing jeans, starched white cotton shirt, and red espadrilles. When she hugs Gabriella, she smells of Chanel mixed with turpentine. Her hair is cut very, very short and highlighted just so. Her figure is trim and fit. She speaks in short, good-natured gusts of energy that often end in exclamation points and question marks. Everything about Elisa is fluffy and intense at the same time, a disarming combination that has allowed her to survive despite her frequent missteps.

Gabriella used to come here regularly. When she was little, Elisa made a point of having her over, setting up a little easel and crafts for her to do during afternoons, her small way of making up for the death of her best friend.

She looks at Gabriella now, and her eyes light up. The girl is beautiful, and Elisa has an artist's appreciation of beauty. "You are stunning," she says matter-of-factly. "You don't look a bit like your mother," she adds happily, the same words she's told Gabriella for the past five years. "But stunning nevertheless."

Gabriella smiles. She's used to Elisa's blunt appeal and she enjoys it. That's why she accepts these annual invitations for afternoon tea. It used to make her feel close to her mother, this reliving of her afternoons in this very place. When they were little girls, Elisa has told her, they would come here after school, lock themselves up in her bedroom, and listen to Journey and Billy Joel. They were avid fans of everything

American—the music, the books, the TV shows and films. Her mother, Elisa told her, always said she would marry a tall, blond gringo, preferably one with a name that ended in a II, III, or IV.

"And she found exactly what she wanted. The perfect man. Gorgeous? Smart? Oh, I love your father," Elisa would say, nodding her head in appreciation as she tipped the silver pitcher, the hot water tinkling down, over the little lattice tea-filled basket and into her white china cup.

The perfect man. The perfect man. The words come back to Gabriella almost as a rhyme as she watches the routine she's watched so many afternoons. That's how she always thought of her father. The perfect man. Why, why would her mother risk losing the perfect man? She looks at Elisa expectantly now, a recurring name in her mother's writings. How much does she know? Gabriella wonders. How much has she shielded all these years behind that happily smooth facade?

"Elisa," she says softly, and something in the tone makes her mother's friend set the pitcher down carefully, put her cup gently on the saucer, and look at her fully. It seems to Gabriella she's anticipating questions she's expected for nearly two decades.

"Elisa, you always said my father was the perfect man, do you remember that?"

"Of course, mi amor," Elisa says quickly, the slightest of furrows marring her Botoxed brow. "He is, in my book. Your mother was lucky!"

"If she was so lucky, then why did she have an affair with Juan José Solano?"

Whatever Elisa was expecting, the question still takes her by surprise, her mouth literally drops open. She looks at Gabriella steadily, weighing the options, considering what to shield from her.

"I know about it," Gabriella intercedes, before Elisa can slather makeup over the reality. "I found her diary. She wrote about it in great detail."

"A diary?" repeats Elisa automatically. "I didn't know she kept a diary."

"She didn't," says Gabriella. "She wrote it for me. But then, she started writing it for herself."

Elisa sighs involuntarily. This isn't a place she wants to be in, telling secrets to her best friend's daughter. Especially *this* secret. She's always felt a pang of guilt, for having tacitly accepted Helena's choices and setting up the chain of events that led to her death.

An accident, an accident, her own mother told her over and over when it happened. "What could you possibly have done?"

But Elisa knows she could have been more adamant in condemning Helena's betrayal of Marcus, because that's how Elisa had always viewed it; not as an affair but as a betrayal. For a second, she has a vision of Helena, dancing with Juan José the night that set it all off, the purple scarf twirling around and around, like a Chinese flag flying over the torches that circled the dance floor.

Everything had looked surreal, almost enchanted.

"I don't know, nena," she says helplessly. "I didn't judge her, because I was in no position to judge." She shrugs, waving her arm. Her reputation as a flirt is notorious; there are at least two substantial affairs attached to her. "I just listened."

"And what did she tell you, Elisa? Because no one wants to tell me," Gabriella says urgently. "No one will tell me, and I need to know. It's eating me inside."

"But, baby, what is it that you need to know so badly?" Elisa says gently. "She's dead now. So what does it matter anymore?"

"It matters. To me it matters. I want to know…" Her voice trails off. She's starting to feel like she's on a merry-go-round, asking the same question and never hearing what she wants to hear.

Elisa looks at her Gabriellita, all grown up now. When the girl was little, she regaled her with endless stories of her mother—how they connived to get extra recess time, how Helena gave her the answers to the algebra quiz that would have made her fail the class, how they played hooky from gym class because they both abhorred basketball, how they were caught smoking in the bathroom and almost received a suspension, how Helena—the brightest, most articulate girl in their senior class—delivered the class speech during their graduation ceremony.

What stories should she tell her now? Elisa wonders, because in her mind Helena is still her luminous Helena, and she can't bear the tarnishing of this beautiful—if defective—soul.

When you're young, everything is so black and white, she thinks. When Elisa was twelve years old, her father left her mother, didn't give her a dime for the rest of her life.

Elisa never spoke about him again, not even to Helena. But when she turned eighteen, she was the one who sought him out, who went to look for her own answers, and found them, imperfect as they were. He took Elisa in, sent her to college, redeemed himself—never entirely—but enough to walk her down the aisle when she got married.

No story, she knows, has only one side to it, and because she knows this, she takes a sip of tea—of tea that has been languishing untouched for the past ten minutes—and tells Gabriella what she knows.

"She always felt constrained by Cali, your mother. It was too small for her, too narrow-minded. For me, too, come to think about it." She laughs. "But I really didn't care. She did, though. She always worried about what was said about her—who knew what. She so badly wanted to go to the States. 'I'm going to fulfill my potential!' she would say. Not in an arrogant way, because your mother was stubborn and sometimes irrational, but she was never arrogant. She wanted to leave and just do her thing and not worry about appearances.

"It baffled me that she would go for Juan José. He was diametrically opposite to her, represented everything she had run away from. And maybe, maybe that's why I never took it seriously. I thought it would be a passing thing, inconsequential? And that is what you should think, too. Because that's what it was. You're tying yourself up in knots over something that was a hiccup in your mother's life."

"Elisa, we're talking about deceit here," says Gabriella, and even to her own ears she sounds prim, judgmental.

"Nena," says Elisa, with an edge and more than a touch

of condescension creeping into her soft voice. "Infidelity is overrated! I should know, I'm an expert on the subject, or didn't you know that?"

Gabriella blinks because, of course, she knows about Elisa's travails, so talked about in this city, but also, in typical Cali fashion, overlooked and swept under the rug; trifling peccadilloes. So many women here sleep with each other's husbands during the day, and at night, they sit together at the club—kiss, kiss, you look fabulous!—pretending everything is okay until someone gets bored and things return to normal.

"My honest opinion, as awful and crass as this may sound, is Helena was away, she saw something in this man, and she slept with him—rightly or wrongly, I'm not going to get into that debate—and she returned to your father and to you. End of story."

"Then, why did she come back, Elisa? Why? Why was she on the plane?" Gabriella asks with urgency in her voice. "*That's* what I want to know now. She had unfinished business. What was it?"

Elisa sighs. "Ay, baby, I don't know. I really don't know. I didn't even know she was coming. But I imagine," she says pensively, "that she just wanted to say good-bye. If I had been in her shoes, maybe I would have done the same thing as well.

"Whatever it was," Elisa continues evenly, "it isn't right for you to attack her when she's no longer here. Everything that happened that year was horrendous. And now, after all this time, to bring it up and make it worse."

"And how do you think I feel, Tía Elisa, about all this?"

Gabriella questions, feeling tears well up in her eyes. "I hate it, too! That's why I want to understand what happened."

"Gabriellita." Elisa leans toward her and takes her two hands in hers. "Think about it—dispassionately for a minute. Had she lived, you would have never known. Your parents would still be married, and you would have never known about this one thing. I'm not asking you to forget, but at this point, I have to ask you to forgive."

Gabriella looks away, clearly uncomfortable, then abruptly changes the subject. "Can I see what you're working on?" she says.

"Of course! Come, come," says Elisa, relieved at the change in subject, getting up and leading Gabriella to the dining room.

It's an oversize oil depicting a tropical rain forest, where branches weave in and out and in and out in endless waves. The two bright eyes are barely visible in the back of the foliage—eyes that follow you wherever you step in the room.

"It's one of a set," explains Elisa. "I'm working on them in blue, burnt yellow, and orangey-red. Really bright, bright hues. They're for the new Bank of Bogotá building, which is all white, so they wanted some contrast."

"I thought you didn't do corporate work," says Gabriella, puzzled.

"Ah, well!" says Elisa dismissively, waving her hand at the inconsequentiality of the question. "Times change. The perception of those kinds of commissions is very different now. I've become flexible at my old age!

"But enough of this talk," Elisa says, putting her slim arm

around Gabriella's waist, taking her back to the living room, looking straight ahead as she questions her. "Is it true what I've heard, that you're dating Luis Silva's son?"

Now it's Gabriella's turn to be caught off guard. "Okay, how did you know?" she asks, half annoyed, half relieved to get it out of the way.

"Oh, nena, everybody knows! And if they didn't, *now* they do, after today's newspaper!" she adds conspiratorially.

"What, what do you mean, today's newspaper?" asks Gabriella with alarm.

"You haven't seen it!" says Elisa, a statement, not a question, as she realizes Gabriella truly doesn't know. "Wait one moment, baby," she says, reaching over the tea set still laid out in the living room.

She delicately rings the silver bell on the tray and the maid appears at the kitchen door.

"Ruby, get me today's edition of *Cali Buena Nota,* please," says Elisa firmly, requesting the photo tabloid that accompanies the daily newspaper, *El País.* It's a feria specialty, printed only this one week, and chock-full of photos featuring the hip and the beautiful.

Ruby returns with the magazine, neatly folded to the right page, which is dominated by a picture of Angel kissing Gabriella and, only she knows, trickling aguardiente into her mouth, minutes before she was almost thrown from the horse. The faces are in profile, but it's clearly her and him. If there were any doubts, the caption below dispels them: "Angel Silva y Gabriela Ricard (her name, misspelled) celebran la cabalgata con tremendo beso!"

Maybe Nini didn't see it, she thinks. Maybe no one of

consequence has seen it, buried as it is on page four. Gabriella suppresses an incomprehensible urge to laugh at the irony.

Yesterday she wanted everyone to know that they were lovers. Today, she's worried over public record of a kiss. Here she is, photographed kissing the man she slept with less than twenty-four hours ago, and there is no one she can happily share the photo with. She feels like burning the damn newspaper.

Elisa looks at her with frank interest, her eyes shrewd in her placid face. "Are you doing this to get back at your mother and Nini, Gabriella?" she asks.

"Of course not!" says Gabriella, pulling her hair back with both hands.

"Of course not," she repeats accusingly, although now she knows. She knows she could have said no on that very first phone call, and Angel, so resolutely proud, would have never called again. After all, you can't say no at the end. You have to say no at the beginning, before it even starts. "He's a great guy," she says quietly. "This has *nothing* to do with Nini."

"Well," says Elisa in a tone that implies everything is settled, but not really. "At least, my dear, your mother was discreet. Because I can't imagine your grandmother is all that pleased, is she? Or has he been able to win her over?"

"She hasn't met him," Gabriella answers, feeling suddenly very, very small.

"Oh?" says Elisa, raising her eyebrows. She starts to say something, but because there clearly is nothing to say, she looks closely at the newspaper picture. "They say he's very good-looking," she allows, letting an ounce of charity into her voice. "A little dark, but very good-looking." She sighs. "It's hard to tell here."

Elisa is dismayed at the turn the afternoon has taken. She's gone from substitute aunt to acolyte to inquisitioner in less than an hour, all roles she detests. "If you like him, then enjoy him, Gabriellita," she says, shaking her head. "It's hard enough to find people you love, or even like, in this life."

Gabriella feels miserable now, devoid of answers, devoid of tea—because she's barely taken a sip—devoid of spirit.

She is in love with him. And she can't even bring herself to say it out loud. Why does loving Angel come accompanied by an apology?

She remembers the first time they made love, on that very first date, high up in the mountains, where he assured her they wouldn't be seen. "Because people never look up. They always watch their feet instead of the sky," he had whispered as he took off her shirt, her tennis shoes, her jeans, her plain white cotton panties because she had never thought to wear black lace on a very first date.

She hadn't thought of consequences then, but now consequences follow them everywhere, as closely as his phalanx of bodyguards.

As if reading her mind, Elisa puts her hand softly on her shoulder. "Things are never that simple, are they?" she says. "Just be careful, okay? He is—well, you know all about him."

If it had been Helena, she would have told them all to fuck themselves. She wouldn't have been ashamed or concerned.

And, thinks Gabriella with sudden clarity, neither will she. "Yes, I know all about him. And he's wonderful. And loving. And I'm going out to dinner with him tonight, Elisa, and I'm going to have the best time. And I want everyone to know it."

Helena

I didn't have the heart to wake Gabriella up, even though she begged me to. She still sleeps like a rag doll, so funny. Her arms wide open, her legs wide open, her mouth open, the covers all tossed aside. I ran a finger down her cheek, so soft, then pulled up the sheet, at least, to cover her up. But she tossed them off, still asleep, before I even left her room.

It was still dark outside when the taxi picked me up.

I've always loved Los Angeles at that time of the day, the fog still clinging to the roofs of the houses, the roses on my front porch heavy with dew. The streets that meander from my home down to the 405 are deserted, but once we hit the freeway, the traffic was already getting heavy, a reminder of this city's perpetual motion. It took me years before I began to think of this as my home, before I stopped feeling like a tourist when I drove to and from the house.

I stared out the window at nothing, wondering exactly what it was I would do when I got to Cali.

For a split second, I was tempted to tell the driver to turn around, because after all, what was the point really? But then we reached the first exit signs pointing to the airport and the moment slipped away, like a hesitant bride who wanted to say no, until finally, she had to say yes.

Gabriella

She chose Azul, the new, trendy Thai place Juan Carlos keeps talking about, located on a second story in Granada, a newly hip neighborhood where picturesque homes have been converted into upscale restaurants and shops, conducive for barhopping and see-and-be-seen outings. It's a beautiful evening, the kind of evening that compels skeptics to stay in Cali. The city is blanketed by the gentle breeze that has swept down the mountainside in the afternoon and pushed the day's heat away.

Earlier, as her grandmother lay reading in her room, the blinds closed against the afternoon sunlight, Gabriella had knocked timidly. Her grandmother's bedroom—with its tall windows and vast bed—has always been her sanctuary, the first place she heads to when she sets foot outside the elevator doors. But in the past week, the closer she gets to Angel, the harder she studiously avoids the beckoning intimacy of this room.

Nini is surprised at the visit, her expression both apprehensive and hopeful. She's been at a loss for the past several days, unable to outright forbid her granddaughter's choices yet reluctant to send her packing and risk losing her entirely.

She justifies her silence, to herself and to Marcus, by rea-
soning that she's already lived through this once, with the
unhappiest of possible outcomes. That she lost Helena when
they were so at odds with each other, the unresolved issues
left hanging forever, still keeps her awake at night.

"Nini," her granddaughter says now, and in the voice she
hears a question and a tentativeness that harks back to a
month ago, when Nini was planning this trip, before everything went awry.

Nini puts the newspaper to one side and looks at Gabriella, trying not to appear too eager or too nervous or too
anxious with this simple visit, this simple little word.

"Sí, Gabriellita?" she answers as neutrally as possible.

"I'm going out to dinner tonight?" says Gabriella, reverting
to her habit of speaking in questions when she's nervous.

"With Angel?" she adds. Swallows.

"And, I wanted him to meet you. I m-mean," she stammers, "he wants to meet you. I wanted to know if he could
come upstairs to pick me up, I mean, instead of me just going
down, and you know, just say hi."

Of all the things Nini expected to hear, she doesn't expect
to hear this, and she stares nonplussed at Gabriella, standing
hopefully at her bedside, not making things right, but trying
to make them better. Her first impulse is righteousness, to
say she doesn't allow people like Angel Silva into her home,
and that she, Gabriella, should know her place.

She can remember another time, when divorces and ille-
gitimate children were studiously avoided, when last names
meant something—a pedigree, respectability, hard-won
through generations of decent living. It has come to this: her

only granddaughter asking for her blessing to sleep with a drug dealer's son.

What would her husband have done? she wonders.

"Gabriellita," she begins to say, and sees the doubt she's feeling already reflected in her eyes. She goes with her heart then, because her conscience is tired of arguing. "Of course. Bring him up. I would love to meet him."

"My grandmother would like to meet you," she tells Angel over the phone, an hour before he's scheduled to pick her up.

"Really?" he blurts out, frankly shocked.

"Yes, really," she says with a smile in her voice. "Don't worry, nothing formal, just a little hi, how are you. Encantado. You know?"

"Why does she want to meet me?" he prods, mulling over this sudden turn of events. From the onset it's been quite obvious that Gabriella wants to hide him from her family, a fact that for him is par for the course, but that he increasingly resents. That uptight cousin, for example, who thought nothing of going to his house and drinking his booze and fondling his friends, but looks the other way when they run into each other. He's tempted to send a couple of his guys on him, just for fun.

"Well, she wants to meet the man her granddaughter is dating!" insists Gabriella. "I think that's pretty normal, don't you?"

"Sure," he says nonchalantly, although he doesn't feel nonchalant. He feels—he admits to himself—overjoyed, but also leery, as if he's about to be tricked.

"Sure," he says again hesitantly. "I'll just get there a little early." He pauses to give himself time to think. "Do I call you when I arrive?" he asks timidly.

"No," she says. "Just tell the guard you're coming to see me, he'll tell you where to go."

Angel hangs up his cell phone slowly. He's going to meet his girlfriend's grandmother. Girlfriend. She *is* a girlfriend. For the first time in months, he wishes he had a confidant other than Julio. For the first time in years, he wishes he had a mother, an aunt, someone other than Chelita, to run this by.

But Chelita is what he has. "Chelita!" he shouts from his bedroom, but Chelita, tuned to her perpetual TV, doesn't answer.

"Chelita!" he shouts again, walking into the kitchen, turning the set off.

"What, what?" she cries, startled, because Angel never screams.

"I'm going to meet Gabriella's grandmother," he says with no preamble.

Chelita looks genuinely puzzled. She's an expert in the complexities of class structure, as shown on the soap operas she tirelessly watches on TV. But it has never occurred to her that her Angel, as rich as he is, could be ostracized. "What do you mean, Angelito? You haven't met her yet?"

To his dismay, he blushes, feeling a wave of embarrassment sweep over him.

"No." He's going to give her the explanation, then stops, because he can't bring himself to say it out loud, especially not to her. "No," he says lamely. "We just never had time."

"Well, put something nice on, mi niño. Take her some flowers. That would be nice," Chelita offers with a smile. "Why are you so worried? She'll love you! How couldn't she?" Chelita says, looking at him with such genuine love, he impulsively goes to her and hugs her, as he used to do when he was a little boy, helping her cut up the dough for empanadas in the kitchen.

"That's a good idea, Chelita," he says gratefully, glad in the end that he interrupted her show.

He goes with the most classic, most generic outfit he can think of: jeans, a starched white linen shirt, and a blue blazer that hides the gun he keeps tucked behind his belt. He sends Julio for flowers, almost going for an outrageously expensive orchid before settling for the safe two dozen long-stemmed roses.

In the elevator, he cradles them in the crook of his arm, adjusting his shirt collar, stamping his feet to make sure the hems of his jeans haven't bunched up around his ankles.

When the elevator door opens, directly into the apartment, Gabriella is waiting for him, wearing the short red dress she adores and would have worn the night she met him had she stood her ground then. She leads him in by the hand, kissing him chastely on the cheek, doing all the things that nice girls do when their nice boyfriends come to visit, a vignette so normal it constricts his throat with how alien it seems to him, like a movie he's paid to see.

"Wow, for me?" she says delightedly, reaching out for the flowers.

"No, no," he says firmly. "For your grandmother."

"Well, how nice," she says, letting a touch of awe and pleasure slip into her voice.

From the hallway, Nini stands silently watching, taking in how tall he is, how assured he looks next to Gabriella's height. And how Gabriella literally sparkles in his presence, how the color of her skin rises, how she tosses back her hair when she puts her hand on his arm, how wrapped up they look in each other's presence. Helena never reacted like this to Marcus, or Juan José for that matter. She was always looking beyond what she had, always thinking she had missed out on something. Had it not been Juan José, Nini now acknowledges, it would have been someone else, and afterward, maybe someone else again. Nini shakes her head, resigned, composes her face, and smooths down the jacket of her fuchsia suit.

"Buenas, buenas," she says now, stepping into the foyer, extending her hand with the relaxed practice of a socialite who can turn graciousness on at the drop of a hat.

"Doña Cristina," he says politely, shaking her hand firmly, not kissing her, she notices appreciatively—kissing strangers is something she tolerates but doesn't take kindly to—and instead proffering her the roses, beautiful roses, handpicked from Impoflores, she can tell from the pink cellophane, the most expensive florist in town.

"I never knew Gabriella had such a beautiful grandmother," he says sincerely, and despite herself, she feels flattered.

It surprises her that he's not awkward or gauche or tacky. But it surprises her more, when she looks up into his green eyes to thank him for her roses, how tenuous his comfort is, how anxious he is to make things right. She wants to ask him who taught him how to dress, how to act, how to say the right things and bring the right gift and look at her with just the right blend of gallantry and respect.

"Won't you stay for a drink?" she asks impulsively, startling herself, startling Gabriella more, startling him completely.

He thinks of the reservation, of the table on hold, just for him.

"We're running late, Nini," Gabriella says swiftly, stepping in. "But maybe another night?" she adds hopefully, a little incredulously.

"We must do that," says Nini briskly. "Perhaps tomorrow? After the bullfights?"

Gabriella looks at Angel inquisitively, a look of unequivocal trust that Nini takes in calmly. This is how she used to look at her husband, she realizes with sudden wonderment, and she wonders just how far this relationship between her granddaughter and Angel has already gone.

"That would be a pleasure," says Angel calmly, smiling his beautiful lopsided smile, somehow managing to look grateful and happy and composed.

"Well then," says Nini, even as she wonders if she's making a big mistake, "I'll be expecting you."

Helena

I slept the entire five hours to Miami, the deep sleep that last night eluded me in my own bed. When I woke up, I felt a new sense of purpose, of my trip, of my return, of my life, really. I could make things right.

I was so absorbed in the thought, I almost walked right past the duty-free shop, a silent reminder that I've shunned not only Marcus, but also my parents, with their quiet, unspoken disapproval sitting heavily between us, even now, months since I've last seen them. I hadn't bought a single Christmas present this season, and the thought has filled me with guilt. I had always delighted in buying for others, carefully selecting the gifts so they're just perfect for each person. It's never about the price, I always say, but about the perfect match; something so unique, they'll know it could only come from me. But in the Miami airport, there was little to choose from. I looked dismally at the generic watches and scarves, and finally settled for something that I knew my parents would, at the very least, use. A liter of Johnnie Walker Black Label for him, a bottle of Shalimar for her.

I walked aimlessly through the store, dabbing on samples of perfume, one brand on my wrist, another on my inner elbow, another on my hands. I've used the same perfume since I was fifteen, after reading about some fabulous star who was always followed by the same scent. I felt like a change now, but I couldn't find anything that defined me now, today. And anyway, I suppose the right time to change my signature scent would be when I'm coming back, not when I'm leaving.

In the end, I boarded my plane with my duty-free gifts and my single carry-on, traveling so very light and so down in the dumps alongside those overstocked, overjolly holiday travelers. I wondered, a bit guiltily, how many people could have better used this seat that I've occupied almost on a whim; people longing to return home for Christmas on this single daily direct flight to Cali, left behind because of my selfish mission.

I tried, ineffectually, to tune out the din around me. The guy behind me was loud and drunk, spewing venom with a Spanish accent, railing about the flight, the stewardess, American Airlines, which sucks, and all Americans, who also suck, and he declared, practically shouting, were naturally stupid and ill informed. Irritated, I put my pen down for a moment, and instead, started turning back the pages.

For the first time in months, I didn't write. I read. And I cringed at my own words, at how explicit, how unerringly honest they were.

Distance definitely makes you bold, I mused, turning the pages slowly, looking at myself as if from a great distance, as my hand involuntarily went up to the back of my neck, rubbed it, up and down. I suddenly wished I had a jacket to cover myself with.

What if Marcus had read this? I wondered suddenly. With new anxiety, I made my way back into the pages, to where it all began, and grabbed everything between my fingers and pulled. But the clump of pages I wanted to purge was too thick and refused to tear under my insistence.

I looked down at the partially bent page between my fingers, and I saw him again in my mind, surrounded by tendrils of smoke from his cigarette as he drove me through the valley.

I smiled, just a little bit, despite myself, tracing the words on the page slowly. It seemed so long ago now. If I ripped the pages out now, I wouldn't have anything left.

Tomorrow. "Tomorrow," I wrote. "I'll deal with it tomorrow."

Gabriella

They are both tall and beautiful, and when they walk into the room, people turn to look. Gabriella's vanity is undeniably stoked, because she feels herself blushing, with something akin to fear trembling in the pit of her stomach, with excitement, with delight at her shared fortune. The irony of the moment doesn't escape her. Things should be the other way around—the public courting first; the intimacy, sexual and emotional, later. She doesn't care, because right here, right now, all the little pieces she's been carrying with her these weeks have fallen into their exact place.

He holds her hand as the hostess leads them to their table, in a corner of the room, a white, bright room, even under the dimmed lights, with sleek, polished, wooden floors and tables with white tablecloths adorned with lilac-colored orchids. The art on the walls is bright and shocking, slates of purples and reds and oranges, against the white walls, everything for sale. She sits against a backdrop of color: a triptych of apples—red over green, green over pale yellow, and pale yellow over red—three separate canvases, bound by a chain link that threads them together at the top and bottom, a celebration of colors whose effect on her is dampened by the appearance of Julio at her side. Julio pulls back his chair to take the seat next to Angel before Angel stops him with just a shake of the head, because this time, this one time, he will sit with only her and her alone, because this is her night.

"At the bar, Julio," Angel tells him quietly, so quietly that only Julio can hear him, but still, he resents the order, resents her. Gabriella knows this in her gut, and for a second, she feels a tinge of remorse, then quickly tells herself that the bar makes so much more sense because it's at the very entrance to the restaurant, because the other bodyguards are there, and because Julio, after all, is a bodyguard, not an uncle, not a father.

"Are you sure?" she asks nevertheless, and Angel only nods yes and sits down next to her, moving his chair closer so his knees graze her thighs underneath the table.

Helena

I woke up to the sound of the pilot's voice, the rustle of passengers. Around me women were reapplying their makeup and cups were being collected.

"Ladies and gentlemen, this is your captain speaking," I heard over the loudspeaker. "We have begun our descent for landing at Cali. It's a lovely evening as we had expected. We'll pass a shower or two on the way in, but at the field right now, it's good visibility, the temperature is two-three, that's twenty-three degrees Celsius, and if you prefer Fahrenheit, that's seventy-two degrees on the Fahrenheit scale. The winds are ten miles an hour from the northwest. It's a very, very pretty evening. I'd like to thank everyone for coming with us."

I fastened my seat belt, straightened my seat back; automatically I checked to make sure everything was in my purse: wallet, passport. I look at the diary, heavy between my hands.

The captain's voice droned on, but the only thing that comes to my mind is the little girl in the bed. My little girl. My Gabriella. Her voice, but it sounds very far away. "How long will you be gone?" she had asked me the night before.

"Just two days, mi amor," I had told her, smoothing her hair back against the pillow.

"Is that a long time?" she asked.

"No. No. It's very short. Day after tomorrow, I'll be back. Today is Tuesday. Tomorrow is Wednesday, and you'll be with Grandma. And on Thursday, I'll be here before you go to sleep. That's not long at all."

"You promise?" she asked me, and I laughed because that's how I used to be, too, when my mother traveled.

"I promise."

"You promise you'll wake me up tomorrow before you leave?"

"I promise that, too," I assured her, knowing full well that if she's asleep, there is no way I'm going to wake her up.

In the darkness of the mountains, I sought out the lights of my Cali, little twinkling dots spaced far apart, then appearing in a wave of brightness as the valley unfolded beneath just ahead, over the mountains. Even now, after all these years, my heart can't help but beat faster in anticipation, as if I were getting close to Disneyland instead of here.

"Again, I apologize for being late tonight," the voice over the loudspeaker continued. "Like to wish everyone a very, very happy holiday and a healthy and prosperous New Year."

I closed my eyes and leaned back, suddenly exhausted. I automatically lifted my right hand to bless myself—in the name of the Father and the Son and the Holy Spirit—and reached, as always, for my locket, the one with your picture in it, but it's not there, of course, because I gave it to you.

"Oh, well," I shrug, and instead bring my hand up to my lips and then lower it, to the hollow of my throat, where the locket should have been.

Gabriella

On their table, a yellow candle flickers next to the orchid, illuminating the red wine that has been poured into tall goblets, the little dumplings that sit untouched, and what she will remember most about this evening, how he took her hands and examined them slowly by the candlelight.

"I don't get it," he says with a trace of awe. "How can you play things like Prokofiev and Beethoven, when your fingers are so delicate? How can something this soft be so strong?"

And those are his last words, because the next instant, he has shoved her hard, and she grabs the tablecloth to keep from falling, but instead, drags it with her to the floor, and the plates and the candle crash beside her, and all she can hear is firecrackers, and she wonders stupidly why he's pushed her and why there are firecrackers inside the restaurant, and then the screaming drowns everything else.

She can't see him. Can't see him draw the gun from behind his waist, even though he knows, as he does it, that it's too late, knew it was too late from the moment he saw them come in and automatically pushed her aside to safety with his left hand. Too late because he was suffused in her, because he trusted Julio to keep him covered, forgetting

Julio wasn't next to him this time. And the shooters didn't count on that, either, because there is the briefest of hesitations before they open fire, as they seek out Julio and find her instead, and in that tiniest wrinkle in time, Angel pulls out his gun and manages to squeeze out a shot, dropping the first one, but already he feels a succession of hard thuds, in his chest and his arm and his stomach, and he's flung back, like an errant punching bag, screaming for Julio.

Julio who went to take a piss, buying himself two more minutes of existence, because his men were the first to go, dispatched with two neat bullets to their heads, clean and simple, their faces slumping down into the bar almost elegantly, everything over so quickly that they never got the chance to reach for their guns. The bartender stepped back, hands up, pressing flat against the sink, but it wasn't necessary, the gunmen were already moving on into a room that still hadn't acknowledged their presence, because they had avoided conspicuous machine guns to fool the guards downstairs, opting instead for little handguns, the kind you can easily hide inside a suit pocket, the kind you can point and shoot, barely causing a ripple, as they've done in this place, where the din of conversation and the familiarity of Carlos Vives's voice singing "Sí, sí, sí, este amor es tan profundo, que tu eres mi consentida y que lo sepa todo el mundo" over the sound system muffled the shots.

Angel recognized the purpose in their eyes the second he saw them standing there, scanning, out of place, out of place. Why hadn't anyone downstairs caught on? he thought. Such a security breach, he would fire somebody over this.

But now, lying on the floor, when he tries to breathe, his

throat is clogged and his chest burns like it has been branded with an iron. He's choking, and when he coughs, bubbles of blood splatter over his linen shirt. He can't hear through the screaming, but above him, he sees the second man, the one he wasn't able to get, and he's standing over Angel with his small but deadly gun raised for his grace shot, because, Angel knows, you always finish the job with a shot to the head, just to be sure.

And then, the bullets start again, a flurry that comes from behind him and strike the man on his face, on his arms, everywhere, the bullets flying across the room, hitting him, hitting everything in their path, hitting the triptych of paintings behind him, which slowly come unhinged, then hurl into the wooden floor, the frames splintering, cymbals reverberating inside his head as the chain collides with the floor.

He can't see, but he knows it's Julio, his loyal Julio, who was right of course about the futility of this vain, stupid, stupid evening, who, quite literally, is caught with his zipper down, rushing out of the bathroom with his underwear flapping outside his pants when he hears the shouts, his semi-automatic cocked, but he can't see Angel and proceeds to spray the restaurant with bullets, cursing himself and them at the top of his lungs—hijueputas, hijueputas, hijueputas—for laxness, for failing to adhere to protocol, for capitulating. As he lowers his gun, a last shot is fired from the ground, hitting him—by pure chance—in the neck.

Julio falls to his knees, his eyes open in surprise as he numbly brings his hand up to the spot just below his jaw, from where blood is now spurting out in short, heavy spasms.

He can't stop the blood, and he feels his life pumping out of him, everything around him a hazy red, like the apples in the paintings that are tumbling to the floor. His last thought is that Don Luis will never forgive him for this. Even if he gets out of here alive, he's a dead man.

Gabriella is buried under the tablecloth, immobile, praying, even though she never prays, except to her mother. But she prays to God now fervently, because she thinks she will really die, because she can't stop her legs from shaking uncontrollably. There are consequences after all, she suddenly thinks, remembering her mother and her flight of doom. How could she have been so arrogant to think herself immune? She is going to die here on this floor, and now she wants God to know that she believes in him, she really does, she will not live a life of perpetual purgatory because one day she fell in love with the wrong boy.

Something crashes behind her, something big and monstrous because splinters fly from the floor onto her bare legs, curled tightly underneath her, and for what feels like an eternity, the noise reverberates across the room until it's gone, completely gone, taking with it the screams and the shots, leaving only Carlos Vives as he sings about the love he wants to share with the world.

She realizes the floor is sticky under her hands, turns them over to find them red and viscous, and although she's never touched blood, not like this, she knows that's what it is, and she stifles the impulse to scream, like they do in the movies, because her instinct to live is much stronger and she doesn't know if there is still evil lurking around her, seeking her—and Angel—out.

His blood, she thinks, his blood, his life seeping under her hands, and she needs to find him, but she can't see properly, because everything is covered by a thick haze and the acrid smell of gun smoke sits heavy inside her nose and stings her eyes.

She hears a cough, and she crawls toward the sound on her hands and knees, her hands leaving imprints of blood on the beautiful wooden floor, and finds him bleeding from everywhere, from his chest and his arms, *oh,* and his stomach, and she tries to stop it all with the tablecloth, but in a matter of seconds it's soaked up again, and she knows she's crying and that's not good, because he'll panic and already he looks desperate and afraid—something she's never seen him look before—but she can't help herself. She's soaking up his blood and he can't muster a word; all he can do is cough, and with each cough, a little more blood leaves him and drips down onto his beautiful white linen shirt, which is now completely ruined, and she can barely believe this helpless man is the same person who picked her up tonight. She thinks, with rising panic, that he's dying, he will die on her, and she can't bear the pain that the mere thought is already causing her.

The smell of blood rises from the floor—she had no idea blood smelled—a sickeningly sweet smell that blends with the burned stench of the gun smoke, and Gabriella, by sheer force of will, swallows the bile that has gathered perilously close to her mouth. Vomit, how could she—it would be his last conscious remembrance of her, her vomiting over him as he lay dying. She searches desperately for her cell phone, using one hand to press down hard on his chest, the other futilely seeking out the floor beneath her, because her phone has to be there, dragged down to the ground with the table-cloth, but there's nothing to be found underneath her frantic fingers, until she sees it, glinting cheerfully underneath the dead man's cheek.

She needs it. She needs to call an ambulance, the police, someone who can save them. Overcoming her fear and disgust, she tentatively reaches for it, never taking her gaze from that face with the staring, open eyes, and when her fingers almost reach it, he releases a slight helpless shudder and blinks.

She lets out a small gasp involuntarily, her hand drawing quickly back before she reasons that he can't do anything to her—he can't move, he's as good as dead—and she angrily inches forward again and in a split second snatches the phone from underneath him and jumps back. She dials 911 before she remembers there is no 911 here, and then she simply begins to shout for help, but she isn't shouting, she's wailing hysterically. She no longer cares who hears, because no one is helping. Why isn't anyone helping? She screams, but no one is moving. The entire room is immobilized by terror, and no one has made the least gesture toward her. They're all hiding and Angel is bleeding, and the blood continues to trickle to the floor, no matter how hard she presses, and he's not even looking at her anymore. His eyes are shut, and his face is now a dull gray underneath his tan.

"They're coming back!" someone cries, and people scramble from underneath the tables, making a mad rush toward the restrooms, the kitchen, anywhere they can hide. Gabriella is left alone with Angel, and all she can think to do is grab another tablecloth, wrap herself inside, and huddle against the wall, curled up tightly, trying to make herself disappear.

She hears the stomping of steps coming up the staircase, swirling about her, the walkie-talkies, the shouts. She doesn't dare move; she hardly breathes. She closes her eyes and clutches her knees tightly against her chest and goes into a place deep within herself, a place she didn't know existed, where there is no time and space. That's how they find her, more than an hour later, long after they've taken him, when one of the soldiers thinks to look at the tablecloth piled against the corner.

Nini

I went to pick Helena up that night. Like I pick up Gabriella. The same flight. The same time. But by nine thirty, it hadn't landed. No one knew what was happening. We waited and waited for some announcement from American Airlines. People went upstairs to the counter. Downstairs. They kept saying the plane was about to land.

I had a bad feeling about the trip ever since she told me she was coming. A two-day trip—right before Christmas! But she said she needed to come. She had some urgent business. But she couldn't stay over the holidays. She wanted to get back to spend the holidays with Gabriella and Marcus.

Your grandfather was with me that night. It's the last time he ever went to the airport. But if it hadn't been for him...

We were getting frantic when someone came running and said the plane had crashed. Well, people went crazy. They ran upstairs to mob the American counter.

Everyone kept shouting, "Where! Where!"

Oh, God. Women were wailing. I felt like I was watching

a movie. I couldn't conceive that the plane had crashed, that Helena could possibly be inside. It was too—unreal.

But there was an ambulance right outside, and my husband stopped them, said he was a doctor. And of course, they knew who he was and they let him go along. He wanted to send me back home with Edgar, but I— I just couldn't do that. We finally decided Edgar and I would follow them in the car.

We just drove and drove. I don't know where the ambulance driver was getting his information. Somebody was probably radioing them. But we drove for hours on that dark highway. I later learned that the plane had crashed just five minutes before landing. I still don't understand how it could have been so far. But it was.

We finally got to the base of the mountain, where the road ended. They said we had to go on foot or wait for helicopters to take us.

Under normal circumstances, I don't think we would have been allowed to go up, but because my husband was a doctor, and there was no one else there—we were the first ones—they let us go on the first helicopter.

We circled and circled. There was so much fog, and it was so dark, it was hard to see with just the spotlight from the helicopter.

There were, oh, God, there were Christmas presents hanging from the trees. Ribbons. Clothes. Jackets and blankets. I mainly remember the Christmas presents and the wrapping paper. There were dolls. A tennis racket. I remember a tennis racket. I was in hell.

We couldn't land. It was too dark, too dangerous. The pilot couldn't find a place to land. So we had to go back to the foot of the mountains, and the soldiers and the Red Cross went back up on foot with flashlights.

We spent the night in the car. I couldn't fathom going anywhere without finding her first. At five in the morning, we went up again in the helicopter. But nearly eight hours had passed. Afterward, when they found the two survivors, they said they thought more people might have been alive, because the crash hadn't been a full-speed, frontal crash. But who *knew*?

It was so cold up there. All I could think of was my Helena, without a jacket. She never traveled with a jacket.

It's quite amazing, if you think about it clinically, what happens in a plane crash. We followed the things. There were objects everywhere. But we couldn't find the people. The soldiers finally found the first ones, almost a kilometer from where we were. There were no severed limbs or anything like that. Thank God. They told us it was because the plane was already preparing to land. The pilot had already put down the landing gear and the plane had slowed down, so the impact wasn't as great.

The authorities didn't know what happened. Later, after they investigated, after the lawsuits, we learned that it had been a pilot error. Apparently, the pilot programmed the automatic pilot to the wrong destination. It's a rare thing, but it can happen. They say that an alarm would have sounded out to signal the pilot that he was approaching a mass, the mountain in this case. He was going to crash against a mountain.

About a year afterward, I ran into one of the survivors—he was a friend of Helena's, as it turned out. He didn't remember anything. He just remembers waking up in the cold. I hope Helena didn't hear that alarm, either.

Every time I get on an airplane, I think about that crash. I think about my daughter, my daughter, fastening her seat belt. Looking out the window perhaps. Combing her hair. And then, I think about this awful, loud siren. I wonder what she thought. I wonder if she knew she was going to die. What could she have thought of at that moment?

I like to think that the alarm never went off, because if it had, Helena would have looked startled or frightened. But she didn't. No one did.

The people I saw, looked...asleep. They weren't burned. Some were bruised but not burned. Some were still strapped to their seats. It was like a giant dollhouse, full of misshapen dolls, with their limbs twisted in the wrong direction. That's what made it look so wrong. And the silence. So quiet. You couldn't even hear a bird chirp. No insects. It felt as if everything had been stunned to death and covered with a huge blanket of sadness.

I couldn't find her. I didn't know what she was wearing, but I kept telling everyone: She has long, curly hair; she has long curly hair. Please find my daughter with long, curly hair.

They found two people alive. Two. I was certain she had to be one of them, because I hadn't felt her die in my heart. I loved Helena so much, I just didn't think it was possible that she could die and I couldn't feel her light flicker off, no matter the distance.

But I was so wrong.

When Gabriella was younger and would try to summon her with that horrible Ouija board, I knew there was no spirit world in which to look for her.

People die, and they die.

That's what I discovered that day. But I didn't have the heart to tell Gabriella that.

For a long time I wondered if maybe Helena was alive after the crash. Maybe she died during the night, and we weren't able to save her. And for a long time I thought I would have known. I thought I would have somehow *felt* her calling me, heard her through the night. But I didn't feel a thing. I didn't hear her call me. I didn't even hear her say good-bye.

I wasn't even the one who found her.

One of the Red Cross medics did. He remembered the hair—with Helena, you told people she had long, curly hair, and then they would actually see the hair and know exactly what you meant—that's what he told me later. He told me he saw them bringing her to the helicopter and he saw the hair. And he ran to get me.

She looked—Oh. She looked so beautiful. Even like that. There was nothing in her face to indicate that she'd been in such a terrible accident. That she had fought against anything. That's been my consolation all these years. That perhaps she never knew what happened.

She was just so terribly pale. Not pale. Gray. Even when

she was asleep, Helena just burst with life. Her soul was too large for that little body. When she was a child, I used to come into her room late at night, and I would just watch her breathe in and out, her breathing trying to keep up with her heart. You could see the blood bubbling underneath her skin. The waking hours were never enough for her.

But there was none of that left when I got her back. As if someone had sucked the life out of her. And, of course, that's what had happened. She was so cold, and so white. I kept rubbing her hands, but they never warmed up.

She was wearing that red gauze shirt and jeans. We never found her shoes.

We took her to Cali right away. My husband called everyone he knew to make sure things went smoothly. So things wouldn't be painful for me. And we buried her the very next day, as soon as Marcus arrived. I never felt she had a proper funeral because there was no time to mourn her properly. But those days, there were funerals every day. Twenty, thirty funerals a day.

My poor husband. In retrospect, I think he might have had that first stroke that very night, but he never said anything. I didn't even know there had been a first stroke until the second one killed him two months later. I just wasn't myself. I missed all the signs, all the details. I didn't take care of him, either.

They called me about her things around the same time. They said they had personal effects that they thought were Helena's. So I went to the airport, to the department of aviation. They took me to this room full of lockers. Rows and rows of belongings in little cages.

They opened one of them and gave me the purse. Wrapped in plastic, with some identifying document. Incredible. A red leather purse, made by hand, survived a crash against a mountaintop. But the people didn't. We are so frail. And we really can't take anything to the grave.

Gabriella

At three in the morning, it's quiet in the hallways of the Imbanaco Medical Center, and even her flat heels click and clack loudly against the bare, antiseptic floor.

She spent the rest of the evening and the next day being questioned by detectives, returning home to a quiet Nini who resignedly watches her pack, getting ready to leave before her vacation is over. All her best intentions have been for naught, she thinks, not saying a word.

Now she has two policemen at her side, as much for her as for him, and when she gets off the elevator, soldiers flank each of the doors. At the end of the hall, where the staircase is, she sees two more.

They are quiet in deference to the other patients on this floor. But they're here for Angel. His face has been plastered all over the news, Luis Silva's only son, miraculously surviving a murder attempt that left three of his bodyguards, two gunmen, and two innocent diners from adjacent tables dead. He took four shots that in one of those quirky twists of fate, good luck, and anatomy missed any vital organs, save for the shot that hit his left lung, making it collapse, making him almost choke on his own blood.

The cops walk her to his door and gesture for her to go inside.

She doesn't know what she expected. She's never seen anybody in intensive care before, and her vision is that of someone simply lying on a bed.

He's not just doing that. He's hooked up to a ventilator, a plastic mask covering his mouth and nose, and every breath he takes is exhaled with a helpless, high hissing sound. An IV drips slowly into his arm, and a feeding tube goes down his throat.

He doesn't look strong or imperious or sexy like this, but thin, so thin under the stiff white sheets. Even his beautiful bronze face is ashen against the white pillow.

Damaged. He is so damaged.

Gabriella wraps her arms around herself, raking her nails hard, up and down her arms, to keep herself from crying.

"Buenas noches."

The voice makes her jump. She hadn't seen Chelita sitting in a corner in the dark room. Her proud Indian features look old now, the face tired, drawn down by the bags that weigh heavily under her bloodshot eyes.

She looks at Gabriella appraisingly, then slowly gets to her feet, and now, Gabriella sees the shotgun that's been lying on her lap this whole time.

"You're leaving," she says, and it isn't a question but a statement, like Angel's statements used to be.

"I have to, Chelita," she says, and despite herself, she hears the defensiveness in her voice. "My father and my grandmother say I have to go. For my safety."

Chelita looks at a loss. And angry.

"He's a good boy. A good boy," she repeats fiercely. "Mi muchacho. He didn't deserve this." She gestures toward the bed, the tubes. "And he doesn't deserve to have you walking out on him. You know that. Now when he needs you."

She remembers Chelita's story. How her husband was murdered. Her son. She imagines her angry impotence and her refusal to back down. But Gabriella isn't Chelita, she thinks. She has other things in the world. She has a life, and she isn't willing to put it at risk, not here, not now, not even for him.

Gabriella steps back before the harshness of Chelita's voice. She's helpless to make things right for him.

"Chelita." She shakes her head. Now she understands what people mean when they talk about being heartbroken. She feels like her heart is truly going to break, it hurts so much. "I can't. I can't. I don't know how to make things better for him. I love him. But this…" She gestures to the bed, but it's not the bed. It's everything; it will crush her. "I can't," she repeats quietly. "I thought I could, but I can't."

She comes close to him and tentatively reaches out and touches his hair, the face whose bones she's memorized, the smooth cheeks that now have a tiny layer of stubbly beard. She lightly grazes it with her fingers, back and forth, trying to bring back his smell, but catching only the whiff of antiseptics.

One afternoon, one of those many afternoons that they spent in his bed, she woke up to find him lying on his side beside her, watching her intently.

"What are you doing?" she had asked sleepily.

"Memorizing your face," he replied.

Then he leaned over and cupped her temples lightly between his palms, holding them there for a few seconds, then running his palms firmly down her neck, her shoulders, her arms, her hands, traversing her body one inch at a time until he reached her feet.

"And now, what are you doing?" she had asked, amused.

"Now, I'm memorizing the way you feel, so I can remember, even if you're not beside me."

She had laughed, but tonight, she remembers that day, and now, she understands what he meant. The bars are up on the sides of his bed, but she reaches out between them, gently touching his head, careful not to move the mask, and slowly goes down the length of him, his broad shoulders, his tattooed wrist, the flat stomach, his legs, strong and warm underneath the sheets. She lets her hand glide all the way down to his feet, trying to make her fingers memorize his long, elegant shapes and his smooth texture.

"And now," she tells his expressionless face very quietly so Chelita can't hear her, "I'm memorizing the way you feel, so I can remember, even when I'm gone."

Angel breathes evenly, and in the silence, she imagines his eyelids flicker, but then the movement is gone as quickly as it came and she's left with the shuttered face again.

She wants to shake him, to make him look up, but after minutes of looking intently at him, all she can muster are words that, even to her, sound pathetic.

"Chelita, please tell him I had to go, tell him I didn't have a choice?"

"You always have a choice, miss," Chelita replies, her voice as leaden as her footsteps as she takes her seat again. "You always have a choice," she says again. "That's the problem."

Gabriella straightens uncertainly. If she doesn't leave soon, she'll miss her flight.

Sensing her impatience, Chelita looks up at her, and in her black eyes, Gabriella sees she's already moved on.

"I'll give him your message," she says simply. "I wish you luck," she adds after a pause.

Gabriella nods.

"Lo mismo, Chelita."

Gabriella stands hesitantly, wishes she had something of more weight to say, because her paltry fifteen minutes with him seem anticlimactic and stale, so different from these past few weeks, the most wonderful weeks of her life, weeks that beg for a big finale, a big musical climax, and not this awkward silence.

But there is nothing more to say to someone that can't say anything in return, and finally she backs up to the door, unable to let go of his face, willing him to open his eyes, to please open his eyes, to look at her, to say something that will make her stay, that will make up for the last forty-eight hours. But only his chest moves, slowly up, slowly down, and the last thing she hears is the shaky hiss of the breathing machine, following her down the hall, all the way to the elevator doors.

Querida Mami:

Ha pasado un año desde que no voy a Cali. One year since I don't see the mountains or the valley or Juan Carlos or my room with your presence inside it.

I've hardly even spoken any Spanish since I've been back, either.

Los Angeles is so strange, a city full of Latinos, and yet no one speaks Spanish. When I open my mouth, they assume I'm a gringa trying to act Latin and they answer me in English. Now my tongue seems to have turned to dust. I stumble over the words.

I called Nini yesterday and told her this. I told her I needed to go back, because I was losing myself.

She told me I had to ask Daddy. She told me even if I had my own money, I still had to ask Daddy.

And she told me to ask you. She told me to ask you, because she won't take me back until I forgive you and move on. She said she has had too much pain in her lifetime to carry the burden of someone consumed by anger. And then she started to cry. My poor Nini. She acted against everything she believed in, for me. For nothing. Just like she did with you. But I suppose that's what mothers do, don't they? When it comes to their children they will do anything . . . Some mothers, anyway.

Oh, Mami, I promise you, I'm not angry anymore. Okay, sometimes I am, a little bit. Do you blame me? On top of everything else, you died on me! And for what? If you could see him now. Oh, if you could see him now. You would laugh at yourself. You would know how silly, how finally insignificant it would all become.

Do you know not a single day has gone by that I don't think about your diary? I have dissected and analyzed and constructed and deconstructed every word that you wrote, trying to find clues in every cadence, some unwritten page to fill the things you left unsaid.

I never told Daddy about what I found. How could I? We only have each other, after all, and what would I gain with that? Nini was right. Some things are just better left unsaid.

Anyway, Mami, the truth is overrated, as you well know.

I sometimes wonder, if you came home to us, and you saw us, and maybe, maybe, decided that everything we were outweighed what you had just found. Maybe you thought that you could make this episode a chapter in the book of your life instead of the rest of your life.

In my book, you find something in us that you didn't find in him. In my book, you decide that doing what's right is actually what you wanted all along.

But you still had to go back, didn't you, to say good-bye.

You probably thought you would never see him again otherwise, and the thought was too terrible to bear; to have found him, and then spend a lifetime praying for a coincidental meeting.

In my book, you went back, for just one more day.

And I want to think that it wouldn't have mattered. That you would have come back to us, like you promised, like you planned, regardless of what you found and what you saw and what you might have thought you needed.

I understand now, because that's what I would have done, too.

I wouldn't have left him behind, regardless of the conse-

quences. I would have stayed, or at the very least, I would have returned to him, for one last good-bye.

But I didn't. I let others decide for me.

And now, Mami. I can't. I can't even find him, and I know he could find me.

The first months, I called every day. Is that what you did, too?

You must have. And I'm certain you spoke, for hours and hours, about silly things, like the weather and the latest movie you saw and where you went out to dinner.

But I had nothing to talk about with him, because he never took my calls. Never. It was as if he had died, even though I knew he hadn't.

He wasn't meant to die that day. That's what the papers wrote after the shooting. Four bullets, none of them fatal. Minute circumstances helped him live—the errant shots, Julio's sudden appearance, and me.

I put him in harm's way in the first place, by taking him there, but then, it turns out, I saved his life by stemming the loss of blood. He must know that, he must know because he knows everything. And yet he still feels betrayed. And I would, too.

I've tried to romanticize it, see? I've rationalized that he doesn't want any contact from me because he wants to spare me. But I'm only fooling myself. I abandoned him, like his mother did. What greater betrayal is there? How ironic, after he taught me to be objective, dispassionate even, about you, about everything. He taught me how to be pragmatic. But for him, everything is black and white.

For the longest time, I left messages on the answering machine, and then I stopped. I felt like I was leaving behind a little piece of my soul, every time I spoke into that blank machine with no face. God knows who was listening to my voice, stealing my thoughts.

The last time Chelita answered, and she told me he had gone back to France for some time, because he was never able to get that U.S. visa to come here. He'll never stop being his father's son, after all. Chelita could have left the conversation at that, but she also told me he sold the piano. And that's when I really knew that there was no going back. That he had erased me completely.

I've kept all the letters that have come back unopened.

Now, I have a whole box of mail that I wrote, but I can't bring myself to read. I actually carry them with me, in a little leather pouch, so they don't get wet or damaged. Like you did with your diary.

Except your pages were meant to be ripped out and burned, whereas my letters are still looking for their reader.

I cling to the notion that one day I'll meet him again, and I'll have them—everything I poured onto paper—ready to hand over to him, to try to make things right.

That's why I now know that you had to go back. That you had to see him. Touch him. Talk to him. You had to look into his eyes and know that your choice was right and fair. Because you couldn't bear the thought of simply waiting for a random meeting, looking around airport terminals and hotel lobbies and at traffic lights, like I do. Thinking you might, just for a second, for the very last time, catch even a passing glance. Wondering, always wondering, like I do, what if?

What if.

I'm going back, Mami. I'm going to seal this letter to you, and take it to the cemetery, to where you lie on top of my grand-father, and even if he hears everything, I'm going to read it to you. And I won't care what they say, and neither will you.

And then, I'm going to burn it, Mami. I'm going to burn it with all those other pages you wrote, and I will start writing my own story. And in time, this will only be one more chapter in that book.

Hasta mañana, Mami.

Te quiero,

Gabriella

Author's Note

Although the characters in this book are entirely fictional, some of the incidents are based on actual events.

On December 20, 1995, Flight 965 from Miami to Cali, Colombia, crashed just outside the Cali Airport, at the height of the Christmas season. Four passengers survived the slow-moving crash, and belongings were found largely intact. I was in Cali at the time with my newborn daughter, and covered the aftermath of the crash for the *Los Angeles Times*. Those articles are public record, as are the transcripts from the flight's black box, including Captain Tafuri's words.

The same year, a notorious drug dealer was gunned down at lunchtime in a popular Cali restaurant. Although he was hit by a hail of bullets, he survived the assassination attempt, only to be killed months later outside of Cali.

The Cali traditions of the feria and the cabalgata continue to be alive and well. American Airlines flight 921 continues its daily evening route from Miami to Cali.

Acknowledgments

This book wouldn't be a reality without the support of many wonderful, giving people.

I'd like to thank my wonderful agent, Kirsten Neuhaus, for believing wholeheartedly in Gabriella and never giving up in her fight to find her a home. I am so lucky my manuscript found its way into her hands. And my amazing editor, Selina McLemore, who tackled this book with so much faith and passion. Every suggestion she made was the right one.

Thanks to Alfredo Santana who saw the potential in this story and pushed me to finish it. Michael Krikorian, who motivated me to begin writing it all those years ago at the *Los Angeles Times*. Luana Pagani, who took the time to read, and whose message on my answering machine meant more than she knows. Rich Isaacson, who not only read, but delivered. Tommy Mottola, who sent "Gabriella" to the Vigliano agency, and, ultimately, to Kirsten's hands. And Lilian De la Torre, who so selflessly and wholeheartedly supports her fellow writers' endeavors, including my own.

Reading Group Guide

1. Do you think this a love story, or a story about mothers and daughters? Could it be both?

2. Do you think the importance of the mother figure is overemphasized in the book? Or do you think the absence of a mother is truly such a transcendental issue?

3. In today's world, is it fair to expect a woman to put her entire life at the service of her child?

4. Do you consider Helena a loving person? Why or why not?*

5. Why Colombia? Do you think setting the story there added something to it? If so, what? Or could the story have been set elsewhere and offered the same impact?*

6. Both Gabriella and Helena are women divided between cultures, language, and upbringings. How important are these factors in shaping who they are and what they do?

*Want to know how author Leila Cobo answered these questions and what inspired her to write the book? Visit www.leilacobo.com to find out.

7. Are Helena and Gabriella ultimately in love with a place—in this case Colombia—and simply looking for someone who will guide them there? Or do you think they fell in love with individuals and ended up romanticizing a place as a result?

8. Is true love doomed if it doesn't happen with the "proper" person?

9. Do you think Gabriella made the right choice by returning home and leaving Angel? What would you have done if you were in her position?

10. What do you think Helena's final intentions were? Was she going to abandon Gabriella, or was she planning on saying a final good-bye to Juan José?

11. Is infidelity overrated? Do you think Helena's affair was understandable given her circumstances? What do you think Marcus knew of her relationship? If he didn't know about it, do you think he could have forgiven her for it had he found out?

12. Does Gabriella truly fall in love for the first time when she meets Angel, or is she merely rebelling against her family for not being honest with her?

Guía para grupos de lectores

1. ¿Cree Ud. que éste es un cuento de amor, o un cuento sobre madres e hijas? ¿Podría ser de los dos?

2. ¿Cree Ud. que en la novela el énfasis en la importancia de la figura de una madre es demasiado? ¿O cree Ud. que la ausencia de una madre es verdaderamente una cuestión transcendental?

3. ¿Hoy día, es justo exigir que una madre ponga su vida entera al servicio de su niño, y no tenga una vida suya?

4. ¿Cree Ud. que Helena es una persona cariñosa? ¿Por qué o por qué no?*

5. ¿Por qué Colombia? ¿Cree Ud. que el ambiente de Colombia añade algo al cuento? Si sí, ¿qué? ¿O podría tomar lugar en otra parte y todavía tener el mismo impacto?*

6. Gabriella y Helena son mujeres divididas entre culturas, idiomas y crianzas. ¿Cuánta importancia tienen estos factores en determinar quienes son ellas y en lo que ellas hacen?

*¿Quiere Ud. saber como la autora Leila Cobo respondió a estas preguntas y que le inspiró a escribir el libro? Visite www.leilacobo.com para descubrirlo.

7. ¿Últimamente, están enamoradas Helena y Gabriella con un lugar—en este caso Colombia—y buscan a alguien quien pueda llevarlas allí? ¿O cree Ud. que se enamoraron con individuos, e idolatraron el lugar a consecuencia de este amor?

8. ¿Está condenado a la ruina el amor si no sucede con la persona "correcta"?

9. ¿Cree Ud. que Gabriella hizo bien regresar a los Estados Unidos y en dejar a Angel? ¿Qué habría hecho Ud. si hubiera estado en su posición?

10. ¿Cuál fue la intención final de Helena? ¿Abandonar a Gabriella o despedirse de Juan José por ultima vez?

11. ¿Está sobreestimada la infidelidad? ¿Cree Ud. que las acciones de Helena fueron comprensibles dando las circunstancias? ¿Sabía Marcus de la relación de Helena? Si no sabía de la relación, ¿cree Ud. que la habría perdonado si lo hubiera sabido?

12. ¿Se enamoró Gabriella verdaderamente por primera vez cuando conoció a Angel, o simplemente ella se rebeló contra su familia porque la familia no fue sincera con ella?

About the Author

Celebrated journalist and former concert pianist LEILA COBO is the executive director of Latin content and programming for *Billboard*, and is broadly considered the ultimate Latin music insider. Leila is a frequent contributor to NPR and has written liner notes for acts such as Ricky Martin, Shakira, and Chayanne. She is also the host of the television show *Estudio Billboard*, which features in-depth interviews with top Latin acts.

A native of Cali, Colombia, Leila holds dual degrees in journalism, from Bogota's Universidad Javeriana, and in piano performance from the Manhattan School of Music. After graduating, she won a Fulbright Scholarship and obtained her masters degree from USC's Annenberg School of Communications. Leila got her start in journalism as a writer for the *Los Angeles Times* and later became the pop music critic for the *Miami Herald*.

Recently named one of Colombia's most influential women by prestigious magazine *Fuchsia*, Leila is a recipient of the Premio Orquidea Award for international journalism. She lives in Key Biscayne, Florida, with her husband and with her children.